Novels by William F. Buckley, Jr.

HIGH JINX
SEE YOU LATER ALLIGATOR
THE STORY OF HENRI TOD
MARCO POLO, IF YOU CAN
WHO'S ON FIRST
STAINED GLASS
SAVING THE QUEEN

William F. Buckley, Jr.

H·I·G·H J·I·N·X

A DELL BOOK

Published by
Dell Publishing Co., Inc.
1 Dag Hammarskjold Plaza
New York, New York 10017

This is a work of fiction. Some of the figures who appear, however, do so under their own names.

Dell ® TM 681510, Dell Publishing Co., Inc.

ISBN: 0-440-13957-0

Reprinted by arrangement with Doubleday & Company, Inc.

Printed in the United States of America

March 1987

10 9 8 7 6 5 4 3 2 1

WFH

FOR ALISTAIR
RENIRA
CAMILLA

H·I·G·H J·I·N·X

ONE

SIX HOURS A DAY were given over to physical exercise, and Blackford Oakes decided he might just as well take the training along with the Special Platoon, the name given to designate the commando group Blackford had been instructed to help prepare.

He had just spent a year in Germany helping to reconstruct a small private chapel. His real purpose in Germany had engaged him in the most heinous postwar assignment he had ever been given—the most heinous imaginable, he had told himself a dozen times during the past two months, waking at midnight in physical and moral sweat. His mind and spirit had had extensive exercise during these weeks, but not his body; so he thought what the hell he might as well get back into prime physical shape, and here was a way to do this in the company of commandos. At age twenty-eight he wasn't yet willing to defer to any presumptive physical preeminence in any group, never mind that over half of them were five years younger and that his sedentary months in Germany might show him up during the first few days. So what?

Actually they didn't. He found himself able to do the forced marches without strain, as also the night work under the barbed wire, the push-ups and the pull-ups, the bayonet work, the whole arduous business. He studied jujitsu for the first time, greatly admiring the resourceful instructor, an English sergeant who had spent the war as a prisoner of the Japanese in Malaysia where he had learned the martial art from a fellow prisoner, an Oriental who had earned the black belt.

The commandos were a cheerful lot and the groaning they indulged in when suddenly awakened in the middle of the night to be given emergency drills in the chill and wet air of late winter in England was all ritual. They were, however young, all of them experienced, all of them veterans of combat, either in the late days of the war or subsequently in Korea. The men did not know what their mission was, only that it would be dangerous (they were volunteers), but they knew from the intensity of their exercises that it would take place soon.

The afternoons were devoted to specialized training. Six men, one each from the six squads, went to Demolition. Six men, again one each from the six squads, to Radio Communications. Six to Medical First Aid. Six to Special Weapons.

The balance—the officers—went with their leader, known to them only as "Henry," into a single-chambered room within the heavily guarded compound.

From the outside the shed looked like an abandoned theater. And indeed, inside the shed the two dozen chairs were arranged in theatrical dimension, forming a circle, the stage in the center. The diameter of the arena was twenty-four feet, and they stared, every day under relentless instruction, at a dollhouse version of the city of Tirana, the capital of the little country squatting west of Yugoslavia and above Greece, a million and a half wretched people so Stalinized by now "as to make Stalin and Mao Tse-tung" (as the first lecturer on that first day put it) "weep in jealousy." Operation Tirana intended, no less, to liberate Albania, the little communist enclave in the Adriatic which, providentially, abutted against no other communist country, now that Tito had declared the independence of Yugoslavia. There were five Albanians, two of whom spoke fluently in English; the other three spoke it well enough to make themselves understood. They would disperse—one Albanian with each of the parachute drops to cope with problems of language, though the operation was designed to make this only a very brief problem—on the way to the sudden change in government. There would be no end of native Albanians at their disposal, the political trigger having been pulled.

One evening at the officers' club Henry sat down with Blackford Oakes at a table by the little bar sequestered for use by the Special Platoon. It was rather like a railroad car in shape. The bar bisected it two thirds of the way down its length, the larger section for the enlisted men, the smaller for the officers, the same bartender serving the lot. Henry, though English, sent back his whisky and soda. "Put more ice in that, old man," he said to the bartender, Angie, who had been brought out of retirement for brief and very special duty. And to Blackford, known at Camp Cromwell only as "Ernie," Henry said:

"I am aware, Ernie, that I am not to ask you anything about your background, and you are not to ask me anything about my background. Shall we practice?"

Blackford poured his beer into a glass and smiled at the large, rangy, weather-beaten, self-assured man in his thirties, with the black straight hair worn longer than commando style, with the teeth white, spasmodically visible given the cigarette he dangled from his tight lips.

"Yes," Blackford responded. "I don't suppose I should even tell you that I am practiced in deception?"

"You may. But you must remember that I am not to take for granted *anything* that is told me here, unless it is told me by Colonel Mac or Joe Louis." Henry's voice was public school English with, as becomes the accent of a professional commando, a light varnish of Humphrey Bogart. "Colonel Mac" was how the company addressed the Ulsterman in charge of the Special Platoon while at Camp Cromwell, the officer who presided over their administrative schedule and their physical training. Joe Louis, the second in command, was a huge West Indian major who was supposed to be addressed as "Major Joe," but cheerfully yielded to just plain Joe Louis when the similarity in appearance between him and the American champion was remarked, on the first day, by Henry. Joe Louis's brother, commando Isaac Abraham Ezra, couldn't, under the rules, fraternize with his older brother at the officers' end of the building, a problem they solved by taking their mugs of beer outside where, impervious to the cold notwithstanding their early life in the tropics, they sat together hour after hour, laughing, talking earnestly and, when the dinner gong sounded, walking together toward the mess hall, parting only at the bifurcation that separated the officers from the men.

"I suppose," Blackford volunteered, "I could

talk to you about the stock market and you might believe I was not deceiving you?"

"The stock market? I say, what's that?" Henry asked, taking a gulp from his glass, stirring the ice with his index finger and rubbing the same finger thoughtfully up the cleft of his bristly chin (Henry was always about one day late in shaving). He reached now into his fatigue jacket and brought out a pack of cigarettes. It was empty. He leaned over to the bar and said to Angie in his distinctively peremptory style: "A pack of Virginia Rounds." He took the pack without comment. Angie knew better—after his initial experience six weeks earlier when he had presented the chit for Henry to sign—than to repeat a gesture that had got from Henry on that first day a frosty, "*You* sign it. I have other things to do." Henry now opened the package and offered a cigarette to Blackford.

"Thanks, no . . . Virginia Rounds! I'll be damned. My father smokes those things. Didn't know you could find them in this part of the world."

"I'd kill for Virginia Rounds," Henry said. "On the other hand, that doesn't say very much, does it, since I kill as a matter of course." He smiled his tight smile and then added, "It's true you can't find them just anywhere, but they're about. I told Angie to lay in a store."

Blackford: "You were asking about the stock

market? You don't know what it is? Well, the stock market is the instrument through which Wall Street dominates all life west of the Democratic Republic of Germany, and east of the People's Republic of China."

"Funny," Henry smiled, drawing on his cigarette, "that under the circumstances I haven't heard of the stock market. Next time you run into it, say hello."

They spent a relaxed hour talking about this and that, with that odd sense of total relaxation engendered by the knowledge of great tension directly ahead. Blackford was dealing, he soon knew, with a commando much experienced, whose conversation revealed traces of general knowledge not associated with bayonets or explosives. And, he saw, the commando chief was by nature impatient. But impatient men can, as his mentor Rufus once remarked, sublimate impatience into the kind of patience required of men engaged in clandestine activity. Someone impatient to find his prey is prepared to await his appearance patiently, hour after hour. When the dinner gong sounded, Henry in midsentence rose to its summons. They ate together, a dinner positively memorable (sole, steak, mince pie), Blackford commented to Henry after dessert, by military standards.

"Ha! I have you!" Henry said with mock excitement. "How would you know it was memorable by military standards unless you had spent time in the military?"

Blackford laughed. He decided he could go autobiographically even a little further without endangering the operation. "Yes. I was a fighter pilot. While I am at the business of divulging my past, I'll go further and say that this dinner is epicurean by comparison with what you poor English boys have to eat at your fashionable schools, and how do I know that? You guessed it, Henry, I was indentured in one."

"When?"

Blackford paused, but only briefly; security was security, but after three years he found himself worrying less about security than about being ridiculous in pursuit of security.

"I was in school here." He was careful not to disclose that he had been at Greyburn. "My parents divorced in 1941 and my mother was remarried, to an Englishman who took me and my education in charge just before Pearl Harbor."

"So that's where the Japs hid you on the Day That Will Live in Infamy. Trust old Tojo. I mean, don't trust old Tojo. I mean, what do you say we take a walk?"

During those briskly cold weeks in January and February Blackford and Henry became friends. They followed the formal rules closely enough so that, under hypothetical torture, neither could reveal anything comprehensively identifying about the other. They experienced each other as professionals with a common cultural background. Henry, Blackford guessed, might have served in a prewar cavalry unit— certainly he had spent time on horseback. He was, oddly, an addict of American baseball who knew and loved more things about the New York Giants than interested Blackford. And he had a clear strategic sense of the importance of the forthcoming enterprise. He was diligently— on occasion brutally—insistent on quality performance from his men. No letting up. No unnecessary physical exposure. No compromise with the camouflage on their faces and hands. Late one afternoon Blackford came on him slapping with open hand and with full force first the right cheek, then the left cheek of one of the younger commandos whose performance had evidently dissatisfied Henry. He was administering corporal punishment, no less, and the junior commando was expected to submit without protest. Blackford's fleeting impression was that the discipline was being exerted with inappropriate gusto. But these were Brits, he reminded himself. And those of them who attended the public schools were used to rough treatment and submissive behavior. Though the episode was distasteful, Blackford accepted it rather as in the spirit of Sparta than of de Sade. He walked by without comment, and though Henry saw him later in the day as they met for a drink and supper, no mention was made of the episode.

Henry was in charge of forty men, each of whom would know exactly what was expected of him. The objective was plain. Within three hours of their landing they would control the communications ganglia of Tirana, "execute" (Would "assassinate" have been the more correct word, Blackford wondered? Nice distinction, he thought, good for a post-cold war seminar someday) a half-dozen top officials of the government, most importantly Enver Hoxha, the bloody Stalinist dictator, declaring Hysni Shtylla, the exiled leader of the patriotic, liberal National Front, prime minister. All of this to be followed in rapid succession by recognition of the new government by the allied powers and, a month or two later, a genuinely democratic election. (Hoxha had a year earlier staged elections at which the vote in his favor had come in at a reassuring 99 percent.) A bold and unorthodox stroke in that, using predominantly Western commandos, trained not in a foreign country but in the heart of Great Britain, it violated orthodox arrangements aimed at coups d'état. But Secretary Dulles had campaigned for the liberation of Eastern Europe. The relative independence of adjacent Yugoslavia and the relative geographical isolation from Bulgaria, the next-closest unswerving Soviet satellite, argued the military plausibility and the geopolitical excitement of a genuine Western salient in the cold war, instead of the tiresome, enervating, stultifying countersalients to which the West had become accustomed in Berlin, in China, in Korea —wherever. Don't push the Soviets, wait till they push, then counter-push. The liberation of Albania would be the dramatic turn in the cold war, the initiative, finally, returned to the West.

Henry and Blackford permitted themselves to fondle the subject, on which they were receiving briefings every day on Operation Tirana. Neither needed to be indiscreet, after all; certain aspects of the operation weren't discussed, for obvious reasons. Blackford was surprised when Henry asked him, "Do you know when in fact we are due to take off?" Blackford could answer truthfully, "Hell, no. I've never seen tighter security than on this one. I doubt Eisenhower has been told."

That night he woke. He looked at the luminous dial of his watch. It was just after four. Blackford tended to sleep soundly, but when he did wake he made it a practice to let his mind wander wherever it chose—an amusement that had been the advice of his mother when he was a teenager. "That way, darling, you will find out what it was that woke you up, then you can deal with it in your mind, and then you can go back to sleep." A kind of one-man Ouija board—Blackford remembered the hours he and his mother, when he was a boy, would sit over the Ouija board and encourage a psychic something or other to move their talismen this way or that, the idea being that the psychic presence would propel the hand toward the correct answer to the questions crowding your mind. He was very much alarmed, on arriving at Greyburn College, to which his stepfather, Sir Alec Sharkey, had dispatched him at age fifteen, to hear the headmaster announce that the boys were forbidden to play Ouija. (Greyburn was affiliated with the Church of England.) A theologian who served as a trustee of Greyburn had declared at a meeting of the board of trustees that the surrender of one's mind to an impersonal force was immoral, arguably an invitation to the devil to take charge of the dispossessed mind. In the years since then Blackford had allowed himself to wonder whether that was the last dogmatic pronouncement ever made by the Church of England, which he had heard described, by one of Sir Alec's cynical old friends, as "the last bastion of not very much."

So he lay in bed and thought . . . and soon his mind turned, naturally, to Sally. Sally Partridge, Yale (almost) Ph.D., specialty, nineteenth-century English Literature, with empha-

sis on Jane Austen. My gal Sal, he had referred to
her a few letters back, intending only to be affectionate. She had replied, " 'My gal Sal' is entirely too proprietary for my taste, Blacky my
boy (and how do you like 'Blacky my boy'?). Are
you aware that Jane Austen's principals referred
to each other as, e.g., 'Mr. Knightley' and 'Miss
Woodhouse' even after they were about to be
engaged?" Blackford had replied that Miss Partridge certainly would not, he had to assume
from their three-year, uh, friendship, wish to be
bound by all the protocols that bound the char-
acters in *Emma*—he was showing off here, as he
wished her to know that he knew where Mr.
Knightley and Miss Woodhouse had figured in
Miss Austen's oeuvre. Thus they corresponded,
she desiring above all things to complete her
dissertation and receive her doctorate—but not,
really (and why should it be necessary?), at the
expense of losing the affection of her "beautiful
Blacky," as she used to call him at Yale until he
laid down a flat, uncompromising prohibition:
"You call me that one more time, Sally dear, and
you will be the ex-girl friend of your beautiful
Blacky." She had laughed; but she knew when
to retreat, though sometimes in her correspon-
dence even now she would tease him about his
striking features and sculpted physique confident that by doing so she would irritate him.
They were well matched to fence in their corre-

spondence and they both enjoyed the sport, even though sometimes they hit below the belt. More often, they were satisfied merely with a caress to reach below it.

So now, in the predawn, he got up and batted out on his portable typewriter a quick note to her, with the usual evasions about what he was up to and, in particular, where he was writing from (she thought him still in Germany), and no evasions about his longing for her.

What now?

Well, Mother, I have a) let my mind wander, b) decided it was Sally who woke me up, and c) coped with that problem by writing to her. But I still can't go back to sleep.

So he put on shoes, pants, and an overcoat and stepped across the hall of the Bachelor Officers' Quarters to the door, and walked out into the cold. It had been stipulated that not even the administrative staff would leave the ten-acre compound save on business, and only when accompanied by another member of the staff, so he would confine his stroll to the area. He walked absentmindedly in the general direction of the officers' mess, muffling himself against the cold.

He noticed, in the radio shed directly across from BOQ, a sliver of light from the window and wondered who else would be up that early. Should he go in and tell whoever it was who was suffering from insomnia about his mother's let-your-mind-loose nostrum?

He approached the window and attempted to look in, but the little tear in the screen, though letting a shaft of light escape, was too narrow to see through. In the stillness he could hear, faintly but distinctly, the telltale *di-di-dah-dah-dah* of the telegrapher, and he wondered what on earth Sergeant Esperanto, the radio specialist charged with the responsibility of instructing the five radiomen attached to the five squads, was doing at that hour. He even permitted himself to wonder whether his curiosity should be official, as well as personal and transient.

He would think about that; and so he resumed his walk, wandering distractedly past the commandos' barracks, past the playing field and the refectory, past the armory. Having come to the boundary of the compound he could go no further aimlessly, and so he followed the large barbed-wire fence in a lazy counterclockwise direction back toward his own quarters, for one final attempt at what would now be time for a mere catnap before reveille.

It was windy, and the gray British cold fingered his neck, and so he fastened the top button of his coat and thrust his hands in his pockets and asked himself—for the first time, oddly—whether he was glad or sorry that he had not been asked to participate in Operation Tirana itself.

If it worked, Tirana would be a most emancipating spiritual event, with infinite strategic implications for the Cold War: a fitting celebration of the first anniversary of Stalin's death, if indeed it should happen that the commandos would set out on March 5. And those who participated in it? Why, they would qualify for King Henry's most celebrated gallery of the gallants ("We few, we happy few, we band of brothers . . ."). If it didn't work, they would perhaps qualify as the century's Charge of the Light Brigade—except for the important distinction that the overseers of this operation were not lunatics, like the Earl of Cardigan. Moreover, when he arrived at Camp Cromwell three weeks ago his spirits had been low, after those long months in Germany. Would he have been revived by joining this expedition?

Would he, if asked, have volunteered? He could not give himself an answer that seemed absolutely reliable.

He was back now by the radio shed, and looked over at the window. The light he had seen was off. He approached the window. No sound. The telegrapher's roll had stopped. Well. Probably something Sergeant Esperanto had forgotten to do the night before and was catching up on.

Like what?

Something. Who knows.

But the question remained on his mind when, back in bed, he finally drifted off to sleep.

The following day, at breakfast, Henry and his squad leaders were informed by Colonel Mac: "Today is D-Day."

TWO

IT WAS JUST after dark when the three
buses arrived for the forty-one men and their
equipment. They were ready, in camouflage
gear, their faces and wrists blackened. "You
won't need this"—Joe Louis took the charcoal
from Isaac Abraham and tossed it under the barracks. He put his huge arm around the younger
man's shoulder and, their heads tilted slightly
toward each other as if they were off to the
ballroom to dance cheek to cheek, the brothers
walked to the waiting bus, the young gladiator
and his older trainer escorting him to the arena.

They had all mounted the buses except for
Henry, who stood for a few moments alongside
the lead vehicle talking with Colonel Mac and
Joe Louis. Henry signaled to Blackford to join
them. Henry was at once calm and discernibly
excited: Blackford knew the feeling. It had
come to him on all three of his missions in
France ten years ago, before mounting his
fighter plane on the way to what could always
prove the terminal engagement.

The colonel and the major now extended their hands and Henry took them, his cigarette between his lips, his beret tilted over his abundant black hair. He reached out then for Blackford's hand and gripped it tightly, his brown squinty eyes alive with excitement. He turned and got into the bus. The caravan moved out of the gate slowly, as to a funeral, and headed the thirty miles to the military airfield where the C-54 transport was waiting for them.

It had previously been disclosed to the eighteen-man training staff at Cromwell that no one would be permitted to leave the compound until the all-clear signal was given. Of the cadre, all but the two cooks and four orderlies knew the nature of the mission for which they had been training the Special Platoon. Knew, then, that if Operation Tirana succeeded, word would come quickly of its success: there could hardly be anything enduringly secret about a coup d'état in a communist country effected by democratic forces. If word did not come, then the mission had failed. In that event it would be a matter of days, perhaps weeks, before they would learn what had happened, the extent of the failure. Knew, concretely, how many of the commandos had escaped, how many had died.

"Figure twenty-four hours if the news is overwhelmingly good. No news in forty-eight hours, the mission has failed. It's that simple," Colonel Mac had said as the buses pulled out.

It had been difficult to sleep that night. The officers, in their section of the bar, speculated endlessly on the variables that might affect the exact time of the commandos' landings. If the planes took off *exactly* at 2300 as planned, and if the March winds were at the prevailing force and from the prevailing direction—and this the meteorologist had predicted for that night—*then* they would begin to land at 0322—about five-thirty in the morning, Albanian local time.

"But hell, Colonel, they're not going to leave at 2300. It will be maybe 2315, who the hell knows?" the adjutant said.

"Who the hell knows?" Colonel Mac repeated. And then, forcing a change in his portentous manner, he turned to his second in command. "Joe Louis. You got any voodoo ancestors? Any witch doctors back there? If so, *ask* them."

The major closed his eyes and with exaggerated introspection bowed his large head slightly. Then lifted it and, with a voice of great gravity, said, "The first commando will reach the ground outside Tirana at *exactly 0329.*

"Now my voodoo ancestor wants to be paid for that piece of information. That will cost you a rum, Colonel Mac."

"Make that a double rum," the colonel grinned.

And so it had gone until, tacitly acknowledging their helpless remoteness from the scene—there was nothing left to do, save to pray—they gradually disbanded. And went to bed, if not to sleep.

If the plan had worked from the first with optimal success, the triumphant radio declaration would have flashed out of Tirana at 1200 local time, 1100 British (GMT) time.

Sergeant Esperanto stood by the shortwave set in the radio shed. But at the officers' club there was also a good strong radio. "If they beam out of Tirana, BBC will pick it up in ten seconds," Colonel Mac had said, twiddling with the dial to get the best signal. "We'll get it right here."

And that had been the longest afternoon.

At five Blackford could stand it no longer and went out for a solitary walk, again passing the radio shed where, through the glass panel door at the entrance, he could see into the room where the light had come from two nights earlier. Sergeant Esperanto was sitting at his desk, the shortwave receiver on; Blackford could hear muffled voices and even the sound of static. He resumed his walk.

That night at the officers' mess, and later at

their club, conversation was forced, and mostly the men were silent, playing cards and drinking beer. At one point Joe Louis spoke.

"Remember, they *could* be regrouping; any number of things could, actually, have just slowed them down." No one commented. If Colonel Mac had been correct in his projections then the mission had—failed.

The following morning after breakfast the physical training director, Master Sergeant "Newt," announced in an imperious voice that there would be a handball game at 1100 for "all" the enlisted men, a game at 1400 for "all" the officers. The winning enlisted team would play the winning officers' team at a Grand Encounter at 1600. The losers would stand the winners drinks after dinner, "all they bloody well can drink!"

It was a welcome diversion.

Blackford didn't know when the idea had come to him, but without hesitation—after observing from his window in his quarters Sergeant Esperanto lope off to the court at five minutes before eleven—he walked out and across the yard to the radio shed.

He entered it, and went through the open door to the room whence the light had shone.

He did not know what to look for, but instinctively he opened the drawers of the sergeant's desk. He knew something of radios, and discovered nothing in the logs of the past few days to arouse his attention. But he did note that although the exact time of all transmissions was carefully noted, there was no entry in the logbook for the early morning hours of two days ago. Or indeed—he flipped the pages back—any record of any transmission at any time later than ten at night, or earlier than eight in the morning.

He spotted the sergeant's jacket, hanging on a hook on the door, and reached into its pockets. From one he drew out a small cardboard-bound telephone directory. He flipped through it: there were perhaps thirty numbers. He studied them alphabetically. Adams, J . . . POR 4377. He looked at each entry, noting nothing more than that most of them were London numbers. His eyes paused over "Claus, R . . . KEN 21881."

Why five digits?

He examined the other numbers, all of them the conventional British three letters followed by four digits.

He took a leaf from the scratch pad on the desk and wrote down, "Claus, R KEN 21881," put the paper in his pocket, and walked out.

Three days later Colonel Mac left a handwritten notice on the bulletin board.

"The gates of the compound will be open at

0700. The staff is at liberty. Make the usual arrangements." He scrawled out his name. And then he added at the bottom of the page, "R.I.P."

THREE

IT WAS THE Albanian affair that finally decided the question for Rufus. He was not by temperament an advocate, but he had to make himself exactly that, an advocate of radical intervention in London.

The Agency had only just begun its postmortem. It would take months and months—these investigations *always* took months and months—to assemble all the data. And under the circumstances surrounding Operation Tirana, some of the data would never be assembled. What was now—ahead of any such investigation—gruesomely plain was this: there were five different sites where the British-American-Albanian team landed. At every one of those sites, "they" had been there. Ready and waiting. Not only that, they had evidently known at which of the five sites Agent One had been scheduled to land. Because Agent One, unlike the others, hadn't been executed right away. The deadly cool Albanian military, no doubt under specific supervision of the KGB, had taken their time in dealing with Agent One. Perhaps a week, or even two—it was a full month before The Album, as they now uniformly referred to it, had come in ("one of the best examples of exhibitionistic sadism *I've* ever seen," the Director had muttered on closing its gory covers). The second to last photograph in that album had shown Agent One seated on a chair, an Albanian newspaper in his hands, the glaring eight-column headline clearly visible. His upper body and head showed bruises and lacerations. His chest was bound by a strap to the back of the chair, but his arms were obviously under his own control as he held up the newspaper dated March 20, 1954.

That was the first of the two final photographs in The Album.

The second picture, the final picture, showed a small hole through the newspaper, which had dipped down from eye level toward the floor. Agent One was slumped forward, a large bullet wound on his forehead. It had been the moment of his execution.

The balance of The Album was devoted to full-face photographs of forty men. Thirty of them were hanging from a gibbet. The others had been shot, some in the head, some in the chest. The Albanian asset, a native of Tirana, had finally been heard from—a full twenty-six days after D-Day. His radio message was re-

markably languid in rhythm, given what he had
to communicate and the hazardous circumstances under which the transmitter must have
operated. The message, delivered in near-pas-
toral tones, was that Operation Tirana had been
"a great disappointment," that "as far as your
contact can establish," all forty-one of the operation's agents that had parachuted into the five
points about the city had been "awaited by the
indigenous military" which had "banded them
together." Some had been shot on being captured. The balance had been driven to the People's Jail and "there, one at a time, they were
hanged on the gallows in the courtyard."

"Who is this character we got out there?" the
Deputy had growled. "Sounds like he was covering a fucking sports event—sorry about that," he
muttered. (People did not use obscenities
around Rufus.)

The Album, unadorned in the brown-paper
wrapping posted in London, had been addressed to the U.S. Ambassador by name. His
deputy had opened the package, alone in his
office, and, examining it, had no idea what it was
all about. He summoned an aide from the Eastern European division and asked if he was familiar with the language in which the headlines
were written.

Yes. "It is Albanian."

"What does the headline say?"

"It says, 'COUNTER-REVOLUTIONARY PLOT
FOILED/INVADERS AND TRAITORS FOUND, EXE-
CUTED.' "

The deputy knew nothing about the operation the epitaph of which had been sent to him
in this cheap leather album. He rose and went to
the ambassador's office—Ambassador Joseph
Abercrombie Little, a portly man of late middle
age. It had once been written in the Hershey
(Pa.) *Chronicle* that J. A. Little knew more about
the manufacture of chocolates than any single
other living being outside Switzerland. He had
been made ambassador in recognition of his devotion to the Republican ideal of worldwide
nourishment. He was reluctant, on surveying
The Album, to betray ignorance similar to his
deputy's of what it was all about. He turned then
to his deputy and told him, in knowing accents,
that he would discuss the entire matter ("It is
deeply confidential, Reginald") with the CIA
station head, Anthony Trust, whom he summoned by leaning over and depressing the
switch that put him in telephonic contact with
his secretary. He nodded to the DCM, who
knew the meaning of that particular nod and
excused himself from the room.

Anthony Trust—tall, slim, young, dark, sharp-
eyed, well groomed, almost playfully cheerful in
expression—came in. Wordlessly the ambassador handed him The Album.

"What do you make of this, Anthony?"

Trust opened The Album. After turning a few pages, the cheer drained from his face. He sat down and continued, slowly, to turn the pages. He dwelled at some length on the final two pages. The ambassador waited impatiently.

"Sir, who else knows about this?"

"Only Reginald. Oh yes—and the Eastern language specialist, What'shisname."

"You will need"—Trust's demeanor had evolved, inoffensively, to that of the senior, addressing a subordinate—"to instruct them most forcefully not to mention to anyone what they have seen."

"Are you familiar with the . . . operation?"

"Yes. Yes, sir."

"What do you propose to do with"—Joseph Abercrombie Little pointed to The Album—"that?"

"I shall need to cable Washington from the Code Room."

"Well, go ahead. And," the ambassador turned his head down as if to survey other, perhaps more urgent matters appealing on his desk for his attention, "if you have an opportunity to do so, you might suggest to your superiors in Washington that I am more useful as ambassador if I have some idea of what is going on around here."

Anthony Trust said nothing, forced out a routine smile, and walked out.

It was six in the morning in Washington when the Director took Trust's call. He had specified that any development concerning Operation Tirana was to be reported directly to him. When, on D-Day plus 1, nothing had come in, the gloom among the officials who had planned it displaced any other concern. The Director, during those agonizing first few days of total silence, very nearly gave up even attempting to concentrate on anything else. He had even had to pinch himself to listen to a discursive soliloquy by the President of the United States in the Oval Office on the subject of the communist penetration of Guatemala. What was difficult in the Oval Office proved very nearly impossible when talking with his brother, the Secretary of State, who desired from the Director "input," as they were then beginning to call it, for a speech he was preparing to deliver to the Council on Foreign Relations on the subject of "The United States and Spain: A Fresh Appraisal." And, following those first few days . . . still nothing. Nothing, nothing at all, about an operation involving forty-one men. Until now. The call from London. The report on The Album.

The Director reached his office before seven.

The three designated officials he had had summoned were there waiting for him.

Rufus spoke. "The very first question, Allen, is: Do we show The Album to the Brits right away or do we bring it over and examine it ourselves first?"

"Attwood"—the reference was to the head of the British MI5—"already knows about the transmission from our asset. All that The Album does is add concrete proof that what we suspected turned out to be so. Gruesomely so. We shall have to let him know—let him examine The Album—right away."

"Yes of course. You're quite right." It was unusual for Rufus—the most experienced, the least impulsive man the Director had ever known, in public life or private—to pose a question as involving serious alternatives and then instantly to acquiesce in the implication that it was a silly question to begin with. The Director made a mental note to probe the matter (What did Rufus have in mind in questioning whether the British should be shown The Album?) when the two were alone.

And so it was resolved. Trust would take The Album to Attwood at MI5, have it copied, and then fly directly, whether on commercial or military aircraft, to Washington with the original.

"I can't pretend I am looking forward to examining the album described by Trust," Allen

Dulles said, rising. "I'm going to have a little breakfast." He nodded at his colleagues, motioning to Rufus to stay as the other two left. "Sweet roll with your coffee?" Rufus allowed his eyes to skim his own paunch, resolved that it was not inordinate in a man sixty years old, and nodded. The Director came right to the point.

"You've got something heavy on your mind, Rufus."

"We all do, Allen." Rufus was appropriately dressed for someone who had something heavy on his mind. But then he was always dressed as if on his way to a funeral. Or, for that matter, to a wedding: dark three-piece suits, gray tie, white shirt. Somehow it fit him, and in any event, no one ever burlesqued Rufus. He had hair only above the ears and at the back of his head. His brown eyes were either sound asleep (that was when Rufus was given over to analysis, parting company with his surroundings as though hermetically insulated from them) or fiercely active, concentrating on what was being said or on what he was saying; analyzing, dissecting, probing.

"Treason is heavy stuff," said the Director, somewhat sententiously. "And treason is our business. So I guess it is fair to say we always have *something* heavy on our minds."

"Yes," said Rufus. "But this is different. Every detail. Every last detail. The penetration by Soviet forces of Operation Tirana is almost unique." (Rufus was too cautious to say about anything that it was "unique"; if questioned on the matter, he'd have commented that only God could know whether anything was "unique.") "We mount the most important countersalient since the beginning of the cold war. A bid actually to split off—to liberate, to use your brother's wonderful, if hubristic, word—an appendage of the Soviet Empire. We are not only frustrated in bringing off the operation, we are checkmated at every technical level. We plan five entirely separate drops. And it appears there were five ambushes there waiting for them. They knew the coordinates of the five different drops. Only one Westerner—as a matter of fact, it was I who selected those five drops from the twenty-five locations nominated as possible candidates for the operation—knew the drops' locations. One man on our side knew all those details. And KBG-Albania knew all those details. A comprehensive job of treason. It isn't a case of one man overhearing one critical conversation, because there never was one critical conversation. What we are facing is a man—a thing—that has got hold of the entire mechanics of our enterprise."

The Director puffed on his pipe and stirred his coffee. "I think you are probably right. So where do we go from here?"

"To the Soviet Embassy, I would say."

And so Rufus disclosed what had been brewing in his mind since it became clear to him—well before the Albanian transmission; before The Album's arrival in London—that Operation Tirana had been a total disaster. Otherwise, *one* of the forty-one special and specially trained agents would have got through. When none did, Rufus sensed that none ever would.

Rufus now argued that a special team physically enter the Soviet Embassy.

"You do mean the Soviet Embassy in London?"

"I do mean the Soviet Embassy in London. London is where the coordination on Tirana was done. The information we need is in the Soviet Embassy in London."

"Which is protected by British law."

"Which is protected by British law."

"Which law we do not have the authority to alter."

"Which law we do not have the authority to alter."

The Director rose. "You are tired, Rufus."

"Forty-one men have been executed, thirty-two of them Americans. A plan to bring about the liberation of Albania and perhaps the beginning of the dismemberment of the Soviet Empire has collapsed. Collapsed miserably. Ignominiously. It was the most important joint U. S.-British enterprise, combining the resources of

42

our respective intelligence forces, since we worked together almost as a single unit during the war. The only dividend of it all is that we have in effect been tipped off that there is *nothing*—literally *nothing*—the Soviet Union doesn't know about our clandestine operations. That tells us one thing: that there is an organized administrative intelligence around somewhere conversant with our most carefully guarded secrets. We need to know who he is, and we need to know what are the techniques he is using. I don't think it likely we can happen on this knowledge without a look at the inside of that building."

"Assuming you were right—I mean, about the need to look inside the building: Why on earth not make it a joint operation with the Brits?"

"Because I don't know how we would do that without alerting the . . . target."

"You're not telling me you suspect Sir Eugene Attwood?"

"No, Allen. I'm not telling you that I suspect him, nor do I in fact suspect him. But who else—how many others?—would Attwood bring into the picture, assuming he were disposed to join in the enterprise in the first place? And it's in the nature of things more . . . difficult if a branch of the British Government gets involved in the violation of British law."

Dulles turned toward the door. "Let's go home."

"Trust is waiting for instructions."

"Will you take care of that?"

Rufus nodded.

They didn't exchange even routine goodbyes. The Director and his principal spymaster were not, really, friends. Rufus was not, really, a friend of anyone, and the Director was by nature reserved. When there were amenities exchanged they tended to be formalistic. Even these seemed somehow out of place on the day they learned about The Album.

FOUR

THE PRIME MINISTER dined alone. *Oh my God what a pleasure it is to dine alone every now and again.* He sipped from his port. *So good.* When at the dinner a year ago he had complimented the Duke of Alba on the fine quality of the port, the Duke had said he would see to it that the Prime Minister received some. The Prime Minister had raised his hand in protest, but such signals were international. *Like the hand wave of royalty.* Anthony Brogan reflected on the internationally practiced, slightly open-fingered, fingers-loosely-bent, counterclockwise-slow-motion royal wave practiced by all royalty—*they can do it for hours. Queen Caroline in Australia last year was on a three-hour motorcade: too damned long, but I'd like to see the Prime Minister last for very long who tells Queen Caroline how long is too long for a motorcade.* He had tried it! *"Prime Minister, if you are suggesting that we exchange duties, I am quite prepared for that. You can come to my office at Buckingham Palace at ten tomorrow morning, and I shall go to Number 10 Downing Street. If you like, we can reverse our roles the same evening at seven. I like to play with my children at seven. When you reenter Number 10, I believe you will find Great Britain surrounded by a more tranquil world. As a matter of fact, I dare to suggest that riding from the Palace to Number Ten you will also happen on a cleaner city with better-behaved inhabitants, though I am by no means certain that you would remark the difference."*

He laughed out loud. *And all that he had said, in going over the plans for Australia, was, "Doesn't that make for a rather long afternoon, ma'am?" Never again. But then I have said never again twenty times in the four years.*

It had been four years since he paid his first call on Queen Caroline, accepting her summons, after the general election, to act as her first minister. There was something about him that was abidingly protective toward her, perhaps some acute desire not merely to please, but to make more pleasing her role, her life. And then perhaps—Anthony Brogan sighed as he sipped again at his port—there was a little innocent masochism there. The Queen took delight in her rebukes, but almost always, after they were administered, her overriding benevolence drew the sting. Almost always. When Queen Caroline was truly exercised, there was missing from her reproaches any sign of a mere gymnastic exercise: she sounded then more like King Henry sending to the Tower a gay blade caught cuckolding His Royal Majesty.

Yes, a jolly good port. When he was advised that the Duke of Alba had sent an entire barrel of it, Anthony Brogan affected to be surprised and dismayed. But after his aide-de-camp left the room, he rang the steward and told him to decant the port into bottles and to send half the supply to Chequers and to place both lots in his entirely private closets. *Nothing more stupid than giving fine wine to people who do not appreciate it . . . I suppose I could have asked Attwood and the American to stay over—it was nearly seven o'clock when the meeting ended. But then, blast it, there are advantages to being chief of government and why not take advantage of them? One is that there is no presumption whatever that the person with whom you are meeting, no matter how high his station, may simply "stay over" for dinner. People who leave the presence of the chief of government, or the chief of state, are simply meant to dematerialize, what?*

And what was to be done about the so-called intelligence crisis? *The fellow Rufus. I didn't need to be privately instructed by Attwood about the reverence in which Rufus is held. They say Ike would side with Rufus against the chief of every NATO power plus the—(hurrah! final plans for it should be consummated early in the fall)—heads of the Pacific powers. I already knew about the legend—Attwood has got rather into the habit of telling me things I already know, including his personal supervision of the deceptive stratagems that persuaded Hitler to deploy his main army one hundred and fifty miles from where our troops landed. Anthony Brogan had been in that room ten years earlier when Churchill recounted the events of that morning. "What does Rufus say? Find out," General Eisenhower had ordered directly. His aide returned within moments. "Rufus says, sir, that the Germans are not expecting you tomorrow in Normandy." In that case, the weatherman having been checked out, General Eisenhower had said (Churchill's rendition of this was wonderfully dramatic): "Let's go."*

But Churchill had a way, in private company, of undermining any appearance of unalloyed admiration for anyone, let alone an American. He had added, "The general's calm was impressive, and we were all grateful that he did not say, 'Let's go, folks.'"

But he must give his attention to what Rufus had said. Rufus would not have communicated any message from Washington without the full backing of the President, and Rufus's message had been that the government of the United

States could no longer combine intelligence missions with the government of Great Britain.

Rufus had said—Brogan reached for the glass of port and then slowly put it down, accepting, instead, another cup of coffee from the butler—*that the conclusion reached by the leadership of the CIA, concurred in by the National Security Council and personally affirmed by the President, was that until the British had "got the matter in hand," there would be a suspension of all sensitive communications—including any technical assistance in the development of the British nuclear weapons system.*

Sir Eugene Attwood had suggested to Rufus that perhaps the problem of McCarthyism, raging in America, had affected the judgment of the American Government. Rufus's reply was rather devastating. "Senator McCarthy was not even aware that Operation Tirana was being undertaken. Senator McCarthy has a slovenly mind. But even Senator McCarthy does not in fact have any idea how profound the problem of loyalty, indeed treason, is."

A formidable point that. There were Burgess and MacLean.—I wonder, why are so many poofs traitors? Though (the P. M. every now and then reminded himself that as the responsible leader of a great empire he should not indulge in silly correlations) *there wasn't anything of that in Allan Nunn May, or Klaus Fuchs, or the*

49

Gouzenko gang, or the Rosenbergs. That head-line in the Daily Mail *last June was memorable: "U. S. Court Says No: Rosenbergs Will Fry To-morrow." Very un-English, "fry."*

The P. M. rose from the table and headed toward the study where the brandy was, and the highly acclaimed biography of his grandfather, which he looked forward to luxuriating in to-night, and tomorrow—*tomorrow morning, I suppose. I shall have to have Attwood come back here tomorrow afternoon and discuss the impli-cations of the American position, and what can be done about it.*

Anthony Brogan groaned at the thought of reporting it all to the Queen at their weekly meeting on Tuesday.

FIVE

BLACKFORD WAS BACK in London, after a three-week vacation following his departure from Camp Cromwell, three weeks in Switzerland with Marta, his ski-mate. He went to the safe house on James Street, where his old friend and schoolmate—his senior at Greyburn, at Yale, and in the Agency—Anthony Trust waited for him with news and a copy of The Album. Blackford stared at its pages and left the room, saying he would be back in a few hours. He spent these pacing the park, in fact, his heart pounding with rage and frustration. He reappeared at James Street early in the afternoon, and said to Trust that he would like to consult with an Agency cryptographer.

"What you got, Black?"

Blackford explained about the night he saw the light in the radio shed, and his subsequent search of the premises.

"Doesn't sound all that suspicious to me."

"Doesn't sound all that suspicious to me either. Are you therefore telling me our cryptographer is too busy to talk to me?"

Anthony laughed, maybe a little nervously, given his old friend's gravity. He picked up the telephone.

When they got back from lunch, Adam Waterman was there. He was young, no older than Blackford. He wore heavy glasses and a tweed coat too large for his slight frame. His hair was long and disorderly, though not self-consciously so. He asked permission to smoke, sat down, and said, "What can I do for you?"

"A couple of questions," Blackford began. He fished the notepaper out of his briefcase and showed it to Adam. Blackford said he thought he had once read that a primitive cryptographic code was governed by a simple inversion in a series of numbers. For instance, *1*2345, if *1* were the governing number, would inform the other party in the know that the correct number was 3452, a single change in the sequence being indicated. Accordingly, *2*2345 would indicate that the correct number was 4523, etc. Had Adam ever heard of such a convention?

"When I was about six years old."

"Okay, so I didn't dream it up, good. Next question: Could this five-digit number, after you worked out all the hypothetical sequences based on the governing number, be checked with the

Brits? To see where the phone numbers are located?"

"We got friends at the Post Office. Sure."

"Out of curiosity, how long would it take to make that check?"

"Day. Maybe two. Let me look at it . . . Hmm. KEN 21881. The governing number, as you put it, can be placed first, or it could be placed second, third, fourth, or fifth. We would be dealing with the number 2 or the number 1 or 8. We'd have to play with corresponding variables with the letters. They may or may not exist. We'd have to try all the possible combinations." Adam pulled out a pencil, leaned over to the pile of magazines on the coffee table, flicked open the pages of *Queen* magazine until he came to an advertisement for a Rover car that gave up a generous display of white space. In a minute he added up the results of his equations. "There would be, depending on whether the letters were transposable, twenty-seven or one hundred and five possibilities."

"I believe you." Blackford grinned. "Full speed ahead."

Adam rose, lit another cigarette, and extended his hand to Trust and then to Blackford.

The following morning he called Trust and said he was ready with a report. They arranged to meet at eleven.

"Turns out only forty-seven possibilities. Two

of the letters were transposable, the third wasn't. Here is a list of the thirty-nine phones with client numbers corresponding to the variables.

One of the thirty-nine telephones on the sheet Adam handed over stood out. It was given as: "UNLISTED. *Private number, Soviet Embassy.*"

"I asked my contact how many private numbers the Soviet Embassy has, and he looked it up: twenty-four. I found out it isn't possible to know in which office of the embassy a given phone is, because the Russians insist on all phones having jacks, so they can move a phone wherever they want whenever they want, just a matter of switching jacks."

Impulsively Blackford reached for the telephone on the coffee table.

"Black!" Anthony Trust rose from his chair. "You're not going to—"

Blackford dialed KEN 8118.

A woman's voice picked up.

Blackford affected a German accent. "May I spikk wit Colonel Bolgin?"

"Who," the voice replied, "shall I say is calling?"

Blackford replied, "An erld friend. I will call later," and put down the receiver.

The three men, all of them standing, did not smile.

"Those poor bastards," Anthony Trust said.

SIX

IT DID NOT surprise Boris Andreyvich Bolgin that *"having nearly broken my neck to get here,"* as the British would put it, he was kept waiting—he looked down at his watch and calculated: kept waiting *three hours and twenty-five minutes.*

It was now nearly one in the morning. He had been offered tea at ten, and at midnight, cheese and white bread. What Boris Bolgin wanted, what he dearly needed at this hour of the night, was some vodka. Quite a lot of vodka. He was proud that no one knew that this had been so with him since shortly after he got out of the camp, just before the war. Having been in intelligence work ever since then, and in charge of his stations for over ten years, he was almost always able to manage to be alone at night, and it was this, really, that made life possible for him, with his impossible job, with these impossible people. He knew it would be the end if ever it were learned about him that that was what he did every night on reaching home: that and his novels, the great Russian nineteenth-century novels that kept his other self, so to speak, pickled; another existence.

But he had certainly made up for his little delinquency, made up for it in terms of service to the Soviet state. And after all, here he was, after midnight, in one of the antechambers of the director of the KGB, on the eighth floor of the renowned Lubyanka Prison at 2 Dzerzhinsky Square, nodding his head, up and down, up and down as he contemplated how much he had accomplished for Stalin during the hours he was *not* drinking, and how much, now—especially now!—he was accomplishing for Georgi Maximilianovich Malenkov, apparently to be the successor to Stalin.

Though, come to think of it, he was not a bit sure how long *that* would last. As chief of KGB-Britain he got to hear rumors about the ongoing contentions, about the great struggles within the Kremlin. It was a hard role for him, that of KGB chief in Great Britain. On the one hand he was expected to know everything going on in the West. On the other hand he was expected to know nothing of what was going on in his own country. True, it was easier to find out what was going on in London and Washington and Paris than in his Moscow. But he could hardly help hearing—experiencing—vibrations of—a mounting division. There was factionalism, spying on one another, the sense that no leader without the strength of Stalin was truly a leader. What was wanted, what was needed, was someone of Stalin's strength without Stalin's eccentric viciousness. Yes, Bolgin mused . . . but what was wanted was probably unachievable. He recalled that during the thirties it was said of the French that they desired an army smaller than Great Britain's but bigger than Germany's.

Meanwhile it was Boris Bolgin's lot to work for the master of intrigue himself. He would not be a bit surprised if the man who had now kept him waiting for *three and*—he looked again at his watch—*almost three-quarter* hours ended up there on top of the heap.

You cannot underestimate Lavrenti Pavlovich Beria, almighty head of the KGB, Bolgin thought. Beria, like the other contenders, had coexisted with Stalin, which showed that he was resilient. More than resilient: he was the cutting edge, forcing others' resilience. And he had mastered the arsenal Stalin required in order to orchestrate his own sadism and his eccentricity. Boris, he thought, be very careful—ever so careful, now that Beria had finally gotten around to calling him in. And remember Beria's uniqueness. Someone had said to him not long ago, "Boris, I think with the exception of Comrade Stalin, you are the only person who knew Beria in 1934 and still knows him in 1954 whom he has not yet executed!"

Yes, 1934. Boris Bolgin knew Lavrenti Beria in 1934. Beria had been in charge of the tribunal that had sent Bolgin off to the concentration camp, for the sin of having speculated, on one occasion, in front of someone, that Marxist dogma, in that it predicates ultimately a stateless society, ultimately predicted a society after Stalin. That had cost him seven years of hard labor, successive frostbites that had permanently contorted his face; cost him his child and his wife, who deserted him. In that special way he had "known" Beria. But Bolgin was a skillful agent as well as a polyglot, and what he had now brought forth in Great Britain made him, well, a hero of the Soviet Union, if not a Hero of the Soviet Union. The latter award would certainly have been given him, to be sure in a private ceremony, except that nobody was giving awards since Stalin's death and nobody wanted awards, because to have received an award from Malenkov might mean, if Beria came to power, that all those who had received awards from Malenkov would next be singled out for liquidation. No awards this season—not from Malenkov, not from Bulganin, not from Khrushchev, not from anyone. That was why Bolgin relished his little pun about being a hero *of the Soviet Union* without being a Hero. Oh God, how he would like a glass of vodka. But even if it were sitting there in front of him, he would not touch it. No. Always the same rule: only at home, or in his hotel; only when his duty was done.

The matronly aide opened the door without knocking. It was by no means absolutely clear that *she* had not had a glass of vodka. Her eyes were bleary. But then—he looked yet again at his watch—it was just after one in the morning.

"Comrade Beria will see you now, Colonel Bolgin."

Beria did not rise from behind his huge onyx desk, an exquisite facsimile of the map of the Union of Soviet Socialist Republics, each republic in a native stone. There were five telephones on one side of the desk. When Bolgin had last been here, six months earlier, you could hardly see the paneling on the four walls for the photographs of Stalin that had decorated the chamber: pictures of Stalin and (in most cases) Beria somewhere alongside or in the background; but also others of Stalin alone. With his wonderful, beatific face, Bolgin thought, a shiver running through his body. The walls were now less crowded, and there were pictures here and there of other functionaries.

Beria nodded his head curtly, pointed to the chair on his right. Bolgin sat down.

Beria came right to the point. "Did you reach the radio operator in time?"

"Yes, we reached him five and a half hours after the American, Oakes, got on to him. We of course approached him very carefully—he was in London, on leave from his unit. We had to see whether he was under surveillance. Surprisingly, he was not. I had plans in the event that he was being watched. He is now safely in East Berlin."

Beria nodded. He then rose, rose in slow motion. And began shouting:

"You bloody idiot, you moron, you brainless pig!"

Bolgin was startled. He had seen Beria-rages before, but he had never been the victim of one. Usually, for the victim, such rages proved lethal. But surely not in his case—not now, in the present circumstances, taking into consideration his quite extraordinary usefulness in London . . .

Bolgin struggled to get in a word. "But Lavrenti Pavlovich, Operation Tirana was a total fiasco for the enemy! Every single one of the agents and counterrevolutionaries was caught!"

"Idiot, that is *exactly* my point. By your thoroughness you necessarily alerted Washington to the extent of our resources. How long do you expect that we can continue to operate successfully through Caruso under the circumstances? The Americans will have to do something now. If you had let a half dozen get away, or be captured later—whatever. But to place an ambush at *all five* of the landing sites when you advised me that no single piece of paper had written on it more than *one* landing site. And then—sublime stupidity—to let that *idiotic* Albanian send an album to London, just showing off! Showing off! Dulles is not a stupid man. He will suspect organic, total penetration. He will suspect what we have. You, by not using your donkey-brain—excuse me, donkey," Beria spoke now in a voice of exaggerated deference, such as he had routinely used on the one occasion when Bolgin had been in the same hall with Beria and Stalin—*"excuse* me, donkey, for insulting your brain by comparing it with Bolgin's!"

The invective lasted a full ten minutes before Beria sat down. Bolgin repeated what he had already stated in a cable: namely, that the Albanian, Firescz, had indeed been instructed to let three agents get away, that on being told about the wretched album Bolgin had had Firescz arrested, that he was at this very minute incommunicado in Tirana, awaiting orders from Moscow on the question of his ultimate disposition. But Bolgin was saying what Beria already knew. Then he simply waited until there was a change in mood. It came quickly. Beria depressed a switch on the side of the desk and spoke the words, "Bring vodka."

Bolgin said nothing. When the vodka came, Beria pointed his index finger first at the waiter, then at Bolgin. This was his way of indicating to the waiter that he was to serve also Bolgin. This was Lavrenti Pavlovich Beria at his hospitable extreme. Boris Bolgin did not dare to refuse the glass, even as he did not dare to drink it. He touched it to his lips, and Beria did not notice, when he poured himself a second dollop, that's Bolgin's glass was undrained. Then Bolgin caught the fleeting smirk on Beria's face. *So Beria knew even that—that Bolgin needed his vodka! Was there anything Beria did not know?*

"Nevertheless you are to return. Your contacts are—I never use the word 'unique.' Useful. And to be in touch instantly with Caruso. He is to continue to supervise the operation. But effective until I shall see to it that no agent—not in Great Britain, not in Europe, not in America—acts on the basis of any of that information. It will continue, of course, to come to me. If I make an exception to the rule, why, I shall make an exception to the rule. But no one else will make an exception to the rule. I anticipate that this ban by us should last at least three months. It will take that long to tranquilize the Americans. How they will account for the completeness of our knowledge of Operation Tirana we cannot know—they will simply have to continue in doubt. Perhaps they will eventually feel it was a curious coincidence that there were troops at all five landing sites. Did the radio sergeant at the camp know the landing sites?"

"No, Lavrenti Pavlovich. What he was able to give us, as soon as the orders were received by the commander of the commando camp, was reports on training activity and, finally, the scheduled time of departure. We did not give him the information on the sites."

"Well. Caruso has got too valuable a thing there for us to endanger. We will do nothing in the next period, nothing more to suggest to the Americans that we are familiar with their internal communications."

Beria then paused and leaned forward, lowering his voice. He said with some drama, "There are important days ahead for our country, Comrade Bolgin. And *absolute* loyalty from you is expected. I mean by absolute loyalty absolute loyalty; do you understand, Comrade Bolgin?"

"Yes, Lavrenti Pavlovich."

Beria stared into his empty glass, essaying nothing. Bolgin calculated that he was safe, and two thoughts brought him great joy. The first was that clearly he was to return quickly to England. The second was that in a matter of moments he would be dismissed, and a very few moments after that happened he would be at his hotel, the Metropole. There, waiting for him, would be his vodka, in the plastic bottles. And at least three books brought from his library. Soon he would be drinking, and reading Chekhov. But he waited, motionless.

It came a moment or two later. "That is all, Bolgin." Boris Bolgin shot up. "And, oh yes, Boris Andreyvich, you are to be commended for your work with Caruso. And"—Beria smiled omnisciently—"for controlling your drinking, if only in my presence." Bolgin looked down at the little, fleshy man, the odious, sadistic, pulp-faced killer-torturer, and said, "You do me great honor, Lavrenti Pavlovich." He bowed his head, and left the room.

SEVEN

THE DIRECTOR GRUMBLED when, at eight in the morning, freshly arrived in his office on E Street in downtown Washington, he was presented with the two-hour-old cable from London.

"You should have got me out of bed on this one, Halsey," he said to the duty officer matter-of-factly. And then, into the telephone, "Call Rufus and have him come in immediately."

Rufus was unbelieving. "Esperanto" had got away *less than six hours* after we had got on to him?

Well, at least it was absolutely clear what now needed to be done. The Director listened to Rufus and approved the plan. And yes, he would speak to the President about that part of it that needed to be communicated to the Prime Minister.

In London, an hour later, Anthony Trust was surprised that the message hadn't come in through his protected telephone line. No, it had come in the form of a written message, sealed, and handed to him by a clerk who had signed for it at the reception desk. Trust was to repair alone to "a telephone you do not frequently use" and to telephone Rufus, in Washington, at a number Anthony Trust was not familiar with.

The communication was made within a half hour. Rufus's voice came in clearly.

"There is one priority above all others. It is that we learn whether Sergeant Esperanto— you have now his real name and his address— left his apartment in London hurriedly; whether there is reason to expect that he was told he had to leave suddenly. Give this top attention.

"Now, I do not desire that anyone other than you should know what it is, exactly, that we are trying to find out. We have arranged through diplomatic channels for a police detachment to accompany you to Esperanto's apartment. The magistrate knows nothing except that the U.S. Government has requested a search warrant on grounds satisfactory to British law to conduct a search for stolen U.S. property. Call Scotland Yard and ask for Superintendent Roberts, give him your name, tell him you have spoken to Washington and are ready to meet the search squad. Then get moving. When you have conducted your search, call me back at this number. Understood?"

"Understood, Rufus."

Number 138 Whitechapel High Street was in the East End of London, a block of six-story flats in a working-class neighborhood. The street outside was a heavily used arterial road running into London. The trucks, buses, and other traffic caused, during that hour in the afternoon, what seemed like a continuous dull roar. There were twelve doorbells. Superintendent Roberts pushed the bell designated as "Janitor."

A very large woman in her sixties appeared, wearing an apron, her gray hair untended but held back by a bandanna. On seeing the officer with the two policemen and the American she took the cigarette out of her mouth, made an exaggerated bow, and said, "An' wot may I do for you, gen'lemen?"

A few minutes later she had opened the appropriate door. Superintendent Roberts turned to Trust and said, "Under the circumstances, sir, you had better handle the questioning."

It transpired that "John Shroud" had lived in the apartment for about a year, had paid his rent (twenty-one pounds per month) promptly. He was often gone, sometimes for as long as two or three weeks, sometimes overnight. A quiet gentleman. He used to have a lady friend who came in every now and then and once stayed an entire week, but she hadn't been seen for several months. As for last Tuesday, the janitor had been surprised to see him leave, a few minutes after six in the afternoon, because that very morning he had complained to her that his refrigerator was not holding the cold and he would be needing ice the following day in particular. ("Supposed he was 'avin' some people in," she commented.) He had come down the stairs, she said, carrying a suitcase, apparently in a hurry, had barely returned her greeting, waved at her, sort of, and she did so hope he wasn't a criminal, but the room contracts had been very carefully made out by a lawyer, and the widow Longstrike had every right to repossess the flat in the event criminal charges were lodged.

Superintendent Roberts thanked her, pointed pleasantly at the door, through which she soon passed, and, under supervision of the police, Anthony Trust began his search.

He had established that Shroud had been in residence for over three weeks; therefore he must have arrived at about the time the cadre had left Camp Cromwell. The question, then, was whether he had left the apartment under pressure of imminent danger, or whether he had simply gone off to meet his next commitment, conceivably to undertake a new mission. As for Shroud's background, Trust awaited the fruits of the extensive research being done under close supervision in Washington by the FBI, and in London by the CIA.

The flat certainly didn't look abandoned. There were two jackets in the closet, a few shirts in the drawer, magazines on the coffee table. And the refrigerator, as the janitor had indicated, had been freshly stocked, including with perishables—milk, eggs, hamburger meat. What was he doing with such goods if he knew that he would not be back soon? Or at all? It would depend, Trust reasoned, on how much of a hurry he was in. If John Shroud suddenly reappeared the next day, or for that matter later today, then what Rufus was worried about was of a completely different order. If he reappeared he would instantly be arrested. On the other hand, if he reappeared it would lay to rest the urgent question: Might somebody have tipped him off between 11:30 A.M. and 6 P.M. yesterday?

Anthony concluded his inspection. By the time he reached the safe house on James Street which Rufus had designated as the provisional headquarters of the "Sergeant Esperanto" investigation, the mystery was cleared up.

Or rather, it had deepened.

Lufthansa, in answer to their inquiry, reported that yes, one man had appeared at the very last moment, asking for space on the eight

WILLIAM F. BUCKLEY, JR.

o'clock flight to Berlin. He had paid for his ticket in cash. He carried a single suitcase, which he said he wished to take with him, as he had "a tight connection in Berlin." He gave his name as John Hightower, carried an American passport, and had filled out the customary immigration form before arriving in Berlin. A teletype to Berlin retrieved his passport number as set down on his landing form.

A check in Washington quickly revealed that no such passport had been issued, in Washington or in an American embassy or consulate.

John Shroud, age thirty-eight, was an American mercenary, a radio specialist who had several times been called on to give training of a kind particularly useful to special missions. He was a member of a pool of technicians loosely affiliated with several government agencies that had been charged with a growing number of special missions ever since the end of World War II or, more exactly, ever since the crystallization of the cold war. There were several agencies in London, Paris, Brussels, and Rome through which one could recruit specialists, usually at a high rate of pay, for almost any job. Shroud had been used for three operations by the CIA and by MI6, having got a security clearance in 1952. He had been a member of the Signal Corps with the Seventh Army that had fought in Sicily and in Italy. He had a Bronze Star, was discharged at

Fort Sam Houston in Texas, had applied in 1946 to a Veterans Administration Hospital for a hemorrhoid operation. And there the trail ended—until his name was given by an agency in London for a sensitive radio assignment involving a search for a submarine that had disappeared off the coast of Scotland with a nuclear inventory. The search had been conducted under unofficial auspices.

"Well, that's it," Trust said, leaning back in his chair. "We'll let Superintendent Roberts continue the surveillance of the apartment in Whitechapel for another few days, but there isn't any point in expecting John Shroud to reappear. He's gone."

The news was telephoned to Rufus, who advised that he was flying in on an Air Force transport and would meet them at the safe house on James Street at ten in the morning. "You are to discuss the matter of Sergeant Esperanto with no one, Anthony."

"I understand, Rufus."

That morning Rufus arrived at the safe house in London looking old, but not for that reason less than omnicompetent. He was greeted with relief, rather as if the chief surgeon had arrived at the operating room and all the attendants instantly knew that that which had been impenetrable would now, little by little, be penetrated. Rufus shook hands (Rufus shook hands with as much thought to what he was doing as other men gave to zipping up their flies). He took the coffee proffered him, stirred it with his spoon held upside down, and the badinage trailed quickly to a halt. Blackford and Trust waited.

"You may have reasoned to what it is that we need to do, gentlemen. But I shall go through the paces in any event.

"We are faced with the most extraordinary penetration of our intelligence system imaginable. Five discrete landing sites—all of them known to the enemy. The time of the landings: known to the enemy. That is a level of coordinated penetration very difficult even to imagine. There is something extra-human to it. More details on that in due course. It operates, moreover, with uncanny speed and precision. And doesn't mind exhibiting this extraordinary technical precision. As witness the matter of Shroud. We reason to his probable connections and a half day later he suddenly leaves—on a plane for Eastern Europe. Gone."

Rufus put down his coffee cup and was silent. He was given to doing this. Not often; but such silences were not interrupted by those who knew Rufus. He began to speak again:

"At 11:06 GMT, Adam Waterman discloses the list of telephone numbers to Anthony Trust and Blackford Oakes, numbers decoded from the key number in Esperanto's phone book. One of those numbers is a private number attached to the Soviet Embassy.

"At 11:07, Oakes dials the suspect number and reaches the office of Colonel Bolgin, head of KGB London.

"At 12:05, a message written by Trust reporting on these events is handed to a coding clerk in the American Embassy, whose name is Gerald Astrachan." All this from memory: Rufus did not use notes.

"At 12:21, CIA-Washington receives the message which was decoded at—I switch now to Eastern Standard Time—at 0745, and was brought into the office of the Director at 0805.

"The Director brings me in and we discuss the matter and alternative ways of dealing with John Shroud—Esperanto. We reach the conclusion that, most important of all, no action taken in London should alert Shroud to our suspicions. We reason, I believe correctly, that Shroud was one part of a comprehensive network, but that at least now we have a link.

"And you know, of course, what then happened. Within five hours of our discussion in Washington, Shroud had left his apartment. Within seven hours he was on an airplane to Berlin. He is now, presumably, in East Germany."

Rufus rose. He walked at first to the coffee pitcher. Then stopped and absentmindedly returned, his empty cup still in hand.

"It means that only a very limited number of people could, hypothetically, have alerted the KGB to our having got on to Shroud. They are:

"1) Blackford Oakes, covert agent, three years with the Agency, during which he was executor of two highly secret, highly sensitive missions." Rufus sounded as though he were quietly addressing a tribunal. "2) Anthony Trust, chief of station, London-CIA. Six years with the Agency, exemplary performance, and recruiter of Blackford Oakes. 3) Adam Waterman, cryptographer, four years of duty, total security clearance. 4) Coding clerk Gerald Astrachan, fourteen years' service including with MI6 on the Intrepid project during the war, total security clearance. 5) The decoding clerk in Washington, eleven years' service, including two years on Air Force One.

"Have I left anyone out, Blackford?"

"Well, yes, Rufus, actually: yourself, and the Director."

Rufus didn't smile. "You are quite right. We are hypothetical suspects. Have I left anyone or anything else out?"

There was silence in the room.

Rufus went on. "Yes. The teletype. All the information we have discussed flowed through the coding room of the embassy."

"Are you suggesting they have broken our code? As obvious as that?"

Rufus answered, "Our codes cannot be broken. Because the codes, at the level we speak of, are changed every day, and no human being knows what tomorrow's code will be because that code is selected from a billion billion possibilities, at random, at midnight."

"What are we supposed to conclude then, if the assumption is that the persons named didn't tip off the KGB?"

"That *without* breaking the code, they are getting our messages."

"How is that possible?"

Blackford regretted asking the question, the answer to which was the towering enigma that had, after all, brought them all together in the first place. Too late.

"We'll have to try to find out. By working at both ends: In the Code Room, at the embassy. And," he sighed, "at the other end. By penetrating the Soviet Embassy."

EIGHT

Sir Alistair Fleetwood stared at the full-length mirror in the bedroom of his considerable suite at Trinity College and straightened his black tie. He paused and allowed himself to wonder *exactly* how Narcissus felt when he looked at his reflection in the pool of water, and adored.

Fleetwood laughed.

"*Sir* Alistair!" He allowed the syllable to pass voluptuously through his lips. Until exactly 12:44 that afternoon he had been simply *Mr.* Alistair Fleetwood: or, to be sure, Professor Alistair Fleetwood when at Cambridge or in the company of academics.

It had been quite a season for him—all of it taking place within six weeks, actually. The call had come that morning six weeks ago—on All Saints' Day, as the musty set at Trinity so quaintly continued to designate the first of November. The electrifying message: The Swedish Academy of Science had selected him for a Nobel Prize. This was to commend his discovery of the electronic formula whose startling success within the astronomical telescope had permitted the examination of the planets and of bodies located light-years away from the earth with the kind of particularity that radio beams never had made possible. When the patent was filed his colleagues at the laboratory were insistent, though he had vaguely resisted, and it was given the name "the Fleetwood Zirca."

In fact Alistair Fleetwood had not been surprised that he had been awarded the Nobel. It had been widely predicted that he would get it. The development of the Zirca was simply his latest success—who could even say with assurance that it would be viewed as the culminating success? Fleetwood was only thirty-eight years old!—in a career that had dazzled first his family, then the faculty and boys at Greyburn College, then the faculty and fellows of Cavendish Laboratories at Cambridge, then his professional colleagues at Bletchley Park, where he had spent four years with the cryptographers introducing novel uses of electrical energy, critically valuable in coding and decoding with near-instantaneous speed. When John Maynard Keynes had visited Cambridge and spent there a few leisurely days before his sudden and unexpected death in April of 1946, he remarked to a friend that Fleetwood was as brilliant a man as he had ever known. Word got about that the

great Lord Keynes had said that about Alistair
Fleetwood, and it became something on the order of an honorific penned after his name. His
talented young student, Bertie Heath, at one
point suggested that "Mr. Fleetwood," as he
called him at that point, engrave his calling
cards "Alistair Fleetwood, C.G.J.M.K." —Called
a Genius by John Maynard Keynes.

Fleetwood, standing in front of the same mirror, would practice an appropriately embarrassed frown for those many occasions when,
introduced as a visiting lecturer or speaker, he
would hear recounted his academic and scientific achievements. He had become quite good
at it, allowing even a trace of surprise to flicker
over his face, as though he was hearing for the
first time the striking record of his accomplishments and, really, was quite surprised, in a detached kind of way. If only they knew what he
was really thinking about this wholly wretched
society and all its frumpery and pomp and hypocrisy. But no one would ever know. Well,
practically no one.

Now there would be the testimonial dinner—
he was due at the master's office in a few minutes, where the round of feasting would begin.
His first night out as "Sir" Alistair. He sat down
on his red velvet couch, opposite the teeming
bookcase that contained, leatherbound, all the
books and scholarly articles he had published

during the past fifteen years, and poured himself a glass of sherry. He reasoned with himself that, in fact, he would have very little trouble in getting used to it all, notwithstanding his doctrinal disapproval of titles. But that disapproval was, again, his secret, and certainly not something Queen Caroline would have had any suspicion of earlier that day, no suspicion at all. If he said so himself, he had to admit it, his comportment had been exemplary. Exemplary!

He had been ceremoniously invited, along with Dame Myra Hess, as he had discovered that day, to stay on after the ceremony at Buckingham Palace to lunch with the Queen. After he knelt and accepted the baronetcy, following the great pianist, an adjutant led them into a large, ornate sitting room. "Her Majesty will be along in just a moment."

And indeed, in just a moment she breezed in, her poodle in her left hand, followed by a lady-in-waiting who took a chair in the corner of the room. Dame Myra and Sir Alistair had begun to rise, but before they were properly up the Queen had descended onto a petit-point couch, and they reversed their movement, reoccupying their chairs.

Fleetwood had seen her often enough on television and was not surprised by the lovely face, the perfect complexion, the fine honey-colored hair, the loose curls held in place by a near-invisible tiara. But he could not exactly have anticipated the eyes. They were dark blue and sent out a bolt of relentless curiosity. Her mind, he had the impression, was forever in high gear, and at this particular moment it was at cruising speed, taking the measure of her newest knight, Sir Alistair Fleetwood. Evidently the Queen was familiar with Dame Myra, and one soon learned that even as a girl the Queen had known the artist, Myra Hess having been a friend of the late Duchess, Queen Caroline's mother.

She took a glass of champagne from the tray and began instantly to speak to him. "Do you know, Sir Alistair, that I haven't the remotest, not the remotest idea of what it is that you have accomplished, for which you have been so systematically honored during the past six weeks? Now Myra here—Dame Myra—I can personally appreciate, because I know that she could, right this minute, put down her glass of champagne, go over there"—the Queen pointed to the far corner of the room—"to that loathsome Steinway—it is loathsome, Myra, and you don't have to pretend it isn't, but everybody around here raised such an unholy rumpus when I suggested giving it away to a museum. They kept sighing," she turned back to Fleetwood, mimicking the royal ululations she described, "that it was after all made in Hamburg especially for Queen Victoria, my great-great-grandmother, on commission by Kaiser Wilhelm, her dumb grandson. Well now, my first reaction when I heard *that* about the piano was, 'Why on earth do we want *anything* in the Palace given to us by that horrible man, my great uncle, who managed to slaughter 750,000 Englishmen, including my father, in a stupid war?' Please take note, Sir Alistair, that it is not only scientists who can remember figures. So I said to Lord What'shisname who watches out over royal treasures here, 'In that case, why don't we give it to the Victoria and Albert Museum? Maybe my great-great-grandmother would be more comfortable having it there? So to speak, as a part of her special collection?' Anyway, *that* Steinway. The tone is terrible, the action is too heavy, and twice I have without success had it overhauled by, of course, the best technicians in Great Britain—in my kingdom, which is how it is appropriate to designate it in Buckingham Palace. Don't you think so, Sir Alistair?

"But anyway, assuming she would consent to play that piano, which Myra is too sensible to do, she would instantly transport us by her skill and poetry. But what can you do to humble intelligences like ours to persuade us that you deserve the Nobel Prize and, now, a knighthood? I mean, Sir Alistair, what is a Fleetwood Zirca going to do for us?"

"Well, ma'am, what does a telescope do for us?"

"Now, that's silly, isn't it? It keeps us from running our ships into the rocks, among other things."

Fleetwood smiled. "The more powerful the telescope, the sooner you know there are rocks out there, wouldn't that follow?"

"Yes, I suppose that would follow, as you put it. But why do I need to know that there are rocks out there, a million miles away, if there is no possibility of my bumping into them?"

"Ma'am, you are teasing me, and I don't really mind your doing so one bit. Because I cannot believe that you depreciate natural curiosity, even if you don't exhibit it."

Queen Caroline smiled, a huge appreciative smile, settling back totally in the couch, mussing the hair of her dog's head.

Just the right answer, she thought. But she mustn't let him have the last word.

"Curiosity leads to desirable ends and to undesirable ends. Are we so glad there was curiosity on how to cause an atom to implode?"

Fleetwood answered cautiously. "One can't tell always, can one, whether a scientific discovery will be used to help or hurt humankind. Scientists are not responsible for the use made of their tools. That is the responsibility of our governors. Offhand I cannot think of one scientist, or ex-scientist, who is a president or prime minister, or even—" he added cautiously, "a monarch."

The Queen smiled again. "Of course, you are correct, and I hope that your Zirca shows us all kinds of things. Perhaps we can do something about the British climate, after we discern how other planets handle their weather? By the way, is the Zirca a state secret?"

"Well, hardly, Your Majesty. You can't award a Nobel Prize for a secret."

"I didn't mean that. I meant: Do the communists now also have a Zirca?"

"Not at the moment. There is, of course, a patent. And your government has not yet ruled on whether its strategic capability will put it on the list of products British manufacturers are not permitted to ship to the Soviet Union and certain other countries."

"Hmm." Queen Caroline acknowledged with a nod the bow of her steward. She rose and began to walk toward the small blue-toned Dresden dining room at the left, followed by her company. "Well, I hope the government decides against giving the Zirca to the Soviet Union. There isn't anything, Sir Alistair, anything at all" —she sat down, the steward having drawn back the chair, motioned Fleetwood to sit on her right, Dame Myra to sit on her left, and nodded absentmindedly at her lady-in-waiting and equerry to take their places—"that the communists will not transform to evil purposes. You could give them Mercurochrome and they would use it to poison somebody."

She continued in her celebrated, animated way, her eyes flashing. "Why don't you invent something," she handed her dog to an attendant, and dipped her fingers in her fingerbowl, " —something that immobilizes everyone in the Kremlin? We'll just manage to plop it into Red Square one day when nobody—nobody but you, Sir Alistair, and you, Myra, and *I*, on behalf of my kingdom—is looking." Queen Caroline's voice reduced to a conspiratorial whisper. "And suddenly—the next day!—the entire government apparatus, all those horrible men—notice, Myra, you don't see any women in the Politburo, do you? *Not one.* I specifically asked that question of my foreign minister as recently as last week. Not one. Though, I admit it, there was that dreadful Ana Pauker in Roumania, whom Stalin was goodhearted enough to purge before being especially goodhearted by dying.—And then the next day, they would all have lost their memory!

"Think of it, Sir Alistair! They would all forget how many people they need to kill during the next few weeks! Forget how many million people they wish they could enslave! What the formulas are for firing their nuclear weapons! What the secret codes are for reaching their spies! Think of it! I will tell you this, in the presence of"—she counted decisively, pointing to each of her guests seated about the table, one after another—"in the presence of four witnesses: *you* invent *that,* and I shall make you a lord. No. I shall make you a duke. Come to think of it, if you do *that,* I shall divorce Prince Richard and marry you! With Myra, here, playing the organ. What would you choose to play at that wedding, Myra? Remember, the Queen of England would be marrying the man who had brought us peace on earth. Wonderful!"

Dame Myra spoke, for the first time. "I shall certainly make myself available for that performance, ma'am. I shall practice 'Amazing Grace,' with 1,001 variations."

"Splendid! It is a covenant. Never mind the Fleetwood Zirca. It will blow away, in memory of the Fleetwood Covenant." Queen Caroline turned to her soup, which was cold. She noticed quickly that none of her guests had begun to eat, waiting for her.

"Oh dear, oh dear. I got carried away, and the soup is cold. Would you like yours reheated, Myra?" The Queen brought her spoon to the tip of her tongue, and gingerly tasted the consommé. "Hmm. Well, not too bad." Without looking up she said, "I beg you, anyone who would like the soup reheated, just motion over there."

It had been a memorable lunch, Alistair Fleetwood thought. No doubt about it. It served, among other things, to fortify his loyalties.

NINE

WHEN, AT AGE eighteen, on completing his first year at Trinity, Alistair Fleetwood was given the Duhem Prize for outstanding academic work, which prize customarily went to a graduating student or, every now and then, to a singular second-year student, his parents felt that they would have to yield to his entreaty, resisted during the previous two summers, to travel in the Soviet Union. "He has, quite simply, earned it," the senior Mr. Fleetwood, the librarian in Salisbury, had said after reading his son's letter. Mrs. Fleetwood agreed, though she didn't like what they had all been reading about the Soviet Union under Stalin, about the show trials and the executions. And so, that night, father and mother went over their accounts and calculated how they might assemble the eighty-nine pounds necessary to give Alistair the month in Russia as a member of the tour sponsored now for the third year by the Cambridge Socialist Society.

The eight students and their guide, Alice

Goodyear Corbett, traveled by Soviet steamship, leaving Southampton early in an afternoon of mid-June, arriving nine days later in Leningrad having, at about midpassage, ambled lazily through the long cool green of the Kiel Canal, as it had been called ever since Kaiser Wilhelm lost a world war and with it the right to continue to attach his name to the canal that joins the North Sea to the Baltic, saving five hundred miles of circumnavigation.

The students were very serious about their month in Russia, and the 12,000-ton *Pushkin* was well equipped with appropriate reading for inquisitive young scholars visiting the Soviet Union for the first time.

Alistair's roommate, Brian Scargill, was a third-year student, the president of the Socialist Society. He took his duties as, in effect, the student group leader very seriously. In consultation with Miss Corbett it was decided that there would be two seminars every day at sea, each lasting two hours. During the first of these Miss Corbett would give general lectures on Soviet life and the history of the Soviet Union. In the afternoon she would teach elementary Russian.

The first day out, in the Channel, they ran into something of a gale. Attendance at the first seminar was accordingly sparse. But Miss Corbett made it without apparent difficulty, as did Fleetwood and two others, not including Scargill who, when late that afternoon he emerged from his stateroom, was volubly mortified that an ordinary storm would stand in the way of his instruction in the great socialist experiment being conducted in the Soviet Union.

Alice Goodyear Corbett was a lithe, pretty, full-breasted, nimble-minded young woman, twenty-four years old. Her father was an American journalist who had been posted to Moscow just four months after the October Revolution, and now was recognized by the community of journalists there as the senior Western journalist in residence. Alice Goodyear Corbett (the convention had always been to use her full name, dating back to when, at age five, asked by a visiting Russian what her name was, she had answered, *"Moye imya* Alice Goodyear Corbett") had attended schools in Moscow from kindergarten and, at first with her father and in due course with others, had traveled everywhere foreigners were permitted to go.

Her early life was confused by the commotions that so absorbed her father professionally but affected her personally. There were the years in the early twenties when she was in grade school and was treated erratically by her teachers, who had not yet been instructed on the proper attitude to exhibit to a young daughter of a representative of the imperialist press. The children, before they reached ideological puberty, accepted her—as a foreigner to be sure, but also as someone apparently as familiar as they were with the ways of Moscow. Alice Goodyear Corbett knew all about their holidays and their history, their museums and their toys. She went regularly to play with other girls, daughters of other Americans and of English and German journalists, but she found, after reaching her teens, that her relations with them tended to be more mechanical than those with her Russian friends. Given her choice, she elected to accept invitations to spend time with her Russian friends.

But then, approaching college age in the late twenties, she discovered, after one incident in particular, that as a foreigner she was generically suspect. She had been excitedly invited to a birthday party by her oldest friend, Olga. The day before the party and after Alice Goodyear Corbett had saved two weeks' allowance to buy a special birthday present, a Mickey Mouse watch, Olga said that her parents had called off the party. Alice Goodyear Corbett stared hard at Olga, who turned her head to one side and began to cry. She confessed that her parents had become afraid of foreigners coming to their home, Comrade Stalin having pronounced recently on the dangers of cosmopolitanism. Alice Goodyear Corbett had replied that she was not Jewish, so at least that particular charge could not apply to her, but Olga was simply confused, and cried some more. There were other such incidents.

Alice Goodyear Corbett reacted by resolving in word and deed clearly to dispel any suspicion on the part of anyone who observed her that by virtue of her parents' background she was hostile to what was becoming the country of her choice. She began to pay special attention during the long indoctrination courses, and consistently got the highest grades in the class, mastering the minutiae of Marxist-Leninist doctrine. In time she was being called upon to give demonstration answers to questions put to her in front of the whole class before visiting teachers from other parts of first Moscow, then other Russian cities. By the time she had graduated from secondary school she had achieved a minor eminence in the student world of Moscow: the perfectly trained Soviet protégée. Some indication of this reached her father (her mother had never managed to learn a word of Russian and simply ignored her daughter's activities except as they involved domestic arrangements). Her father passed it off as the kind of thing precocious children tended to do—involve themselves in their own culture—and paid little attention to it. Besides, he was himself sympathetic with what the Soviet state was trying to do and not entirely decided whether, when time came to retire, he would go back to Virginia. Perhaps he might just stay on in Moscow.

While a second-year student at the University of Moscow, Alice Goodyear Corbett had been called surreptitiously to the inner sanctum of the Party, located in the Student Union Building, and proudly informed that close observation by her teachers and others had persuaded officials to pay her the supreme honor of extending to her an invitation to join the Communist Party which, if she accepted, would mean that she shared an honor with only three percent of the Soviet population. The principal condition attached to her membership was that on no account was she to divulge this development to anyone, especially not to her father or to her mother, because although they were known to be friendly to the great revolution, if it became known that their only child had become a member of the Party this would embarrass him with his employer, the United Press, perhaps even bringing about his recall to the United States and depriving the Soviet Union of a useful commentator.

Alice accepted the honor with great enthusiasm. During her two trips home to Virginia during the preceding five years she had become practiced in defending Soviet policies. Much of what was alleged about Stalin's Russia was, quite simply, a lie—for instance the charge that the defendants in the great purge trials were any less than flatly guilty, as charged, of treason. She was happy to think of herself as a consolidated member of an international movement, the great purposes of which would be to remove war and the causes of war and social and class antagonisms from the earth forever.

Alice wrote poetry, and her poetry included paeans to the Soviet state and its leaders, though she had had on more than one occasion to face the metrical choice either of substituting the name of a new leader in place of the name that figured in her original lines but was now exposed as having been treasonable or, if she couldn't find another leader with the requisite number of syllables to his name and ending with the same sound as the deposed leader (she was not able to find someone to substitute for Zinoviev), she would have to toss the poem away. But she had now the equivalent of a little book of poems, dedicated to Soviet leaders, to Soviet cities and villages, to Soviet schools, and to some of her Soviet teachers. One day, she dreamed, when her father's professional interests would no longer be jeopardized, she would publish these poems. What pleased her most was that she had been able to compose them both in Russian and in English, taking here and there the necessary linguistic liberties.

While doing postgraduate work in Russian history, she had been approached by her cell leader and told that Comrade Pleshkov of Intourist desired to see her. The meeting took place late that afternoon in what had been the groom's cottage of a czarist prince, on Herzen Street.

It was wildly exciting. The idea of it was that every summer until further notice she would escort a half-dozen or as many as a dozen British students, bringing them from England for a month's tour of the Soviet Union. Mrs. Pleshkov explained that Soviet policy was to encourage a true knowledge of the country by intelligent young people from abroad, particularly those who had shown interest in communism. On top of her regular duties—to lecture to the students, to expedite their travel arrangements, to coordinate their programs—she was to keep a sharp eye out for any student who inclined sufficiently toward the great communist experiment, of which Russia was the matrix, to qualify for possible recruitment.

"Do you mean—actually to invite them to join the Party?"

"Yes," Mrs. Pleshkov said in her husky voice, taking a deep draft from her cigarette. "Yes—of course, you will in each case check first with me so that we can conduct appropriate investigations. But I have that authority, to extend membership. And we can hope that some of the young people will in due course show themselves willing to go further."

"What do you mean, Comrade?"

"The imperialist world—as you know, Comrade Corbett—is always poised to do damage to the socialist revolution. We need help from within Great Britain from young people who are loyal to humanity, not to decadent imperialist regimes."

"You mean, spies?"—Alice Goodyear Corbett's calm, matter-of-fact request for elucidation showed that she was not in the least troubled by the nature of her proposed commission, let alone shocked by the idea.

"You might call them that, yes. 'Friends of the Soviet Union,' I would prefer to call them: foreign friends of international socialism. These young men and women will, when they graduate, branch out and take positions in the armed forces, in the foreign service, in the academies: it would be good to know that our fraternity is always growing, that everywhere—everywhere in the world—there are friends of the Soviet Union."

Alice Goodyear Corbett said the prospect pleased her in every way. Among other things it appealed to the poet in her, the notion that, using her own informed intuition, she might discern which students especially to approach, which other students to let alone.

The first of the Intourist Tours for the Cambridge University Socialist Society had yielded a harvest of two students whose fidelity, tested now for two years, had been established. Granted, there had been a slight problem with young Greenspan who had exuberantly volunteered to assassinate King George. But in Moscow it was judged, however tentatively, a satisfactory enterprise, and it was now established procedure that on their return to Cambridge, those students deemed worth cultivating would be put in touch with, and thereafter serve under the direction of, unit leaders. Both of them, after the first summer, had commended the recruiting instincts of Alice Goodyear Corbett; the second year, three of eleven student tourists accepted her discreetly proffered invitation.

The experience, moreover, had done wonders for Alice Goodyear Corbett, whose self-confidence had blossomed and whose very appearance took on a special, arresting aspect: a handsome, passionate young woman, alight with enthusiasm, confident of her ability, shrewd in her insights.

Alice Goodyear Corbett decided the very first night, when the *Pushkin* was rolling wildly in the cranky seas of the Channel and most of the ships' passengers stayed in their staterooms in varied forms of queasiness and outright distress, that the young man from Trinity who had completed only his first year at Cambridge was the most attractive prospect for the Party of all the students she had mixed with, and before the evening was over they had engaged in sprightly conversation. She discovered that in his subtle, almost childish way (he was, after all, only just eighteen), the slim young man with no trace of a beard on his face, a light sprinkle of faded freckles reaching from his nose to his hair, so quick to grasp nuance, to expand and improvise on subjects only tangentially touched upon, so phenomenally knowledgeable on the subject— the communist enterprise—in which Alice Goodyear Corbett was an acknowledged expert, that notwithstanding his almost exaggerated youth, Alistair Fleetwood was really the senior presence in the group. She was at once perplexed, intrigued, and excited. It was almost midnight, and the bar was all but empty. She asked him if he would care for a nightcap, or would that overstrain his stomach? He answered that his stomach was perfectly fine, and ordered an orangeade. She touched her glass of vodka to his orangeade and said, "You will have a wonderful adventure during the next month, I promise you, Alistair."

"Oh, I am quite certain that is the case, Miss Corbett. You know, that is, after all, why I came.

That, combined with the intelligent disgust anyone has, or should have, who knows England as I
know England. But we need not go into that:
the class system, the public school snobberies,
the grinding poverty of the working poor. It is
possible that I could teach you something about
my country that you don't know. But I am so
pleased to be here under your guidance! I look
forward especially to learning Russian from
you."

They said good night, and even walked out on
deck for brief exposure to the howling wind.
Alistair Fleetwood insisted on escorting her to
her cabin, on reaching which he bowed his head
slightly, smiled, and said he would see her tomorrow at the seminar. "Or maybe even before
that, if you are at breakfast." Alice Goodyear
Corbett smiled, and on sliding into her bed was
mildly astonished to find that that young man—
that child! she insisted on putting it that way, in
self-reproach—had actually . . . aroused her.

One month later they were again aboard the
Pushkin, having traveled two thousand miles
within the Soviet Union. Mostly, of course, they
had been in Moscow and Leningrad. The reactions of the young Cantabrigians, Alice Goodyear Corbett reflected, were not very different
from the reactions of the first and second
groups, the one last year and the one the sum-

mer before. Two or three were traveling, really, only for the sake of the adventure, their curiosity limited to what Alice Goodyear Corbett quickly grew to recognize as the "exciting" historical sites: Lenin's Tomb, the Kremlin, the house in Leningrad where Rasputin had been killed, the prison where Lenin's brother had been held before he was hanged—that kind of thing. The embalmed Lenin was to be expected: it came first with foreign visitors, even as with Soviet pilgrims. But beyond these obvious historical sites, "they are more interested in the guillotine that cut off Marie Antoinette's head than in the French Revolution," as she said, compressing her criticism in one report to her supervisor. These students were visibly bored during the hours and hours and hours spent in factories and agricultural collectives where, by contrast, the ideologically motivated students took copious notes, cluck-clucking over what they were assured was the relative backwardness of comparable British and American enterprises.

Jack Lively, a vigorous young man of twenty who played rugger at Cambridge, was a socialist, Alice Goodyear Corbett suspected, largely because his father was a prominent leader of the National Union of Mineworkers. Jack Lively made it clear from the moment he landed in Leningrad that he expected a little romantic diversion. Alice Goodyear Corbett told him that that kind of thing did not go on under socialism; to which Lively, who was reading anthropology at Trinity, said to Miss Corbett, a) that she couldn't really be right about that, that what she called "that kind of thing" happens everywhere on earth; and b) if in fact socialism has come up with a system in which "that kind of thing doesn't happen," why, said Jack Lively, he would need to reconsider his commitment to socialism.

Most of the group—the conversation took place in the little bus on the ride to Nagornski, so that they might witness with their own eyes the freedom of religion given by Stalin's government to those "quaint old monks," as Alice Goodyear Corbett put it—sided with their guide. But later, in their hotel room, Brian Scargill confessed to Alistair Fleetwood that though he had sided with Miss Corbett, in fact he thought that probably Jack Lively was correct.

What brought on the concrete problem was when, a few minutes late for breakfast the following morning, Jack Lively, sitting down between Scargill and Fleetwood, smiled lasciviously as he dug into his ham and cheese and said, "You know that blather old Corbett was giving us yesterday about how in Stalin's Russia there are no you-know-whats?

"Well," he smiled, "she was wrong. And this one"—his eyes closed sweetly to suggest satiety and then opened again, the eyes now of the accountant—"was hardly dear, unless you want to call one package of Dunhills and one quid expensive. Say, do you think old Corbett would go along with the idea if I persuaded Tania— yes, 'Tania'—to join us for the rest of the tour? I'm sure she'd be glad to. Besides," Jack Lively was enjoying himself hugely, "there is great advantage to be got from my suggestion, because as in the Soviet Union all things are owned in common, Tania would, I am certain, be happy to oblige the rest of you. Though—" he stopped dramatically, "perhaps not you, Fleetwood. She would probably take one look at you and figure you wouldn't know what to do in bed, and she is not a licensed teacher."

Alistair Fleetwood, though he gave no signs of it, was heavily challenged by this dose of raillery and condescension from Jack Lively. On the one hand he was totally loyal to Alice Goodyear Corbett and felt honor-bound to believe everything she said about life under socialism. On the other hand, his scientific intelligence taught him that facts, among them those that had to do with (ineradicable? Was this defective loyalty to Marx-Lenin?) human appetites cannot be denied by ideological asseverations, and evidently Jack Lively had had a night out with a professional. He was, also, secretly amused and titillated by the fantasy of a traveling tart with the Cambridge Socialist Society Intourist trip through the Soviet Union. If such perquisites were advertised, he was sure there would be more volunteers for the next tour. But above all he was sensitive to the implication that he was not really old enough to be experienced, perhaps even too naïve to be conversant with basic biological formulae.

But meanwhile he had to say *something* to Lively. So he shot back, "Oh really, Jack. So you found someone who breaks the rules. Whoever said there are any societies anywhere where some people don't break the rules?"

Lively was not going to leave it at that. "There are certainly a lot of people who break the rules in Russia, you can say that again. At the rate at which they are executing traitors, Fleetwood, breaking the rule must be a very popular thing to do."

On this point Alistair became truly defensive. "Do you have the figures, Lively, on the number of Roundheads executed by Cavaliers? Or the number of heretics killed during the religious wars of the seventeenth century? When you get around to doing that research, come see me about the Moscow trials."

He recounted, later, the whole conversation to their guide, who told him he had handled the challenge perfectly. "You will be hearing a great deal of that kind of thing. It is not unanticipated. *Stalin is trying to change human nature!* Such a challenge, such audacity, calls for great strength of will."

Alice Goodyear Corbett was by now, though speaking slowly, addressing Alistair in Russian. He had directed his mind to the problem of learning the language with the same intensity with which he had directed that formidable apparatus to scientific inquiry. Scargill and one or two others had learned a few phrases, and could order a meal or a taxi—or, in the case of Jack Lively, a woman of pleasure, however unlicensed. By the time they had completed the tour, back in Leningrad, Alistair Fleetwood was speaking regularly in Russian not only with Miss Corbett but with guides, drivers, and waiters. When the tour came to an end, she had made her selection of the three students she would press. First and foremost, of course, Fleetwood. Second, Brian Scargill. And also (she permitted herself an invisible sigh) Harold Abramowitz, that tall, ungainly, dull young man with the clipped black hair and the mustache struggling to flower but still straggly even after almost thirty days of studied neglect. But Harold Abramowitz's devotion to communism was positively fanatical, and Alice Goodyear Corbett felt she could count on success with him.

They would have seven days on the *Pushkin*, the morning and afternoon seminars continuing, as on the trip out. Even so there were myriad opportunities for two people to sit down in a corner of the dining room, or in the library, or in one of the three sitting rooms, or on deck. She would approach them one at a time, of course. Everyone she approached always thought himself uniquely singled out, so the demands of security were fortified by vanity.

Curiously, it was Alistair Fleetwood about whom she was most apprehensive. This was so, she forced herself to admit, because she was a little bit in awe of him. The speed with which he was learning Russian was merely one example. His natural air of authority extended to all matters. Normally, when recruiting someone into the Party, the seniority of the recruiter is utterly plainspoken. Her authority rested in her established status as a party member; as a graduate of the University of Moscow; as a linguist; as a longtime resident of the Soviet Union, and yet . . . she felt that perhaps he would be difficult for her to manage. There was that impalpable sense that he knew more than she.

The first night out of Leningrad was festive. A century earlier a French nobleman had written that there is always the inner urge to celebrate on the day you leave the Russian frontier. There was no way, Alice Goodyear Corbett comforted herself, to blame *that* on the communists. But the phenomenon had certainly not changed with the advent of communism. That first night the passengers aboard the *Pushkin* were given Russian champagne, and vodka, and caviar, and zakuski, including a wider variety of meats and cheeses than they had tasted during the whole of their stay in Russia. During dessert, Alice Goodyear Corbett said to Alistair that she would like to have a few moments of private conversation with him, and what about after dinner?

"Of course, Alice." The students had been asked so to refer to her, after the formal end of the Russian part of the tour. "Where?"

"Well, we could take two deck chairs—it is quite warm. Or perhaps find a corner in the lounge where there isn't too much noise."

"It's going to be noisy everywhere," Alistair said. And then he looked up directly at her, his eyes wide open, and said, "Why not in your stateroom?"

Alice Goodyear Corbett paused, but did not avoid his young, searching eyes. She felt instantly exactly what she had felt when Grigori had asked her, in her final year at the University of Moscow, to come to his room after the birthday party: the impulses she felt racing through her blood were unmistakably the same. Grigori, dear Grisha, gone now to the army . . . But this *child!* Yet such an extraordinary young man.

She hesitated, and said, her voice now entirely feminine, so different from the lightly stentorian voice of Alice Goodyear Corbett, tour leader, "If you like."

"Fine." Alistair, rising from the table, was not apparently surprised. "I know the room number, and I will meet you there in a half hour. Maybe I will bring a surprise. No, not maybe: I will bring a surprise. A present for everything you have done for us."

How very much thought he had given to this present. Quite simply, the most he had to give. And Alistair Fleetwood had been aware for many years that what he had to give was more, much more, than what others of any age, let alone his young age, had to give. He felt positively ennobled by the proposed act of generosity, but also tender in the knowledge of whom he stood now to patronize with his largesse: Alice Goodyear Corbett was a very special teacher, a very special specimen of the new revolutionary. And a very beguiling . . . woman.

She debated exactly how she would be dressed. She compromised by simply removing her jacket, leaving herself with skirt and blouse. And by using a quarter of her precious supply of French perfume, and brushing back her hair. The cabin, slightly larger than the ordinary cabin, was large enough for a desk on which she could do her paperwork. There was a flat couch on the porthole side, running the width of the cabin. And, opposite, the single bed with the protruding struts, so that it could be made into a double bed when there was double occupancy. She adjusted the reading light over her desk, and the light over the couch, and the single chair next to it, on which she was sitting when he rapped on the door.

Alistair Fleetwood entered carrying a tray with a bottle of champagne, two glasses, and a small package wrapped in red ribbon. He was dressed as at dinner, in white duck trousers, white shirt, and double-breasted navy blue jacket. He looked sixteen.

His eyes were bright as he opened the champagne, but told her she would need to wait before opening the package. It didn't occur to Alice Goodyear Corbett that she had any voice in the matter, and when she looked at him, glass in hand, she saw that his expression was at once excited and entirely composed. She drank down half her glass, and then told him what was on her mind. She was beginning to go on—her packaged recruitment line was extensive, about opportunities to serve the people, humankind, peace: she had never known it to consume less than a full hour. But after a few moments he interrupted her.

"Of course, Alice. I want to help and I will help, and I will help in every way I can. You do not need to press on me the idealistic nature of what you are talking about. I knew this early on, and I *felt* it in Russia."

She smiled, a smile lit with pleasure, surprise, and awe.

"Now," he said, "you can open the package."

Alice Goodyear Corbett said, rather flirtatiously, "I am glad it is wrapped in red. That is an appropriate color today."

Alistair Fleetwood said nothing.

She opened the package, and bared: a condom. She looked up at first startled, but in moments flushed, submissive. She knew now that her young charge was every bit in charge of her.

"Driving to Nagornski one day, Jack Lively told me that if I were to find myself in bed with a woman, I wouldn't know what to do. Well, I have an idea what I would do, but I do need instruction. And I would like to have that instruction from someone I like and admire as much as I do you, Miss—you, Alice. And I am also aware—I am widely read in extra-scientific literature, you know, Alice. I am widely aware that the most precious present a human being can give is her—his—virginity. You shall have mine," he said, in a voice that cultivated gallantry.

Alice Goodyear Corbett rose, turned off the study light, and sat down next to Alistair Fleetwood.

TEN

WHEN ON AUGUST 23, 1939, the news
came, Alistair Fleetwood was for an instant unbelieving. But there it was, and later editions of
the papers even featured a ceremonial picture:
a smiling Nazi Foreign Minister von Ribbentrop
signing the accord with Soviet Foreign Minister
Molotov. Fleetwood could not know directly the
reaction of the communists in Cambridge, or
even in London, because by design Alistair
Fleetwood had become estranged from them.
His very first instructions, on returning to college after the summer tour with Alice Goodyear
Corbett five years earlier, had been to dissociate
himself emphatically from the communists he
had once associated with, and, gradually, even
from the socialists: indeed, from the political
left. So that by now it had been more than an
entire college generation since he had mingled
with the hard left community, either students or
faculty; over four years since he had mingled
with the little clots of fellow travelers among the
students and his colleagues (he was on the

faculty). Even the Russian he had learned, he was encouraged to let lie fallow. He greatly missed those fervent evenings with the select few, the brainy idealists who recognized that the Soviet revolution was the twentieth century's way of saying no to more world wars, to imperialism, to the class system. But he was ecstatically engaged in that experience in his underworld life, even if apparently withdrawn; no longer the exuberant first-year socialist who had gone up to Cambridge in 1933.

On August 23 the whole of the British press descended on Harry Pollitt, the General Secretary of the British Communist Party. But he had declined to make any comment at all: and left-leaning apologists for Stalin in Parliament, most notably Denis Pritt and Harold Laski, were not physically present when the House met in an uproar over the news. Winston Churchill observed that perhaps Joseph Stalin had suddenly discovered that Adolf Hitler's party was called the National Socialist German Workers' Party and had discerned the bond between the two ideologies. The Moscow-leaning members of the Socialist Party were in deep distress. The Communist Party was torn.

Not so Alistair Fleetwood. After the initial shock, his mind went to work. It was, by character and training, a mind that could juggle relationships, reducing them to abstractions as required, so that what emerged was on the order of correlations of interest, rather than wrenched static relationships. And by the time his young dinner guest, Bert Heath, came by, Fleetwood was thoroughly at peace with his own analysis.

Obviously Hitler's fascism was a strategic menace to the international communist movement. Clearly Stalin had acted out of prudence. This was hardly inconsistent with Marxist-Leninist theory or practice. Lenin, during the New Economic Plan period, had gone so far as to encourage isolated pockets of capitalism, among other things to attract to the Soviet Union Western scientists who would depart leaving their skills behind.

Bertram Heath, to whom now Professor Fleetwood handed a glass of whisky, arrived in white heat. Heath swallowed his whisky with a single gulp, and Fleetwood knew it would be a long, long evening. No matter. He would prevail. In the first place he was used to prevailing over problems. In the second place, he could, with all due respect to Bert Heath, persuade him, though he was only a single year his junior, of, well—Fleetwood faced it—anything. Not a reflection on Heath's malleability, rather a reflection on Fleetwood's strength of mind and on his singular capacity to satellize. And then too Heath found Fleetwood engrossing. He was, with Fleetwood, in the company of a man he could not bully and had no desire to bully. Fleetwood's intellectual achievement was too outstanding to be thought competitive. His subtle understanding of the great and noble reasons to hate England, Great Britain, the Empire, the West, the whole imperialist-bourgeois world, was a flame they had in common. Heath would have killed for Fleetwood. To be sure, he'd have killed for a lot of people. But for Fleetwood, he would take pleasure in killing.

Via radio, Fleetwood had been in regular communication with Alice Goodyear Corbett. Her father, two years earlier, had retired from journalism and, with what looked like a world war on its way, returned with his wife to Virginia. Their daughter elected to stay on in Moscow "to continue her scholarly researches," as she put it to them and, indeed, to her friends. In fact she had become a full-time KGB operative, and Fleetwood was one of her charges in Great Britain. It had greatly surprised her that he had never evidenced any impatience, or even restiveness, under her supervision. Whatever her orders, Alistair Fleetwood followed them with near-jubilant docility.

Fleetwood's career had continued on its spectacular course, and by the time he was in his twenties he was widely regarded as among the most inventive and productive scholars in the general field of electricity and electronics in the world, in constant demand at convocations of scholars pressing the frontiers of the relatively young science of electronics.

He affected only detached interest in the worsening situation in Europe, the Sudetenland crisis, the Munich Conference, the obvious preparations Hitler was making for war. He posed as only a bystander of sorts. During this period, he had been made aware by Alice that a clandestine group of Cambridge students was "in very close touch with us." It amused him that one of these—"The Apostles," they styled themselves—might actually approach him, thinking to energize him ideologically, perhaps with the view to interesting him in the common proletarian struggle. For that reason he allowed a kind of dull glaze to come over his eyes when political discussion was entered into. And, soon, though a very young man, he was treated as something of a scholarly fuddy-duddy, and more or less left out of any spirited political discussions.

No one had ever condescended to Alistair Fleetwood, to be sure. He had long ago begun to publish, and showed an originality, a comprehensiveness of knowledge, an interest in the productively esoteric that attracted not only national and international attention but inevitably the presumptive respect of associates even much older. "When Alistair's mind is engaged," a colleague had said of him, in the refectory of Trinity one day, "which is most of the time, he would not notice an explosion in the corner of the room. But he would notice a political discussion, and when that happens, before your very eyes he simply dematerializes." Fleetwood rather enjoyed the drama of his great imposture, because during the whole of that period he spent many hours doing his chores for his Alice: silly things, he often thought as he compiled clippings revealing the political attitudes of people he had been told to monitor—politicians, professors, newspaper reporters. Indeed sometimes he reflected that special pleasure was to be got from the relative tedium of his work for the Party. "A kind of mortification of the intellect," he once dared say to Alice, who once went so far as to reveal to him, which was not to abide by the protocols of the profession, that more often than not it was not she who dictated what Agent Caruso, as his code name had it, was supposed to do. "Never mind. One day one of your services will perhaps even transform the struggle!"

"Take your time, my dear Alice. I am not hurrying you," he answered.

Fleetwood had made it a point to cultivate scholarly connections in Stockholm. And there he would frequently go, as would Alice Goodyear Corbett, her superiors in the KGB acquiescing in the arrangement on the grounds that Fleetwood would certainly prove extremely useful to them and was evidently disposed to continue to act through the young Soviet-American. In Stockholm the two would pass each other in the lobby of the Grand Hotel as strangers. They would meet in his suite, usually beginning with dinner; or if his formal commitments made that impossible, then later. And there they released their passion. One night he told her that he thought he would turn his mind to a formula that would express with electrical symbols the energy consumed by the average act of love. "In our case, I would multiply that by a factor of ten." She smiled as she lay by him, stroking his hair, telling him how happy she was, except for the long periods they needed to spend apart. Their shared idealism was a form of communion.

Alistair Fleetwood replied that he believed war lay ahead of them and that the single privation he could not stand was the thought of a prolonged separation. "What will you do if there is war?"

"Whatever I am asked to do," she replied. "Perhaps they will want me in America. Perhaps they will want me to stay where I am. That will depend."

"You must never let them come between us."

She agreed, and every time they were together they renewed their pledges to each other.

His first nonclerical commission had been the recruitment of Bertram Heath. Actually, the initiative had been his. Fleetwood had been attracted to the tall, rangy Wykehamist who devoted himself equally to physics, soccer, and politics: the quiet, determined young man with the even-featured straight face and the steady brown eyes that signaled what was coming before the laconic twenty-year-old got out what was on his mind.

It had been well after Fleetwood himself had retreated from overt left-wing activity that he noticed, from reading the daily *Union Reporter,* the Cambridge student newspaper, Bertram Heath's name cropping up in the sports section as a rising star in soccer, and in the Cambridge Union as a fiery socialist speaker. During Heath's second year, he qualified to participate in a seminar guided by Fleetwood prompting, in a matter of weeks, a fascination with the strikingly gifted young scholar by the only slightly younger student which begged for social intimacy. This came first with Heath staying after class to pursue answers to one or two questions that especially vexed him. This became, a fortnight later, an invitation to take tea at a local café. Fleetwood reciprocated with an invitation to drinks on Tuesday night at the Fellows' Lounge. A month later they were sharing an evening meal at least once every week.

Heath, Fleetwood learned, was highly mobilized on all the requisite issues: the problems of the working class, the threat of Hitler, the hold of the New York bankers on commercial life, the insensitivity of the government of Neville Chamberlain, the class structure that was so especially evident in the public schools including the renowned school from which Heath had graduated. Fleetwood permitted himself certain hospitable resonances when the young man spoke, and very gradually permitted him to know that he was, however silently, in sympathy with his basic positions, but had been too preoccupied with his professional researches to devote the time necessary to master the whole problem of international politics, and now he was encouraging Heath in effect to instruct Heath's brilliant mentor, an imposture he was sure would not be resented if the decision was finally taken to engage in recruitment.

He did notice about his young friend that he was less than charitable in his attitude toward those who disagreed with him, or indeed toward those who got in his way in any matter, whether it was a student competing with him for the higher grade in a physics paper or a soccer player on the other team or a Cambridge Union orator who disagreed with him, particularly if the form of that disagreement was patronizing. Timothy Bethell, defending the policies of the British Government, had remarked a few weeks earlier that such criticisms as were being made of "the speaker" (it was Bertram Heath) would "lighten the political burden of the nation, especially if, as a consequence, he were to devote himself exclusively to soccer, in which activity he is said to excel, perhaps to the point of failing to recognize that he is in this chamber supposed to treat arguments other than as footballs. They really are different things, Mr. Heath." There was great jubilation in the chamber, most of it at Bertram Heath's expense.

The following night, returning from a convivial supper with friends, Timothy Bethell, rounding the corner of Trumpington Street to approach his college, was accosted by a large man wearing a mask who proceeded to administer a beating so severe as to result in Bethell's hospitalization with a fractured jaw. There was great commotion at the college, and suspicion instantly fell on Thomas Brady, the boxing champion of Clare College, whose steady girlfriend of several months had only the week before been annexed by Timothy Bethell. Brady was asked informally by common friends to account for his whereabouts at the time of the assault, and although he pleaded most vigorously his innocence, in fact he had no way of proving that he was on a bus returning from London where he had done nothing more mischievous than go to the cinema. Some believed Brady, some did not. Alistair Fleetwood did.

The time had come, Fleetwood decided late that spring, and he dutifully consulted Alice Goodyear Corbett, asking her permission to proceed.

It had been a revelation to Bertram to learn that in addition to everything else the man he admired most in all this world was also in fact a clandestine revolutionary, wholly mobilized behind the cause of the working classes. He joyfully accepted a commission as a revolutionary colleague. They spoke for hours on end about the excitement of their common purpose. It disappointed Heath only to learn that he would need to submit to the same discipline Fleetwood had submitted to, namely to recede from his firebrand mode as socialist and fellow traveler. But he was willing to do everything necessary to qualify fully.

So that by the time he was in his final year, Bert Heath had crossed the aisle to the Liberal party in the Cambridge Union, and his high BTU former colleagues thought him a spent case in whom the fires of idealism had burned out. Though they conceded that nothing else in

Heath had burned out: he had become the captain of the soccer team, and was regarded as certain to win a first in physics.

Bert Heath was in Cambridge that summer doing a research project under the supervision of Fleetwood, and they dined together twice, sometimes three times a week in the suite Fleetwood had already begun to aggrandize with a cook-butler who served tolerable food, and a young but discriminating wine cellar. They ate now in the airy dining room, the windows on the side open to let in the summer air. Bert had been heatedly denouncing the pact, Fleetwood patiently counseling him to wait wait wait, that the wisdom of it would one day transpire. He acknowledged that communists would now be on the defensive everywhere, but that what mattered was not such setbacks as these, but progress in major, historical terms. That, he reminded his impatient and severe young friend, "can't be measured by today's headlines." And then, of course, the headlines a week later brought news that Hitler had invaded Poland. And forty-eight hours after that, the government of His Britannic Majesty George VI declared war, for the second time in a generation, against Germany.

The Army Recruiting Office ruled that certain categories of scholars should not be drafted into the army: they would be more valuable performing special services. Fleetwood fell instantly into such a category, Heath marginally. Fleetwood was asked to report to Bletchley Park where he learned that he was to help with the whole cryptographic enterprise. He had his misgivings, which he confessed to Alice by radio. He was not disposed to help an imperialist power in a fight against Adolf Hitler so long as Hitler was an ally of the Soviet Union. She counseled him to protect his cover by agreeing to serve. And while there at Bletchley Park he could keep Moscow informed of all technological developments that might prove useful, meanwhile being as sluggish as he thought he could get away with in contributing to the war effort against the Soviet Union's ally.

Fleetwood spoke with Heath about coming along into the Government Code and Cipher School. Bert Heath on the one hand longed for more active work, but could not envision himself fighting on air, land, or sea against an ally of the Soviet Union. So he permitted Fleetwood to exercise his considerable influence to bring him into the bustling operation at Bletchley.

At Bletchley, Fleetwood learned what he could from his fellow scientists, but mostly he absorbed himself in a series of experiments about which he spoke little, even to Bert Heath, who throughout the long period that lay ahead of them was manifestly demoralized. Heath was frequently late in coming to work. He was seen at the local bars with different women who, after a few days, were given the option of sleeping with Bert Heath or being dropped by him like a stone. He calculated one night, as he left the hotel room he had hired for two hours, ahead of the American WAC lieutenant who would leave a decorous few moments later, that his rate of scoring came to about fifty-fifty, and those were reasonable odds. He cared nothing for any of the women he spent time with. His mind was occasionally stimulated at Bletchley, and he became a skilled radio operator, bringing his considerable knowledge of physics to his aid in helping to solve special problems.

Thus it went for two abysmal years, past the fall of France, through the Battle of Britain, through the bombings and blackouts, the shortages and rationing, and the general dreariness. His superiors no longer thought of him as a brilliant young scientist capable of creative work. It could be said that they lost interest in him. But all that changed on June 22, 1941, when Adolf Hitler's armies invaded the Soviet Union.

A week later, Fleetwood was working feverishly on projects directly related to the war effort. And one week later, Bertram Heath was receiving basic training at a camp for commandos in the south of England.

ELEVEN

IT HAD NOT been easy.

"You'd think we were asking to inspect their ladies' boudoirs," Anthony Trust said, stretching his legs over the coffee table.

"Interesting idea," Blackford replied.

"Maybe *that's* where The Spook" (as they had taken to calling the vegetable-mineral-animal they were looking for) "is hiding."

"If so, Anthony, you'll be the first person to find it."

But Rufus had entered and the schoolboy banter, at which they had had considerable experience since they had been, indeed, schoolmates at Greyburn College, ended abruptly. Trust removed his legs from the table.

"It is set for ten tomorrow morning," Rufus reported, sitting down opposite. "I began by asking our friends if Pulling and Spring could study the electronic schematics but they said," Rufus paused, as though taking a deep breath before elaborating a profound ambiguity, " 'No.' " That was as theatrical as Blackford had ever seen Rufus. "It became necessary," Rufus said, back now in his understated mode, "to pursue the matter."

The "matter" had gone all the way to the P. M., and finally Anthony Brogan simply overruled MI5 head Sir Eugene Attwood, who had several times remarked that in modern history no one had ever invited a foreign power, never mind how friendly, to "ransack" its private communications facilities. The Prime Minister assured Sir Eugene that "ransacking" the Code Room was hardly what the American specialists intended to do. The fact was, a monstrous leak had been unmistakably deduced, the result of which was that the passage of all American intelligence communications and high security information was as of this minute suspended, pending the elimination of that leak. "It has to be in our organization or in theirs, inasmuch as the leaked information passed through both arteries and no other."

Attwood finally agreed to cooperate, but only after wresting from the P. M. the promise that two equivalent British experts be present when time came to "sweep" (having capitulated, he now used a gentler word than ransacked) U.S. Embassy quarters. Moreover, as a matter of pride, the American Embassy would be first: "We are, after all, sir," Attwood had reminded the Prime Minister, "in Great Britain, not in America, and I should think the presumption would be not that the host country was delinquent in security matters, but that the foreign country was. So we should begin by inspecting *their* quarters, and only *then*, our own." Brogan sighed and said he would make the suggestion to Rufus, who said that was fine by him; he had no interest in the matter of precedence. And so, on that Monday morning, Bruce Pulling and Hallam Spring of the CIA arrived with Rufus and Anthony Trust at Number Two Grosvenor Square, where they were met by two agents of MI5.

The two British technicians were amiably treated by Hallam Spring as first they waited in the reception room, and then rode up on the elevator together, entering the Code Room without any discernible tension. This would not have been so if Bruce Pulling, a short, hairy man in his thirties, had met them alone, because Pulling had a distracting habit, whatever the company he found himself in, or the circumstances, of leaning over and making notes on his notepad, causing light banter to come to an excruciatingly self-conscious halt. But while his colleague made his notes, Hallam Spring chatted.

There they were: in a simple enough, utilitarian room, but a room designed to receive and to transmit data of trivial but also of momentous consequence. Rather like the room that holds the electric chair, Anthony thought: all of the support systems are outside.

No files cluttered the room. Just the two chairs for the two clerks (top-secret material was never handled by only a single employee). A steel table running across two thirds of the middle of the room. The transmitting unit, set on its own table on the left against the wall, adjacent to the paper shredder. The other walls bare. Not even a picture of President Eisenhower.

On the table at the center, the teletype machine, its electric wires running down to an elaborate electrical socket-grid underneath. Immediately on its right, the encoder; on its left, the code-to-print transcriber.

The number one communications clerk would receive from the embassy official the sealed message to be transmitted. The clerk would open it and place it flat on the table beside the keyboard.

He would then type out the message, which would emerge—on oily yellow inch-wide scrolled paper, with perforated dots that corresponded to the letters being typed—from a slot on the left of the machine onto a horizontal three-inch open tray. Gravity would impel the paper, on reaching the end of the tray, down onto a stainless-steel receptacle on the floor.

After the message had been typed out, the

number two clerk would collect the scroll of perforated paper and feed it into the third machine, which looked like a large electric typewriter. The perforated tape would activate the typewriter, which would type back the message on regular office-sized paper, on a roll that issued out of the back of the machine, once again dropping slowly into another receptacle.

When this operation was completed, clerk number two would pick up the printed copy and read aloud to clerk number one, who would check what he heard against the original. When there was an error he would stop the reader, make the correction on the teletype, and the reading would resume.

When the clerk-reader had finished, clerk number one would take the numbered corrections from the roll and apply them over the indicated lines (every line was numbered)—a routine splicing operation.

The edited tape was then fed into the encoder, whose internal arrangements changed once a day, pursuant to radio impulses reaching it from Washington.

Clerk number one then took the encoded paper and walked to the heavy transmitting unit to the left of the table. He inserted the roll into a slot at waist level, and a tractor feed chug-chugged the scroll through the mechanism. As this was being done, an identical roll of paper was emerging in the office of the State Department or the CIA, depending on the designated destination.

Meanwhile, clerk number two was feeding the noncoded tape into a shredder. After the encoded roll had been ingested by the transmitter and returned through a second slot below the first, that roll was also fed into the shredder.

The original message was put back into the envelope, resealed, and a button inside the Code Room depressed. The duty officer outside would reply with the signal for that day, a signal divulged to clerk number one only after he had gone into the signal office for duty.

On hearing the proper signal, clerk number one would open, from inside the Code Room, the heavy steel door, and return the sealed envelope to the duty officer, who would take it for filing in the principal vault of the embassy, located in the basement, about which someone had once said that a force "on the heavy side of Hiroshima" would be required to open it forcibly.

There are rote procedures all secret service sweepers have in common. They begin by searching for electronic bugs. Never mind that the four technicians knew that audio bugs were not the suspected problem. They began searching for them even as a physician, called in to attend to a cyst, begins by taking the patient's blood pressure. As a matter of professional deference, the Britishers, following Pulling and Spring about, did not make identical soundings —that is, if the Americans found nothing under the lamp light, the British team would assume there was nothing under the lamp light. Occasionally they might go further, for instance by taking readings on the steel wall with their electrical impulse recorders at shorter intervals than Spring and Pulling. But that kind of thing is done unprovocatively.

Then the major job began, the careful disassembly of the four basic electronic units: the teletype, the encoder, the code-to-print unit, and the transmitter. Were there any extraneous wires there? Any hidden tubes that might be used for transmission? Any suspicious circuitry? On the transmitter: Was there anything, really, to look for, given that it was fed tape already coded, and that that code was assumed to be unbreakable? A Soviet radio disk, catching and recording those transmissions, lacking the code, would be helpless in trying to penetrate those signals. And that code, assuming that by extraordinary enterprise the Soviets succeeded in getting its key, would expire at midnight that night.

So having one by one exonerated the three other instruments, when it came to the transmitter mostly they just sat and stared at it. Conversation gave out. They found themselves leaning against the wall, three of them, while Pulling sat on one of the chairs, writing on his notepad.

They had found nothing.

And, at Leconfield House on Curzon Street where three hours later they completed a similar search of the British installations, they found: nothing.

Rufus received the report fatalistically. At least, under present arrangements, he had a little time. Because, effective two days before, no clandestine messages of substance were being sent from Washington to London. Either to the U.S. Embassy or to Leconfield House. The volume of transactions was not reduced; it was contrived to send classified material of a noncritical kind. Scheduled, in about a week, would be a transmission revealing that Counterintelligence had discovered the identity of a particular KGB agent working with the United Nations and traveling frequently to London. Rufus would time what happened next, and note how long it would be before that agent, whose identity and activity had been detected a year earlier but who had proved of no particular use to the CIA, was recalled to the Soviet Union.

And so Rufus began to conceive an elaborate plan. But, difficult though it would undoubtedly be to execute, the burden was great to expose The Spook. Whatever it was. Whatever he was. Whatever she was. Whatever he-she-it was.

TWELVE

RUFUS'S PLAN called for Blackford's going to Washington. He had informed Blackford that he would serve as Rufus's personal aide in developing the plans for the operation and in coordinating with Anthony Trust and his small but highly trained staff. The evening before the day of his planned departure, Blackford went to Trust's apartment on Baker Street and from there to a neighborhood restaurant Trust spoke about with some enthusiasm.

Still, their spirits were low. The ignominious failure of Operation Tirana continued to fester, and the continuing insecurity of the existing situation was a reminder of their humiliation and of the terrible ends that had resulted from a security failure for which, by definition, they—not the enemy—were guilty. It is a government's duty to provide for its security. Sure, Rufus had a plan, not all the details of which had yet been disclosed. But would even the penetration of the Soviet Embassy yield the secret? Short of holding a dagger up to the throat of

KGB chief Boris Bolgin, neither Anthony Trust nor Blackford Oakes knew what could be done.

And, in the meantime, top secret U.S.-British communications were being transmitted as if by pony express. An urgent communication by President Dwight Eisenhower to Prime Minister Anthony Brogan had either to be telephoned directly over the protected line or else written out and transported physically across the ocean and hand-delivered.

Both official London and official Washington deemed this a singular humiliation, and if Rufus hadn't solemnly decreed that until further notice no reliance was to be placed on conventional electronics, President Eisenhower would have pounded his fist on his desk in the Oval Office and ordered Allen Dulles to reinstitute regular communications via regular channels. He was tempted by one of his advisers who argued that the tragedy of Tirana had to be the result of one of those awful coincidences: a single mole, accumulating the diverse data from here and there, putting them all together, and delivering the package to the KGB. There was, he insisted, no other possible explanation. But Eisenhower agreed to go along with Rufus. For the time being.

Rufus had not specified what his plan was, but it was known that he had something in mind that required patience and a continued irregularity of secret communications between Washington and London.

"We'll do as asked, and see, right?" Anthony Trust sought, during dinner, to put the matter out of their minds as they sat down at the small table, the candle at its center, over the traditional red-checkered tablecloth. There was the faint and all the more appealing smell of wine and herbs and cooking butter, and the genial concern of the maître d'hôtel to leave his clients happy. The braised chicken and petits pois were fine, the claret excellent, the mille-feuilles sensational.

And so they moved on. The residual frustration imposed a certain drag on their mounting spirits so that it took longer than usual to reach overdrive. But they would do so.

When professionally burdened, his old friend Anthony, Blackford knew, tended to turn his mind to stimulations unrelated to the world of getting and spending and the cold war. And, as ever, Blackford was bracingly acquiescent. For one thing it was very much worthwhile just listening to Anthony Trust in his romantic mode, if only for the sake of listening to Anthony Trust in his romantic mode. He was very good at it, and it was heavily contagious.

Anthony was just one year older than Blackford. They had met as the only two American boys at Greyburn College, in 1941: Anthony a shrewd, urbane senior whose precocious social skills had got him named a prefect by the time Blackford Oakes, the irrepressible young Yankee, arrived, causing by his informality something of a sensation, which had culminated in the ironic scene of Blackford being physically held in place by his fellow American while the headmaster applied a savage beating with a birch rod to punish Blackford's insolence. Trust did his formal duty, but then risked his prefectorial standing by acting as an accomplice in Blackford's altogether unauthorized departure from Greyburn.

They had coincided again at Yale, the one (Anthony) a junior, the other a sophomore. In due course Anthony Trust recruited Blackford into service with the CIA.

Anthony Trust was something of a sentimentalist. Unmoved by facile pain, by quotidian vicissitudes; but deeply moved by genuine pain, and positively outraged by sadistic pain. It was, he once confessed to Blackford, primarily for that reason that he devoted himself so completely to the political struggle against communism. "Every time the spirit lags," he told Blackford as they fought their way clear of the inscrutable problem of the Comprehensive Mole, "I pick up a book on a particular shelf in my library. I have another sequestered library shelf: it chronicles the atrocities of the Nazis.

"Do you know of Rolf Hochhuth? He has a play. I've read it. It will hit Broadway one of these days, hit it big, I predict. It's called *The Deputy*, and makes out a case against Pope Pius XII. The thesis is, the Pope didn't do enough to alert the world to the evil of Adolf Hitler. I want to know: How would Rolf Hochhuth (or his followers) treat the same Pope—or the present Prime Minister of England or the President of the United States—if he used the kind of language Hochhuth thought appropriate to use against Hitler, but used it now against Malenkov, successor to Stalin? And, in fact, many of them never even approved of tough language against Stalin." Anthony Trust was gripping his glass.

"Anyway, when my spirits flag, I pick up one of those books. I'll give you just four or five titles —you know them all. *I Speak for the Silent. The Captive Mind. I Chose Freedom. Darkness at Noon.* Tchernavin, Milosz, Kravchenko, Koestler, and twenty-five more. Then I reach out and I pick up *The Diary of Anne Frank*, but I say to myself: 'The people who did that to her are dead or in prison. We managed that! We finally reduced the Thousand-Year Reich to one bunker and an automatic pistol, and Hitler took it from there. The remaining bastards we dithered over at Nuremberg before hanging them (should just have shot 'em, Black, and then hanged them). There is no such thing anymore as a Nazi threat.

But the *other* bastards are doing it all the time. Every year there is another book I add to that shelf." His smile was grave. But then, and this quality in Anthony Trust Blackford cherished, it was gone—flash!—in a moment. Replaced by a smile that Blackford or anyone else could only describe as, well, joyful—lascivious, though that perhaps is a word unfairly freighted against those whose keenest sensual distraction happens to be carnal.

Anthony Trust was at once deeply in love with women and resigned to the knowledge that, in the absence of engaging any one woman in an eternal embrace, they were capable, on a quite casual and, so to speak, disposable basis, of yielding intense pleasure, pleasure he made certain to reciprocate. Anthony had started to talk about the Bag o' Nails, a London "gentlemen's club," here defining a collective of particularly attractive ladies of pleasure. Blackford leaned back and listened to Anthony Trust, who went on as though extemporizing the last, elating act of *South Pacific*.

"They are all very attractive, but Hilda—well, she is quite unique. Let me tell you . . ."

Blackford, of course, listened, without reminding Anthony that if Blackford had perfect recall, he could give back a dozen accounts of unique Hildas in Anthony's life.

But Anthony—dark and slim, and intense

now, his white teeth flashing in a curious way in synchronization with the expressions on his face, at once of awe, of love, of pleasure, of admiration—talked on. Of course, he said, poor Blackford, who had been away all that time in that lonely castle in Germany (Anthony knew better than to protract any reference to Blackford's preceding, heart-rending mission) had never met Hilda, and of course such a meeting must be effected *this very night!* given that no one knew exactly when Blackford would be back in London.

Three hours later they were in the suite Hilda shared with Minerva: two bedrooms, the living room between them dimly lit by lamps covered in only barely diaphanous pink, the walls hung with nineteenth-century prints of lush nineteenth-century fops in rustic setting, the furniture highly varnished, heavy in design, with here and there a touch of silver—an ash tray, a cigarette case, a little flowered vase.

Anthony, at the club, had talked very nearly nonstop, as Hilda had done—sometimes, it seemed, simultaneously. They managed to communicate with each other without any apparent difficulty as, Blackford knew, a single telephone line could mysteriously accommodate simultaneous transmissions from both ends, tapped in concurrently without interference to either of the two parties, who received their messages on their own receivers apparently uninterrupted.

But soon Minerva and Blackford, sitting with their champagne at the table at the Bag o' Nails, were engaged in their own conversation. They quickly and quite sincerely exchanged compliments, managing this without any sense of routine. Minerva was a slight but voluptuously beautiful blond young woman with sprightly green eyes that turned, at least on that night, very quickly from cynical to skeptical to—enraptured. Blackford Oakes, she said to him after a half hour, was the most beautiful man who had ever entered the Bag o' Nails. "Not as beautiful as Tyrone Power," she qualified this in a spirit of intellectual rectitude. "Nobody is as beautiful as Tyrone Power. And do you know, he was here once? And do you know, *that* was the one night I was not here? I was visiting my mother in Sussex. But Hilda was here, and Hilda said—no. She said nothing. Truly. She never spoke about it. She just sighs when you mention Tyrone Power.

"But even though you don't look like him, you are, really, Charles" (neither Blackford nor Anthony ever used their own names except in last wills and testaments, letters to their mothers and to alumni records offices, to which they regularly lied about their professional occupations), "so *beautiful*. Really, I hope soon Hilda will suggest we go home."

Soon Anthony did, and the four of them shared the living room for a few minutes, after which they separated. And in due course, in that charmingly vulgar room with the thick quilt bedcover tossed playfully on the floor, the music (Strauss) (Johann) coming in softly from the automatic record player, the mirror on the ceiling, surrounded by the faded wallpaper with the dozen dreamy-eyed copulators weaving in and around flower trees and vines and waterfalls, the paper exactly framing the mirror ever so lightly tinted, Minerva was giggling as "Charles" expressed his affection for her, though she knew, as he did, that, released from the springs of passion and finding a more appropriate mode of speech, he would speak rather of ardor than affection; but then her giggling ceased, and she groaned out the pleasure they both felt, the appreciation of each other's bodies, an appreciation mature in the knowledge that tomorrow it—they—would be nothing more than last night's memory, last night's voluptuous, memorable memory.

The Pan American flight connection to Washington required of its passengers that they check in one hour early, and Blackford did so, Anthony Trust at his side helping with the bags. He retained in his own briefcase, to hand over to Blackford for delivery in Washington, a sheaf of

139

classified papers. But he would not release the papers—The Rule—until the time came for Blackford to board his flight.

They had a cup of coffee at the airport restaurant and touched conversationally on the morning's headlines, which spoke of the Kremlin's obsessive demand on Western heads of state that they meet in a summit conference. Their idea of a conference was to consider Soviet objections to the scheduled independence of West Germany. Flight 112 was now called and Blackford, taking from Anthony the sealed brown envelope and putting it into his own suitcase, got up. Together they walked out toward the gate.

Blackford passed by the large newsstand and paused to buy a paperback to take with him. As he leaned over the book racks he heard the voice.

It said: *"A pack of Virginia Rounds."*

Blackford froze. That voice. He shot up and turned toward the man handing over the ten-shilling note to the saleswoman. He was looking at a large man with a full beard, a cap over his abundant black hair, dressed in a loden coat and black corduroy pants. Blackford stared at him.

"Henry!" he said.

The man turned abruptly as his change was being dropped into his open hand. His eyes rested only fleetingly on Blackford, then back down to his open hand. He muttered, "You must be mistaken. Good day," and quickly left the newsstand, his pack of Virginia Rounds still on the counter.

Blackford closed his eyes for a second. He looked up. Anthony Trust was at the other end of the magazine rack, idly scrutinizing the display.

Blackford grabbed him by the sleeve and whispered tersely, *"Listen! Mayday mayday mayday! See that man—"* he pointed to the stranger, now halfway across the large terminal. *"Follow him; whatever you do don't lose him.* I may be wrong, but I don't think so." Anthony Trust, trained agent, reacted instinctively, sprinting away without even muttering goodbye.

"This is the last call for Flight 112/Pan American Clipper to Washington D.C., with a stop at Santa Maria in the Azores. All aboard Flight 112 to Washington."

Blackford hesitated. Should he cancel?

He was tempted to dump his briefcase and run at full gallop across the terminal.

Briefcase.

Rufus.

The vital documents.

Stranger. Hallucination? . . . *My* Henry, after all, is dead. I've seen pictures of him dead . . .

He boarded the airplane, took his seat assignment, removed his jacket, sat down, and shut his eyes.

Henry? Henry, the commando leader of Operation Tirana. Henry, who had been first tortured, then shot, the whole of it photographed. Could Blackford have been mistaken?

As he persuaded himself that it was irrational to believe that that was Henry, his mind closed on a certitude: That, it said, *was* Henry. Henry of Camp Cromwell.

He could not stay seated. And so walked to the rear of the airplane and entered the head, merely to pause there and walk back. Five hours to the Azores to refuel. Then seven hours to Washington. At the airport at Santa Maria he would try to get through to Anthony Trust. He did try, but was firmly advised by guards that through-passengers were not allowed into the terminal area where the public telephones were.

It was three in the morning London time when Blackford called in to London from the airport in Washington where the Stratocruiser's passengers passed through Customs and Immigration. He asked Anthony Trust breathlessly:

"Did you trail him?"

"Yeah. He checked in at the Goring Hotel. We've got a surveillance team there watching him. You may be on to something 'cause I had to practically destroy an old lady to get a cab to keep sight of him. Now, pal, would you do me the favor of telling me who it is I practically killed myself and other people to trail? Was it Molotov?"

"No. That was the chief commando of Operation Tirana."

Blackford could hear the pause. Followed by the cluck-cluck.

"You've got to be mistaken. The guy they called Henry? He was executed."

"In that case he's risen again."

Another pause. "You sure, Black?"

"I'm as sure as I am that I am talking to Anthony Trust. Now: Grant the hypothetical possibility that someone has been studying your voice for years, trashed you an hour ago, has been lying in your bed waiting for my phone call, so I'm not really talking to Anthony Trust but to an impostor. Grant it was hard to see the Henry I knew through that forest on his face. But the size was right, the eyes were right, and the voice was *unmistakable*. And he was flustered enough to forget the cigarettes—the Virginia Rounds that Henry smoked at Cromwell. And after that"—Blackford was becoming impatient—"to take off pretty goddamn rapidly."

"I'll say it was rapid. I had to gallop to stay up with him. You headed for Rufus?"

"You bet. Now listen, that guy is the key to

everything. Don't for God's sake let him get away. I'll talk to Rufus. Get him to call London and get out a warrant. Never mind on what grounds. Just tell me, Anthony—*reassure* me—the guys you got out there are good men."

"They're the men we rely on."

"Okay. I'll call you back after I see Rufus."

Blackford dialed Rufus's number. No answer. He closed his eyes in concentration. He needed orderly thought. It was three in the morning, internal clock time.

He dialed another number and got the duty officer at the CIA. He carefully identified himself, giving the requisite signal that communicated that he was on emergency business. He was put through to the Deputy Director, interrupted in a bridge game in Georgetown.

"You don't know me, sir, but I am Blackford Oakes and I just flew in from London on instructions from Rufus. Something is up that's a real emergency. Do you know where Rufus is?"

The Deputy said no, he did not: he knew only that Rufus was back from London. Nor had the particular alarm gone out that requires specified officials to log in with a central clerk where they can be found at any hour. Could the Deputy himself help Oakes?

Blackford thought, and concluded it would be too complicated to brief the Deputy on the need to get a London warrant for arrest that suited the demands of this situation. He would take his chances perching outside Rufus's apartment.

He signed off and told the taxi driver to take him to the nearest rent-a-car. In a few minutes he was driving a Ford sedan. Again he telephoned Rufus; again there was no answer. He drove to Lee Street, the quiet street in Alexandria where he and not many others knew that Rufus dwelled. He walked into the ground floor and placed a folded note in the slot of Rufus's mailbox. It read simply: "I am waiting for you in a Ford sedan across the street—Blackford." The alternative was to confront every figure that came in from the dark into the apartment house, to see if he was Rufus.

It was a long and agonizing wait. But shortly before midnight, as Blackford was dozing, there was a rap on the windshield. Rufus.

They drove together to the CIA building at E Street. It would be, in London, a few minutes after five in the morning. The objective, Rufus had said, would be to have the police at the hotel by seven, it being unlikely that "Henry" would be leaving his room before then.

Rufus did not hesitate to wake the director, who approved Rufus's plan. He called London and roused the ambassador. Joseph Abercrombie Little did not like to be seen merely as a link in a chain that led from somewhere he did not know to somewhere else he did not know, and began to make this point to Rufus until Rufus cut him short by telling him that the Director of the CIA desired the arrest to take place by seven in the morning, namely one hour and forty-five minutes from now.

The ambassador, taking down the details, said he would call Rufus back.

In a half hour he did so.

He had roused Sir Eugene Attwood and relayed the request. Sir Eugene had called back fifteen minutes later to say that the relevant judge and magistrates "and God knows who" were being mobilized, that his legal aide was right now drawing up papers alleging a violation of the Official Secrets Act and other national security violations, and that they knew a judge who in the past had proved amenable to the need for extraordinary judicial exertions designed to expedite the work of MI5—Ambassador Little was beginning to enjoy all this, and almost hung up when suddenly he remembered the one datum missing: He had not been told who it was who was supposed to be arrested, and where he was to be found.

Rufus suddenly recalled that Blackford had not given him that meticulous information. He turned to him, hand over the receiver: "Where is Henry staying, and what name is he using? Do you have his room number?"

Blackford replied. "He's at the Goring Hotel. But damn, I don't have the name he's using. We'll have to get that from Trust."

"Call Trust on that telephone"—Rufus pointed. "I'll keep the ambassador on the line."

It took the operator several minutes to get through to London. But Anthony Trust answered the phone.

"Anthony. Black. What name is Henry registered under, and do you have his room number?"

"Hang on a minute." Trust was obviously going for his notepad. "It's . . . Desmond Daugherty, and the room number is 411. Everything going all right?" Before answering him, Blackford gave the information to Rufus.

"Yep. We hope to have the police there with a warrant by seven."

"That's less than an hour off."

"We don't fool around."

"Well then, what do you call what you did with Minerva last night?"

"Oh shut up, Trust. Where will you be when the bust happens?"

Anthony hesitated. And then, "Makes sense, I think, to go to James Street, since we're not permitted to use the wires at the office."

"Roger. I'll call you there."

Rufus was off the telephone. "There is nothing we can do now until London calls us."

"Rufus," Blackford said, "is that picture album where you can lay your hands on it?"

Rufus nodded, rang the duty officer, and together they descended to the vault. Rufus was back in ten minutes. He pointed to a chest-high table above which hung a flexible light. From a drawer he brought out a large magnifying glass.

They turned the pages quickly, past the gibbet scenes to the picture of Henry sitting strapped on the chair, holding up the Albanian newspaper. Rufus examined carefully the bruises on the right side of Henry's face.

"Could be real, could be faked. But the photograph doesn't reveal facial swelling. Perhaps a pathologist could tell the difference." He flicked quickly over to the next page. It showed Henry bent over, the bullet piercing first the newspaper and then, apparently, the victim's forehead.

Once more Rufus examined the photograph in detail.

He shook his head. "Impossible to say whether there is actual identation, as when a bullet passes through. Here, Blackford, you have a look."

"There's something protruding, I can see, from the forehead. But that could be anything. Inked putty. A bit of cereal. Just can't tell."

The telephone rang. Rufus picked it up. Blackford looked at his watch. It would be 7:15 in London.

Rufus listened. "Yes," he said. "Yes." His eyes narrowed. "Thank you, Mr. Ambassador. We'll be back in touch." He put down the telephone. And paused before addressing Blackford:

"The police knocked, then entered the room with a passkey. It was empty. An overnight bag was left behind. There was no identifying material anywhere. They are taking everything personal to the laboratory for examination and will report further in a few hours."

Blackford Oakes, still standing over the photograph table, gritted his teeth. He felt rising in him a sensation that was absolutely novel: A total personal revulsion against another human being he had only a few weeks ago thought his friend and brother-in-arms.

"Rufus"—he spoke softly—"let me go back. I want to go after Henry myself."

Rufus paused, then nodded.

At nine in the morning Blackford was aboard Pan American's Flight 823, Washington-London. They didn't need to schedule a stop in the Azores; the wind was with them.

THIRTEEN

THE LARGE STUCCOED study on the second floor of the safe house at James Street became Blackford Oakes's laboratory. He felt after two weeks as he assumed that biographers begin to feel. Granted the special problems of biographers who deal with subjects who are dead. On the other hand, biographers' dead subjects aren't usually inconspicuous. He wondered idly how many lives of Julius Caesar had been written . . . Dead a couple of thousand years, yes. But more of the people who surrounded Julius Caesar thought to record his words and deeds, and reactions to them, than had devoted themselves to recording the thoughts and deeds of:

Bertram Oliver Heath.

Yes, that was the full name by which "Henry" had been baptized. Imagine baptizing such a monster, he permitted himself to think, immediately reproaching himself for sacrilege. It had been right to baptize Stalin. And Hitler. Perhaps, baptized, there would be less theological red tape in dropping them into the inferno.

The study, under Blackford's supervision, was well organized; the project—so to speak, the reification of Henry—well under way.

He was born in Sussex, the second of three children and the only boy. His father, Daniel Oliver Heath, a qualified chemist, owned and operated an apothecary at Seaford. He was still alive, though not so his wife, who had died in a car accident while driving to a celebration on V-E Day.

Daniel Heath, on being approached to talk about his son, resolutely refused to do so. "I am not in touch with Bertram, and not inclined to talk about his youth." Inquiries in the neighborhood revealed that there had been an estrangement many years ago, toward the end of Bertram Heath's career in Cambridge. The older sister, Patricia, had married an American bomber pilot and gone to Los Angeles to live. Interviewed there, she said that she had maintained perfunctory touch with her brother— "Christmas cards, that kind of thing"—that, really, she hadn't known him very well, inasmuch as he had gone to Winchester at age nine and "was only home for the hols."

By the time he matriculated at Cambridge, Patricia Heath had taken a job as a secretary in London. It was there, during the war, that she met her pilot, with whom she eloped, which marriage made it possible to follow him abruptly to America when he was wounded over the skies of France. Her sudden departure from London had simply ended her relationship with her brother Bert, "except for, you know, I do send him a birthday card and as I say a Christmas card, and every now and then he sends me one." But she gave the matter serious thought, anxious to help the interviewer. He was from a law firm, the caller had told her, and was attempting to expedite a small bequest made on behalf of her brother, whom they had not been able to locate. "He always gives the same mailing address: P.O. Box 378, Knightsbridge, London SW3. You know, Bert moves about a good deal. I think he maintained his ties to the commandos even after the war. But I have never had any of my cards returned, so I am certain that is the right address. Do let me know where you find him, and give him my love and tell him to write."

Bert Heath's younger sister Priscilla was unmarried and helped her father run the shop. She was ten years younger than Bert. Approached during her father's lunch hour, she wanted to know, "Why are you being so persistent? Is he in trouble? He never comes here, you know. He and my father don't get on. And, really, I never knew him." She was cooperative, however, and volunteered to look in her mother's family album to see if there was anything there that might help the insurance company looking for Bert to find him, to answer questions about the car that had been stolen from him some time ago.

The album contained report cards from his little grammar school (he had done very well in all his subjects), a letter from the headmistress advising his parents that young Bert was very intelligent but also very headstrong, and a little bit of a bully with the younger boys.

There were, then, the report cards from Winchester School. Once again he had excelled in his schoolwork, but there were complaints— again, about bullying. And there was a letter from the headmaster reporting that he had had to punish Bert for going without permission to a local pub where he was detected, having first lied about his age. In addition to the caning administered, the headmaster reported, Bert Heath was put on probation for ninety days. The final entry pertaining to Bert in the album was the letter from the Admissions Office of Trinity College accepting his application for entrance in the fall of 1936. Opposite it was a picture taken on the day of his graduation from Winchester. Slim, serious, a prominent jaw, a trace of haughtiness in the carriage of his head.

George Callard, the retired headmaster of Winchester, invited in to tea the pleasant young solicitor who had asked if he might interview him to ask a few questions on behalf of a client to whom Bertram Heath had applied for employment. Dr. Callard, silver-haired, rotund, and genial, served the tea and reminisced. Certainly he remembered Heath, remembered him very well; he had after all been nine years at Winchester. A very gifted scholar and a first-rate soccer player; indeed, he had been the captain of the soccer team. "In fact, you will find—I think my memory is correct on the point—that he went on to be captain of the team at Cambridge."

The retired headmaster then put down his teacup and leaned forward, lowering his voice slightly. "Is this entirely confidential?" he asked.

"Absolutely," the young solicitor assured him, discreetly fingering the little wire recording machine in his pocket to make certain it was running. "No one except my client will ever know of our conversation."

"Well," Mr. Callard said, "I should tell you that six weeks before graduation, Heath got into trouble. He was a prefect, you know—at Winchester it is very nearly inevitable that you become a prefect, if you become the captain of the cricket team or the rugby or soccer team—something of a tradition. Even so, I considered intervening to prevent his election (the boys elect their own prefects at the end of the fifth-form year). This is so because twice, when he was a fourth- and then a fifth-former, I received complaints that he had bullied some of the younger boys. At Winchester, complaints of that nature get referred to the prefects, and I saw to it that this was done, and I would assume that they administered a beating. But when at the end of that year he was himself elected a prefect, recalling those complaints I viewed his election with some misgiving.

"And," Mr. Callard lit his pipe, "unfortunately my fears were realized. In the Michaelmas term —it was just before Christmas, I believe—I had a most irate telephone call from the father of one of the boys, himself a Wykehamist, who told me that his son, a third-former, had been savagely beaten by a prefect named Heath. I investigated, and indeed the prefect was Bertram Heath, and the beating was indeed inordinate— we ordered the school doctor to investigate, and I give you his judgment of it.

"In any event, I immediately relieved Heath of his authority as a prefect. There was some sentiment among the faculty that the incident should be reported to the admissions department at Cambridge—Heath had just then been accepted at Trinity—but I thought it better simply to reprimand Heath, which I did. Most severely." George Callard nodded his gray head knowingly.

"And I am certain I did the right thing. He had a quite brilliant career at Cambridge, studying physics, or science of some sort. And then he went off to war. But then everybody did, didn't they? You would perhaps have been too young." George Callard smiled the smile that says well now, we're glad that subject is over, are we not?

At Cambridge three tutors were found who remembered him well. But they all said much the same thing that Harry Bacchus said, who had taught chemistry to the class in which Heath had distinguished himself. "There was only one figure at Trinity who mattered for Bertram Heath, and that was Alistair Fleetwood. He spent all his time with Fleetwood. To be sure, they were very nearly of the same age—Fleetwood was preposterously precocious, you must know. Anyway, Heath worshipped him. And Fleetwood was very generous with his time, giving him a great deal of individual coaching notwithstanding that it was all very time-consuming and that Fleetwood was then at work on one of his important research projects. Don't waste your time with me, or anyone else at Cambridge. Go see Alistair Fleetwood. Oh yes—'Sir' Alistair Fleetwood it is now, of course."

But Fleetwood had declined to be interviewed. His secretary had said over the telephone, "Sir Alistair very much regrets, but he simply does not have the time to discuss his former students. You must know that they add up to perhaps over one thousand. No. No. No, sir, it does not matter in the least whether it was a particular student with whom Sir Alistair spent a great deal of time. He has spent a great deal of time with a great many students. Sir Alistair has to answer categorically: He will not give interviews in the matter. Thank you very much," and she hung up.

A letter addressed to Sir Alistair Fleetwood by a well-known firm of London solicitors divulged that an American foundation was considering an application for a grant by a physicist who had listed Bertram Heath as a possible collaborator. The foundation required evaluations of all prospective collaborators by their former tutors, which evaluations had to be given personally to the solicitor, and might he therefore schedule an appointment with Sir Alistair? The request was answered by a printed postcard which read: "Sir Alistair Fleetwood regrets that his studies make it impossible to grant your request."

Two technicians who had worked at Bletchley Park during 1940 and 1941 remembered Bertram Heath. One said only that Heath's dependence on Fleetwood was manifest, and that for all intents and purposes Heath had been Fleetwood's apprentice. The second added that

Heath seemed very bored with the work at hand, that he tended to arrive late for work in the morning, and that he had acquired a reputation for being something of a dissolute, patronizing the local bars, often with a girl. "Arse-chaser, he was," a laboratory technician said. "But remember, he was only twenty-two, twenty-three. Went off to the commandos, you know. Don't know what they did to him. Or he did to them. Not a very genial gentleman. When he had a hangover he dealt with us as if we had force-fed the alcohol into him the night before. Never bothered to say much, except the absolutely required 'Good morning,' 'Good evening.' Ate either with Fleetwood or alone. You have, of course, seen Fleetwood?" The visitor said it was down on his list to talk with Sir Alistair.

The War Documents Office revealed that Bertram Heath had served with the Eighth Army in North Africa, and that he had taken part in the invasion of Sicily. There he had been wounded by shrapnel. The medical report revealed that six pieces of metal had been removed from his body, leaving scars, including a four-centimeter horizontal scar just below the hairline at the back of his neck. By the time he recovered, the war was going into its final phases and he was sent to a training camp for commandos. The reports there from his superior officers gave him excellent grades as an instructor, but promotion to major was denied on the grounds that "Captain Heath is given to occasional acts of severity so extreme as to damage the morale of the trainees. He has three times been reprimanded on this account, and on one occasion threatened with a summary court-martial." Bertram Oliver Heath was discharged from the army on September 10, 1945.

General Rory Islington had been put in charge of Operation Tirana by its architects. He was a veteran of skeptical turn of mind and accordingly received the young officer cautiously. The young man appeared in naval uniform, presented his papers, and said that he had been assigned by MI5 to write for the archives a highly classified study of the background of the commando team sent to Albania, perhaps to be published "a generation or so down the line." And the first question of course had to do with the leader, who had been known as "Henry."

The general personally examined the papers of the inquiring MI5 historian and picked up the telephone to verify from Sir Eugene Attwood himself that he was permitted to give out details on this highly sensitive mission. Satisfied, he leaned his long, heavy frame back on the armchair and said, "What exactly did you want to know about Heath?"

Well, the young historian said, "What did he do after he left the British Army?"

"We have incomplete records on that. But we used him three times, on three important missions, all of them successful: one in Yugoslavia, one in Vietnam in cooperation with the French, another in Morocco. Always we contacted him through his box number in London. He was a brave and tough officer. Two of the operations I mention involved hand-to-hand engagements, in both of which he was wounded, his antagonists killed. His men respected him and feared him—he executed one man, on the North African mission, when he refused during a fire fight to carry out orders. We needed for Tirana someone highly intelligent, which Heath was: He was trained in physics at Cambridge before the war. Someone who had had parachute training: Heath taught parachute work toward the end of the war. And someone who kept his mouth shut, and there had never been any security problems there. Oh, he would go out drinking and wenching every now and then, but there was never anything more. To this day, as far as we have been able to determine, the Russians know nothing about the three missions Heath was involved with."

The MI5 clerk wanted to know if, in the files, there was any record of any address other than the post office address?

General Islington stood and went to a six-foot-long strongbox. He opened it and pulled out a file. He returned to his chair and opened it on his lap. "Before that first mission—that was 1948 —we had him complete a form. After the question: 'Where have you lived during the past three years?' he wrote down, 'Mostly in London. I stay with my fiancée in Old Windsor when she is in residence (she is an airline stewardess). I have frequented many hotels in London, and have traveled several times to the continent.'"

"That is all that's there?"

"Yes. Ah. There are notes on the margin, evidently by the security checker. On the margin is written, 'Questioned, Captain Heath gave (reluctantly) the identity of his fiancée. She is Renira Williams, employed by BOAC. Check with Miss Williams confirms relationship with Heath.'

"There," said General Islington, evidently pleased with himself. "Not too much to go on. You will not, of course, need to know the nature of the other missions, but at least you can fill out a memorial paragraph or two, I should think?"

Tracing Renira Williams had been time-consuming, but she was found to be living in a small house in Old Windsor, near her family home, and working as the matron at a Jesuit boys' preparatory school, St. John's, affiliated with Beaumont College, the public school to which the younger boys mostly went when they reached the age of thirteen or fourteen.

The Reverend John Paine, the headmaster, received the solicitor who told him he needed help in checking on the credentials of an applicant for a confidential position, and that the name of Miss Williams had been given as a reference, and might he interview her?

The short, stocky priest said of course he would have no objection to this, so long as Miss Williams had no objection.

But first, the visitor asked, a question or two about Miss Williams. His records showed that she had been an airline stewardess?

"That is correct. But before she went with BOAC she had spent a year at a nursing school, so she is qualified to run our little infirmary. If a boy is seriously ill the doctor comes over."

Did Miss Williams spend nights at St. John's?

"Most of the time. Her family lives nearby and occasionally she will leave after the boys are gone to bed and will be back by breakfast time in the morning. She has, of course, a day off every week." The priest then rose, shook hands with the solicitor, and said he would send in the matron.

A few minutes later, Renira Williams walked in.

She was a handsome woman, erect and heavy-set. Dressed in a nurse's stiff white uniform, she wore a small cap on her rich brown hair. A tiny red cross was sewn above the trim little pocket above her left breast. She greeted Blackford Oakes with poise and sat down.

"Father Paine says you have some questions you wish to put to me? What about?"

"About Bertram Heath."

"Oh," she said guardedly. "What about him?"

"He has applied for a position, and the client of our legal firm" —Blackford extended a card identifying himself as "George Benton," an associate of "Whitelock & Entwhistle," solicitors, at Gray's Inn Road, London— "has asked us to— well, to make the normal investigation."

"How did you get my name?"

Blackford gave the same story he had given to the headmaster. "Why, Mr. Heath evidently gave your name as a reference."

"He did not. You are lying to me."

Blackford managed to look surprised as he reached up and pulled distractedly on his two-week-old beard. "Why, Miss Williams, I am most surprised at this. I have simply assumed that he gave your name, because your name appears on the list of the four or five people I have been instructed to consult. It could be, I suppose, that one of the other references gave your name; it would be in the file I have here." Absentmindedly, he looked into the little folder.

"Look," Renira Williams said. "Let me be direct. Is your firm willing to pay for information?"

Blackford seized the moment. The tone of his voice changed. "Yes," he said. "My firm is willing to pay for information."

"In that case, meet me at the Nell Gwynne Tavern at Windsor at nine-thirty."

"I shall be there. Thank you."

Blackford walked out the main door, down the steps to his car. It was very nearly dark. He opened the door, and thereby caused a bucket of water perched on the car roof and tied to the door handle to tumble, dousing him with its contents. He heard the squeals and giggles of boys from behind the brick wall running to the side of the school building. He thought briefly of giving chase, instead wiped the water from his face with the sleeve of his jacket and called out, "Nice aiming, boys." He drove off.

FOURTEEN

ALISTAIR FLEETWOOD returned to his
apartments late after the dinner in honor of Albert Einstein. Fleetwood had been designated
to give the first toast, and he was pleased, when
he rose to speak, by the wall-to-wall murmur of
appreciation, not unmixed with awe. He had
spoken of Einstein's humbling of the universe, a
universe which had succeeded over so many
centuries in outwitting the mind of man—until
it came upon the mind of Albert Einstein.

A lot of that kind of thing, Sir Alistair chuckled
internally, the sort of grandiloquent nothing-
ness that works so well with people who are
expecting profundity, and will find it, never
mind the merit of the thought. (Einstein, Sir
Alistair liked to think, hit on a very bright idea in
his early twenties, and dithered for most of the
rest of his life, but all that dither was interpreted
as profundity, and Sir Alistair was willing to go
along with the game, indeed thought it professionally self-enhancing to do so.) But Fleetwood
had gone out of his way to indite a few sentences

the meaning of which he knew would be understood by not more than a dozen of the hundred guests there: a nice, recondite cadenza on the subject of the choreography of wavelengths, which exercise would there and then reemphasize him as a part of that elect fraternity that could speak to Einstein in his own special language. After that, he turned his esoterica into a single metaphor that suggested the preeminent concern all civilized persons must have for peace, and—Sir Alistair Fleetwood smiled just a bit as he turned the key of his door—the crowd had, well, demonstrated the rare satisfaction they had taken from hearing such . . . poetry, from their very own Nobel laureate.

Inside, he took off his black tie and jacket and laid them down on the armchair in his living room for Jackson, his manservant, to pick up in the morning, press, and hang up. He went into his large, book-lined study, in one corner of which he kept his formidable collection of radios. (He boasted to his friends that he had not paid an overseas long-distance telephone bill in years, so proficient was he with the use of ham radios. "If I wish to speak to Paris, God save me, I simply ask a fellow ham operator in the area kindly to 'patch me in' to the desired number, to introduce the vocabulary of the fraternity!") He went to the little wire recorder he had preset to tune into Radio Moscow at nine. This was, after all, a Monday, Alice Goodyear Corbett's day of the week. He wound the wire back, flicked on the switch, and continued undressing as he listened to what had come in on the 7.150 MHz frequency. It began as always with the top of the news:

"Soviet authorities today delivered identical notes to Great Britain, France, and the United States, proposing a Big Four summit conference to take place in August or September in order to pave the way for the European Security Meeting already suggested by Soviet authorities to the three nations on July 24." The announcer continued for five minutes, mostly on this development as yet another indication of the dogged priority attached by the Soviet Union to a peaceful world.

Then came the gravelly voice of the woman with the personal announcements, mostly devoted to an account of awards given to workers who had distinguished themselves in one way or another. "Nikita Kholkov" had received an award: which meant that at eight the following morning Fleetwood must tune in on MHz 3.008. He yawned, but had no need to set his alarm. He always woke early, and tomorrow morning he would need to begin to work on the Rede lectures he was to deliver in October.

The following morning, across an unusual amount of static, he tuned in on the humdrum voice giving the humdrum messages. He singled out the one intended for him, along with the code number. It was "eleven." That meant: go to Stockholm. The number was repeated three times: "Kholkov eleven eleven eleven."

The repetition—eleven, three times—meant that the need was very pressing.

He turned to his desk and looked at his calendar. It was relatively uncrowded for the three weeks remaining in August, before the beginning of the next term—it would be easy enough to put off the two or three casual engagements he had for lunch and dinner. And going off to Stockholm never presented any ambient curiosity. His academic contacts were kept lively. There was always work to do in Stockholm.

But mostly he had to look forward, in Stockholm, to Alice Goodyear Corbett. To think of it! Almost twenty years since, as an eighteen-year-old, he had met her. And, even now, when he was with her he felt biologically eighteen years old, and otherwise something like a god, which is how Alice treated him, assuming there were any such things as gods. It was as basic as that she truly worshipped him, and in her hands he found his own natural self-esteem wonderfully warmed. No one could speak quite as Alice spoke of Alistair's singularity. Of his towering intellect. Of his contributions to human knowledge and to the advancement of social idealism.

And—of his personal irresistibility. His manly body, his extraordinary eyes, his . . . He forced himself to stop, else he'd have needed to reenter the shower.

By ten his travel arrangements were made. He used his ham radio to telephone a colleague in Stockholm who passed along the word to the right quarter about his impending arrival.

Alistair Fleetwood spent the afternoon of the following day in the laboratory of the University of Stockholm, where he was a frequent visitor. He surveyed the logs kept by two graduate students studying the metamorphosis of radio wave patterns in space, made a few comments in a notebook, spoke over the telephone with a fellow astrophysicist. Two of his colleagues invited him to dine, but Fleetwood pleaded fatigue, told them that night he would eat in his room, retire early, and be the life of the party with them the following night.

He reached his room at six, called room service, and ordered smoked salmon, roast beef (Alice loved roast beef, which was hard to get in Moscow). A bottle of red and a bottle of white wine, coffee ice cream, and aquavit—for two. "Serve me at eight," he added. "At eight exactly." He put down the telephone and went into the bathroom to shower.

He did this, and then brought from his travel

bag the cologne, picked up his dressing gown and looked at himself in the mirror, both with his dressing gown on and with it off. He was pleased by both sights, even acknowledging that he was tucking in his stomach just a very little bit. But he weighed only 180 pounds, which was not heavy for someone nearly six feet tall, and he wondered whether anywhere in the world a Nobel laureate looked quite as—well, noble was not such a bad word for it, though Alistair Fleetwood hated puns. He felt mounting anxiety in his loins, and for a fleeting instant, but not for more than an instant, he wondered whether Alice would let him down. Surely she had got word of the time of his arrival? And she always took such pride in the promptness of her own coordinated arrivals when he answered her frequent biddings to come to Stockholm. He took the bottle of sherry he had bought at the airport, opened it, and at that moment heard the knock.

She came dressed in a white blouse and flared orange skirt, her dark hair in braids around the back of her head, her ample bosom alight with excitement reflected in her eyes and with a smile on glistening lips. They kissed passionately. "Oh my darling Alistair, my handsome, brainy Alistair, the little boy I took all over the Soviet Union . . . Just think that only a very few years ago you were a student, and now—well, now you are quite simply the most exciting, and the most handsome, young physicist in the world. Everybody knows that. What they don't know is that you are also the greatest lover in—in—"

"The spy world?" Alistair Fleetwood proffered, laughing. And then, "Hurry, hurry, dear Alice, don't keep me waiting now. It has been two months."

A separation of two months was for Alice as heavy a privation as it was for Alistair. Since that summer before the war, she had come to think of him as something of a flower she was herself responsible for nurturing. She had presided over his formal initiation into manhood. She had enlisted him in the great struggle for the world. And she had found herself in the company of a man who year by year, month by month, almost day by day, suggested the towering limits to which one human being could go. Her little eighteen-year-old, whom she had taken from museum to museum, now a Nobel Prize winner! Now the instrument of the most formidable intelligence breakthrough in history!

She went happily into the bathroom. He drew down the shades in the bedroom and moments later was waiting for her in bed. She came to him, and he wondered whether it was possible that she could have added to her inventory of knowledge on how to pleasure him. She was resourceful, and adamant, and adoring; and she whispered, as they locked together, her devotion to him, to his great genius, to the great debt the world owed to him; and he knew bliss, unaware whether what he heard in his ears or what he experienced in his loins gave him the greater pleasure. Soon, he moaned. And she fell silent, her lovely, loosened head of hair on his chest.

Fleetwood looked at her and reflected that she was a very special vessel of delight. She managed a fluent combination of talents, he thought. She knew how to appeal to his mind, by saying things he liked to hear—liked to hear them because after all they were true: He was a scientist, and he knew as a scientific fact that he was abnormally good-looking, and very probably a genius. And then she had a true appreciation of his body. The combination of skills she used, with her hands, her lips, her breasts, were perfect orchestrations of a tribute to his remarkable body. Yes, Alice Goodyear Corbett was really quite remarkable, a refreshing contrast to the perfumed mini-delights he satisfied himself with in London. And then, behind it all, they had the spiritual bond in common, that great and exciting struggle in which they had joined against Western hypocrisy.

It was very nearly too much, Sir Alistair thought contentedly as he reached over and turned on the bed light. It was twenty minutes before eight.

"I have ordered dinner for the usual time. A dinner fit for a queen. Fit for you, my dear Alice. My dear Alice Goodyear Corbett. I am glad that I do not remember the name of that Russian yokel you are married to."

"Ah, my darling. That is, really, a professional relationship. Not to be mentioned in the same breath with yours and mine."

When the doorbell rang, she rose and went into the bathroom.

Fleetwood let the waiter into the large living room adjacent to the bedroom. After the dinner, he poured them each an aquavit and then said, "All right now, Alice Goodyear Corbett. What is going on?"

She was grave now, as she began.

Although she had been in the company of the head of the KGB a total of four times, starting when Alistair Fleetwood had confided to her what he thought he could accomplish, she was always terribly nervous in his presence. And when, three days ago, she had been instructed to go to him at midnight, she found herself wondering whether he might actually have in mind something—personal. The idea of anything personal with Lavrenti Pavlovich Beria did not appeal to her, "not one little bit, Alistair."

But just in case, acknowledging the realities—

that if he was determined to take her, she could hardly resist the head of the KGB—she went to him after taking a hot shower, using some perfume, and taking precautions.

"I mean you can never absolutely tell. But on my way to the Kremlin I reminded myself that he likes routinely to keep very late hours. Between you and me," she said to Alistair, "it is quite widely thought that he does this because Stalin always did it, and of course there are those who believe—I would not mention this to anyone but you, my darling—that he would not mind stepping into Stalin's shoes, in case, for instance, Malenkov failed, or whatever. Anyway, I was told to be there at midnight, I got there at eleven-thirty, and he called for me at one-fifteen!"

"And then?" Alistair Fleetwood asked, anxiety audible in his voice.

"And then he came quite quickly to the point."

"Which is?"

"Well, Lavrenti Pavlovich says that an agent of his in whom he has supreme trust has told him there are reasons to believe that counterrevolutionary activity is being conducted by a highly placed Soviet official. But someone so highly placed—he did not, of course, disclose the name —that the KGB cannot proceed against him as it would against ordinary suspects. Nothing like tapping his telephone or surveying his mail, that kind of thing. Apparently this official gets most of his communications right through the Kremlin coding machine. And it is an urgent matter of state security to detect him in this pursuit. Lavrenti Pavlovich told me"—Alice's eyes were wide open, her grave face very grave, her voice now lowered so that Alistair had to strain to hear her—"told me that this official could be a mortal enemy of the Soviet State."

"Mortal enemy? How can there be a mortal enemy, dear Alice? There is no such thing as a 'mortal' enemy of history. It is history that is working on our side. There can be *setbacks*—of course. But nothing *fatal*. Nothing *mortal*."

"Well that was the word he used—*smertel'nyi*, which is the Russian for 'mortal,' 'fatal'—"

Fleetwood interrupted her. "Dear Alice, do you not suppose I now know why I have been summoned?"

"Of course, dear Alistair. And the question is, can you supply a Zirca for Lavrenti Pavlovich?"

Fleetwood sighed. "My darling, it is most awfully intricate. You know that I had to put it together myself. I must have spent—oh, two hundred hours on it. The parts alone need to be hand-made. The testing, the refining, the fine-tuning . . ."

"He said to tell you that the entire resources of the Soviet State are at your disposal."

"The entire resources of the Soviet State wouldn't save me five minutes' work." Alistair Fleetwood seldom passed by opportunities to acknowledge the singularity of his achievements. Normally in the course of drawing attention to himself, he would not disparage the Soviet Union, but the scientist in him had just now been provoked. "Those chaps—" he said heatedly, "Tamm, Sakharov, Cherenkov, Frank—have become very skilled in manufacturing hydrogen bombs, and I am aware that they are working on a missile, and perhaps one day, not far away, a satellite. But they are heavily dependent on Western scientists, people like me—well, there aren't, exactly, 'people' like me, except Einstein, Teller, Oppenheimer maybe. Yes, people like us. But you know, on the whole, Soviet scientists have not yet learned how to make, well, shredded wheat. Help *me* with a Zirca? Help Michelangelo paint a ceiling?"

"Oh darling, we rely on you so heavily. But I must tell you that Lavrenti Pavlovich stressed that there is nothing more important than this mission. Your contribution could be critical, he said. I will avoid using the word you say is anti-Marxist, but suppose that he is correct, and that this counterrevolutionary official could deal us a devastating blow." Alice Goodyear Corbett was becoming fiery in her delivery. Alistair Fleetwood remembered how, twenty years ago, lecturing to the young Cambridge socialists, she had spoken of Leon Trotsky. "You will do it, won't you, Alistair?"

"There is an obvious alternative, Alice. Quite obvious."

"What do you mean?"

"Use the one that is already made."

She drew a deep breath. "I have to admit, I had not thought of that."

"Well, you should think of that. Especially since as we both know, we are not even acting on the information we are currently getting."

"That doesn't mean it isn't valuable."

They spoke, probed; and left it that she would return and make the counterproposal.

"But what if Lavrenti Pavlovich says he can't spare the existing model?"

Alistair Fleetwood sighed. "I suppose I would need to reorder my schedule for the next month or two."

Alice Goodyear Corbett embraced him.

"But understand, you are seriously to raise with him the alternative."

"I promise."

"Do you promise to make me go to sleep tonight blissfully?" The Nobel laureate adopted the manner of a ten-year-old boy asking for a lollipop.

Alice Goodyear Corbett led him by the hand to the bedroom.

FIFTEEN

THE PRIME MINISTER sat stiffly in the back of the Rolls-Royce. His Foreign Minister was seated next to him. They drove through St. James's Park toward the Palace. He made an idle observation about the weather (it was sunny and warm, and Dahl Breckenridge observed that it was sunny and warm) concerning which the P. M. took no notice. Anthony Brogan knew that the session with Queen Caroline would probably be the most painful of any of the weekly meetings since he became Prime Minister. He knew, moreover, that the Queen did not welcome third parties at their meetings. Even so, his bringing Breckenridge along was bound to ease his burden, which was why, through the Queen's aide, he had solicited her agreement, perfunctorily granted, on the constitution of this particular meeting. There were moments with the Queen when it was very nearly impossible for the P. M. to say *anything*. Breckenridge was a phlegmatic type and was sure, when heavy weather came, to calm things down in his own unexcited, unexcitable way.

The Prime Minister's car advanced through the Main Gate, as usual. The inspector poked his head at the window, saluted, and waved the car on into the inner courtyard.

They emerged, the steward opened the King's door, and they moved into the antechamber. The Queen's equerry bowed slightly, said good morning, and led the two top officials of the government up the staircase to the Queen's Audience Room. While they walked, Dahl Breckenridge said something complimentary about the Palace decorations. Once again the Prime Minister did not comment, so they continued the balance of the way to the Queen's Audience Room in silence.

Queen Caroline rose as they were ushered in. She was wearing a deep-blue long-sleeved dress and a light pigskin belt. Her familiar pearls caught the sunshine coming in from the window facing the courtyard. With her left hand she held her poodle, Furioso; with her right, she shook hands with her ministers, then motioned them to sit down in the two leather-bound armchairs. She sat opposite them in the larger chair, putting her dog down on the empty seat.

She ignored her Foreign Minister. "I suppose, Prime Minister, that you will remark on the excellence of the weather? On the grounds that otherwise I might not have noticed it?"

"Well, ma'am," the Prime Minister made an earnest effort at geniality, "it would be positively—*ungrateful*—not to mention such weather, wouldn't you agree?"

It was immediately obvious that carefree remarks about the weather were not being received this day at the court of Queen Caroline. She looked vaguely out the window, stroking her dog. "Interesting formulation, that. If I say that I *do* agree—that it would be ungrateful not to mention the weather—then I am acquiescing in an implicit agenda. Am I correct? One begins by saying good morning. One moves next to the question of weather. That is convention. Conventions are necessary, I agree. But to invest in conventions an extra meaning, as you have just now done, Prime Minister, by suggesting that to do otherwise than to express one's gratitude for such weather is disdainful . . . ?"

She turned and stared at him, and then smiled, picking up the dog and massaging his arched head. "Disdainful toward the God who willed us this good weather? It is always appropriate to express our gratitude to Him. But since it is unlikely that He was the efficient cause of today's weather, then we are being grateful to what? To a chance concatenation of elements over which we have no control, and which are in any case insensible to any gesture of approval or disapproval from us."

The disconcerting thing about Queen Caroline when she went on one of these jags, the Prime Minister ruminated, was that she managed it all without malice. She was amusing herself, working her resourceful mind, draining the meeting of the kind of routinization which so many of her predecessors (he had gathered) had invested it with. There was no alternative than to wait it out; and it was dangerous, very, very dangerous, to let the mind wander: she demanded exact attention to what she was saying . . .

"On the other hand, if I *disagreed* with you, you would harbor in your mind—don't contradict me now, Prime Minister—you would harbor in your mind the suspicion that your sovereign is simply insensible to the episodic niceties of nature. That would undermine me in your eyes. Obviously I would not wish to be a party to any attrition in my own reputation with my own Prime Minister, now would I? Would you?"

Anthony Brogan sighed. But that sigh was not detectable. Visibly, he smiled, and chuckled a little bit, and said nothing. It would be over soon, this—rite of passage—that so regularly preceded the matters of state, which were the staple of the weekly meetings.

"But let it pass, let it pass, Prime Minister. Yes.

It is indeed a beautiful day. And I trust you are feeling well.

"Oh, speaking of feeling well, I cannot imagine that British farmers are feeling well, on receiving the news that you plan to cut the farm subsidies. Doesn't it appear to you awkward, not to say wrong, to cut farm subsidies so soon after cutting the tax on luxuries? I acknowledge that ours is a conservative government, but I shouldn't think it likely that it would continue for very long in power if you give out the impression that you are engaged in transferring income from poor farmers to rich diamond merchants?"

The Prime Minister carefully explained that the luxury tax was being reduced from 75 percent to 50 percent, while the farm subsidies were being reduced by a mere 16 percent. The Queen listened, put the dog down, then smiled in the way she so often did, as a punctuation mark indicating that she was prepared to move on to the next matter at hand.

She turned, for the first time, to Dahl Breckenridge. "I am always pleased to see you, Mr. Breckenridge, but I must suppose that there is some special reason for your accompanying the Prime Minister here today?"

Anthony Brogan broke in. "Ma'am, we have come to the conclusion that there is tension among the leaders of the Soviet Union in their struggle to consolidate power—"

"Stalin has been dead for over a year."

"Yes, ma'am, but he was almost thirty years in power, and there are never orderly arrangements set up to provide laws of succession for tyrants. In any event, we—the Foreign Office, after extensive consultation with our people in Moscow and elsewhere—are convinced that Mr. Malenkov is, of all the major figures in the Kremlin, the most disposed to a foreign policy that would conduce to amicable relations—"

"Who wants amicable relations with the Soviet Union?"

"Ma'am, I did not mean 'amicable' in that sense. I meant amicable in the sense that we are not at war with each other. May I continue?"

Queen Caroline nodded her head.

"It has been most discreetly suggested to our ambassador in Moscow that the hand of Mr. Malenkov would be considerably strengthened if"—Anthony Brogan breathed deeply—"if Your Majesty were to receive Mr. Malenkov after he addresses Parliament, which it is our proposal to invite him to do."

Queen Caroline's large blue eyes grew larger. She reached for Furioso and plopped him on the adjacent cushion.

"Are you *seriously* suggesting that I receive the prime tyrant in the world, whose entire country is mobilized to suppress the freedoms of Eastern Europe, so the Soviet Union can get on with the business of attempting to suppress our own freedoms—that I *receive* that monster?"

"We are attempting, ma'am, to conduct a foreign policy that best guarantees the protection of our freedoms."

Dahl Breckenridge broke in. "Understand, ma'am, that the tradition is very ancient that a chief of state—"

"Malenkov is not a chief of state. He is chief of government. Voroshilov, Chairman of the Presidium of the Supreme Soviet, is the chief of state."

"To be sure, ma'am, you are of course technically correct, but Malenkov is acknowledged by all the world as the principal political figure in the Soviet Union. And the tradition has always been that, if such a figure is invited to address Parliament—which we propose to invite him to do—that ceremony is followed by *some* contact with the British sovereign. Ordinarily this would be a state dinner. We are not asking for that. Merely *something*—perhaps tea at Windsor Castle? Something that would assure that he didn't think himself—snubbed."

"My dear Prime Minister, do we really desire that he should not think himself snubbed? Why should he not be isolated from civilized company, if Comrade Malenkov would be so gener-

ous as to assume that my company is civilized—
sometimes, I concede, an arguable point. Prince
Richard would definitely hesitate before committing himself on the question. On the other
hand, His Royal Highness Prince Richard will
hesitate before he commits himself on *any* question, save that any human being whose skin
color is other than white has reason to loathe the
British Empire for all the dreadful things we
have done to them, like trying to give them
civilization—" Queen Caroline's strictures
against her husband's affinity for what the winds
of change in Africa were bringing on were common knowledge.

"Well, ma'am, we have resolved that the
House of Commons' invitation should be extended. But to extend the invitation is to convey
a certain message that not only is incompletely
conveyed if you are unwilling to receive Mr.
Malenkov, it is worse: the departure from convention would *stress* that—*exclusion*. And that is
the opposite of the impression we seek under
the circumstances to give. The likeliest alternative to Mr. Malenkov, for instance, is Mr. Beria
of the KGB, who is the most dangerous man
alive, with designs on West Germany that could
lead to general mobilization. And there is Mr.
Suslov the dogmatist, and that wild man Khrushchev . . ."

*   *   *

The exchange lasted another half hour, during which the Queen attempted to make the point that social and political exchanges should be distinguished from each other, while Breckenridge and Brogan argued that on this occasion there was no way in which this could be done.

The Queen said, finally, "Well. You appear to make it quite plain that we are talking not about royal folkways, over which I have—still—a certain tenuous authority, but about political mores, which are the business of the House of Commons. Very well. You will grant that the season in London this summer will prove confused. We began it by welcoming Dr. Billy Graham, who holds his evangelical revival meetings here, warning against the evils of communism. We learn in the press that Mrs. Donald MacLean has written to her mother from—somewhere. She did not divulge where she is hiding her husband, who happens to be a traitor in the employ of the Soviet Union, which is no doubt rewarding him for stealing what secrets we have left. Do we care? Indeed we do: I read that the Boy Scouts have just finished expelling a member on the grounds that he is a member of the Young Communist League. And to cap all of this, it is proposed that I entertain this Hydra at Windsor Castle. It is, really, all rather confusing, is it not?" Suddenly she raised her hand, arching her eyebrows. She was not through:

"I wonder if I might," Queen Caroline grew ostentatiously solemn, "while at it, have an ecumenical tea of sorts at Windsor? . . . Yes! We could invite Mr. Donald MacLean, the communist Boy Scout Mr. Malenkov, and then ask Dr. Billy Graham to say grace before we pass the crumpets. Yes! Yes indeed! Does that appeal to you, Prime Minister?"

Anthony Brogan chuckled with nervous relief, as he bowed his head and rose, together with the Foreign Minister. Queen Caroline stood, Furioso in hand. She smiled.

"Good day, Prime Minister. You have noticed, have you not, that it is a lovely day?"

SIXTEEN

PRESIDENT Dwight David Eisenhower listened. Attentively, for quite a while. He became fidgety when his Secretary of State was reciting the biography and probable performance, should he come to power, of the fourth on the list of top Soviet figures, Nikita Khrushchev. Finally he interrupted.

"Do you know something, Foster? I don't think our people have the remotest idea how long Malenkov is going to stay in power—one month, one hundred months; who is coming in if he goes out: Beria, Bulganin, Suslov, Khrushchev, Molotov—it's all conjecture. I read Walter Lippmann on the subject—you may laugh, but twice a year I read Walter Lippmann. Doctor's orders, only twice a year. Anyway, he was gassing on about what I take it they now call—Kremlilologists? That right?"

"Kremlinologists," John Foster Dulles corrected him.

"That's it. Kremlinonogists. Anyway, they do nothing but study the comings and goings in the

Kremlin, and the idea is they can predict everything that happens. I would like to know *one* thing: Why is it that if they can predict what happens, *I* never get told what happens? I mean, who told me Malenkov was going to succeed Stalin?"

The President permitted the silence to predominate in the Situation Room. He rather relished it, and took the opportunity to look languidly about the table at the graven faces of the Secretary of State, the Secretary of Defense, the Chairman of the Joint Chiefs, the National Security Adviser, the Vice President, the Director of the Central Intelligence Agency.

"Okay. So nobody knew. So what do they know now?"

"It isn't," the Director of the CIA spoke up, "that we know who is going to win in the struggle for power, Mr. President. But we do know that there *is* a struggle for power. And we are pretty much agreed"—he paused, as if to invite opportunity for dissent on the point—"that is, we have a general idea that Malenkov is on the . . . softer side of the question. Clearly Beria would probably precipitate a crisis quickly, particularly since we know about his designs on West Germany—and the other contenders are mostly unknown, though of course Malenkov can hardly be thought of as an open book."

"You mean that everyone else you mentioned

would probably leave us worse off?" The President turned to his Director of Central Intelligence. "Is this surmise, Allen, or is it something more than that?"

"It's something more than that, Mr. President."

"Well, all right. I don't need to know the details. Speaking of details, anything on the British leak? I am informed that if I wish to consult with the Prime Minister, I either have to call him on the telephone, which I don't enjoy doing—Brogan can't say good morning in less than ten minutes—that, or send him a postcard written in invisible ink, or whatever."

"No, sir," Allen Dulles spoke again. "Nothing concrete. We are working on it, but we don't yet have an answer. It's a rough one."

"Goddamn shame, that Albanian operation. Goddamn shame. So where were we? You've got hard evidence, Allen, that Malenkov ought to be humored right about now?"

"Yes sir." Allen Dulles looked over at his brother, the Secretary of State, who took the lead.

"He has been pressing for a summit conference. The objective is plain: The Soviets wish to delay the formal recognition of West Germany, and—"

The President interrupted him. "I don't believe in summit conferences. You know that.

And did you spot the vote in the Senate day before yesterday? No? Not bad: the vote was eighty-eight to nothing to give me a free hand on West Germany."

"Yes, Mr. President. You can recognize West Germany. Your decision would be final as it affects this country. But of course Mendes-France is doing his usual this-ing and that-ing on the subject."

"What about the Brits?"

"I've consulted with Brogan," the Secretary of State said. "They're willing to invite Malenkov to address the House of Commons. They don't much like the idea of a summit conference among the Western powers. Brogan figures the Soviets would find a way to use it to stall the whole German question."

"How can they stall it if I can recognize them tomorrow?"

"They can't. But they hope to divide Europe in the matter, and get France to refuse to go along. Our thought was that something—some gesture, this side of a summit conference— would serve our purposes. A gesture in the direction of Malenkov, without accepting that Western summit he's been insisting on."

"What do you have in mind? You're not going to suggest we invite him over here? Joe McCarthy would really like that! That would be the end of the censure movement against that bastard. That is just plain out." The President spelled out the word, o-u-t.

Dulles spoke. "Perhaps, Mr. President, it would accomplish our purposes if I were to go to Moscow. We could then arrange for Breckenridge to go, perhaps after Malenkov comes back from London or even before; then apply joint pressure on France. It wouldn't look like a summit or even like a mini-summit if we went separately. But it would accomplish what we think Malenkov wants, namely that the musclemen in the West are willing to court him a little."

The President turned visibly thoughtful. He looked up at his National Security Adviser. "Bob, on the McCarthy business. When do you think the Senate will censure him? I mean, they will, won't they?"

"The betting, sir, is about fifty-fifty. There's an awful lot of mail objecting to censure, and he's got himself a hell of a lawyer, Edward Bennett Williams. And Williams has Brent Bozell working with him, and writing McCarthy's speeches. He and Bill Buckley wrote the book *McCarthy and His Enemies.* Blows the hell, between you and me, out of most of the charges that grew from the Tydings investigation. So just can't say."

"Hmm. I'd rather announce a Dulles trip to Moscow after McCarthy was censured. How urgent is all this business? I mean, can it wait a month or two?"

Allen Dulles spoke up. "It's hard to say. But it does seem to be coming to a head."

The President rose, followed by his council members. He nodded to Allen Dulles. "Stay a moment, Allen." To his other advisers he gave his half smile, and they walked out. The President shut the door and sat down alone with his CIA chief.

"I guess I do want to know. What you referred to. About how we know what Beria's intentions are."

"We have a solid asset, Mr. President."

"Where?"

"Right there."

"You mean . . . in the Kremlin?"

Dulles nodded his head, slowly, gravely.

The President cleared his throat. Evidently he wanted to hear more. Dulles continued:

"He works in the Kremlin. We hear from him as often as every two weeks. This has been going on for six months, and we've checked out everything he has told us. Some of the material isn't verified, some of it isn't verifiable. But three hard items have checked out absolutely."

"And he tells you Malenkov is wobbly?"

"He tells us Beria is pressing, the KGB is becoming all-powerful, and the line being advanced is that Malenkov has been too sweet with the West and hasn't got anything out of us. The idea is that the meetings we're talking about would fortify Malenkov."

"This—agent. Commercial proposition?"

"We're depositing money in an account in Switzerland. Not large sums, but the kind a prudent man would ask for. My guess is, either he simply hates Beria or he hates the whole system. Hard to say. And here's one for you: He's married to an American."

"What's she do?"

"She works for the KGB."

"That must be a cozy arrangement. Does Mrs. Asset know what Mr. Asset is up to?"

"We don't know."

"God. World wars are easier than this, I sometimes think."

The President stood. "I'll think about it. You'll hear from me, Allen."

SEVENTEEN

BLACKFORD OAKES was at the Nell Gwynne Tavern at nine-fifteen. It was uncrowded. Its customers, relaxed, convivial, appeared to be regulars, natives of Windsor, though there was a studied quaintness in the decor and in the menu handed to Blackford, when he sat down at one of the tables, that suggested a play for tourists who came by to see Windsor Castle, or parents who came to take their Eton collegers out to lunch on weekends.

It was warm, and even smoky, though no charcoal grill was in evidence. Blackford spotted, at the far end of the dining area, a table shielded by a wooden partition from the larger bar-dining quarters. He rose, slipped the serving girl a ten-shilling note, and said, "Someone is meeting me here. We'll have a little more privacy in the corner. Is that all right?" The pert young waitress pocketed the bill and said, with just a suggestion of a mock-American accent, "That's okay, sir. As you like," and followed him to the corner. He sat down and ordered a beer. "Oh, and do you have one that is cold?"

"Yes, sir. We serve a lot of Americans at the Nell Gwynne."

Renira Williams was punctual. She took his hand formally, and sat opposite. Her nurse's uniform had been removed, and she had put on makeup. She was indeed a handsome woman. Her manners were direct, her self-assurance manifest. Blackford did not doubt that she was a veteran of a thousand BOAC flights, nor was he concerned that the urchins at St. John's would give Miss Williams much to worry about. He doubted that *she* had been doused when she stepped into her car. Blackford signaled the waitress, and Renira Williams ordered a gin and tonic.

"Well then, Mr. Benton. You are interested in Bert Heath?"

"That is correct. My clients are interested in knowing something about him."

"Who are your clients?"

Blackford pulled out the card, as he had done previously.

She stared at it. "Well, that doesn't mean anything to me. But I am not going to call them up tomorrow to verify that you are on the level. And do you know why?"

Blackford said, as though amused by a hypothetical question, that no, he did not know why.

"Because I don't particularly care whether you are or you are not. I suspect you are not, for the very simple reason that Bert never plays it straight himself. You never know what he is up to. Oh, you find out eventually what he is up to where you are concerned. But what he does when he disappears for weeks and months at a time I haven't the least idea, and the only time I asked him it cost me a black eye." She sipped from her drink. "Oh yes, please let's get the other business settled first. How much do you propose to pay me for information on Bert?"

Blackford said that his clients were certainly prepared to compensate her for her time, and something besides, but that the actual sum would depend on how useful her information proved to be.

"By 'useful' can I assume, Mr. Benton, you really mean 'damaging'? If I told you Bert Heath was a full-time choirboy, that wouldn't be worth much to you, now would it?"

Blackford reasoned that it would not subvert the essential gravity of the conversation if he permitted himself to smile. Which he did. She returned it, but cynically. "It happens that I am in need of some money. St. John's is not a munificent employer. What is it you most wish to hear about?"

Blackford was not quite ready to say that he wished most to know where Bertram Heath was. The cover story was that he was being considered for employment. His clients presumably knew where the applicant was. So he said, "When did you last see him?"

"You have not mentioned a figure."

"Suppose we agree that for your trouble tonight I will pay you fifty pounds. In the event that the information we get from you turns out to be especially useful, I shall send a check for another fifty pounds."

Renira Williams's smile was genuine. "Very well. And I shall have another gin and tonic, please. The bar here is better than the one at St. John's."

She had met Bert Heath, she said, lighting a cigarette, on a BOAC flight from Rome about four years ago. He had flirted with her. She had admired his looks and manner, and agreed to meet him for dinner the following evening.

This had led to a long romance. She lived in a small cottage in Old Windsor, one mile from the house where her parents lived in retirement. "Bert had a flat in London, and sometimes we stayed there. Sometimes we would go to Old Windsor. This had to be done carefully, because of my parents, though they never come to my cottage; I go to theirs. But of course, there are neighbors.

"We had two passionate years. It wasn't ever

easy. My job with BOAC kept me out of England half the time, and his job kept him on the move. I suspect he had something to do with the military, legal or illegal I don't know. But often in his bag there'd be a copy or two of a magazine, forgot what it was called, but I flipped through one once and they were advertising guns and the kind of thing you would want in a military situation. My guess is that Bert is a soldier of fortune, I guess you would call it. Do they call it that in America?" Renira Williams wished her interrogator to know that it was entirely clear to her that whether or not he was actually associated with a British law firm, he was clearly an American.

"Yes," Blackford said. "Same thing."

She drank deeply from her glass. "Bert was always asking me to marry him, and when I'd say yes—you know, in the sort of situation in which a girl tends to say yes—he was always postponing it. Then the business of last March happened."

"Last March?"

"Yes." Renira paused in her narrative, stirring with her finger the half-empty drink. "I was scheduled out on a long haul. London, Rome, Cairo, Salisbury, Jo'burg. Eight days there and back, counting required time off. He said that by the time I returned he would have a wedding license, and we would 'stitch it up'—his words.

In Rome we had engine trouble. The mechanics worked three hours before the flight was canceled. I was directed to return to London and wait there for the schedule to resume. There was just time to catch a westbound BOAC Super Connie. I got to London about nine, went to phone Bert and thought no, I'll surprise him. So I went to the apartment—naturally, I had a key —and opened the door. He was having at it right in the middle of the living room with this . . . very young girl—lights on, music playing, whisky bottle at their side."

Renira Williams paused. "This is not a story Father Paine would want to hear."

Blackford said nothing.

"I don't know what I did. I think I reached for the bottle of whisky and tried to smash it down on his head. He caught me up, of course—he's a strong bastard, Bert—and then he started in on me. Gave me one hell of a beating with his open hand—I mean, one hell of a beating. I guess I passed out. When I woke up, they were gone. There was a note on the door. I keep it. It brings me down to earth. I look at it, maybe once a month." Renira Williams's voice was subdued now, strained. She reached into her pocketbook and brought out an envelope and handed it to Blackford. He pulled out a piece of paper on which had been scrawled in ink, "Get your ass out of my apartment—B."

Blackford said nothing for a moment. Then, "Nice guy," he said, returning the envelope. "Is that the last you saw of him?"

"Yes. I had to go to a clinic for treatment, missed my flight schedules for three weeks, and was bumped—BOAC was looking for reasons to trim back. I looked around the home town area and got the position at St. John's. Life there is less exciting than it used to be, but it has its compensations."

There was no other way to proceed, Blackford decided, than more or less directly. But he took a slightly circuitous route. "I am very sorry, Miss Williams. And now I need to advise you that my clients have in fact lost contact with Bert Heath, and wish to be in touch with him. Where is he?"

"Ah," Renira Williams's face brightened. "So that's it! You people want to hunt him down! He's wanted by somebody? For something. If it's for murder, I hope it was that blonde on the floor. No—" Renira Williams was serious again. "Actually, I don't want him hurt. At least, not permanently." She looked up at Blackford. "Do you know, Mr. Benton, or whatever your real name is, I don't think you are a mobster aimed at gunning Bert down. Just a feeling. May be wrong." She took the initiative in signaling for the waitress to bring her another drink, and Blackford ordered a second beer.

"Well, you have his apartment number, don't you?" she said.

"He isn't there."

"Funny. He's had that apartment for a long time. Of course, he goes off for long trips, too. How long has he been away?"

"He hasn't been seen for six weeks."

"That's a fair amount of time for him to be away. Is his apartment emptied?"

"There is evidence that he doesn't intend to return there. Is there anyplace else you can think of that he used to go?"

Renira Williams thought. "No," she said slowly. "No. He never told me where he was going. But then . . ." she paused. "Yes. Just after Christmas he went off on one of his missions, and a week later I got in the mail, in Old Windsor, an insurance receipt. One of those policies you buy at the airports, you know, so many thousand pounds per half crown you put into the machine. Old Bert must have put a half-dozen half crowns into the machine, because the policy—the accident policy, payable if Bertram Oliver Heath was killed as the result of an airplane accident between Date A and Date B—read, 'Pay the sum of twenty-five thousand pounds to' "—she mimicked the wording of a check—"and on the line for the beneficiary he had written out, 'Renira Williams, 2 Sunnycoate Lane, Old Windsor, Berks.' But then there was fine print, something like, 'In the event the designated beneficiary is deceased, please specify alternative beneficiary,' and Bert had written out a name, and an address.''

"Do you remember that name and address?"

"I do, as a matter of fact. I had completely forgotten about it—though I still have that policy, somewhere, in my cottage. But looking about the newspapers a month or two back I saw a picture of one of our scientists, introduced at a speech as a Nobel Prize winner. I thought, well now, this is a coincidence. Same chap gets twelve thousand pounds from the King of Norway as would have got twenty-five thousand pounds from Lloyds of London, assuming Bert had been killed, and I had died or been killed. There can't be two people called Alistair Fleetwood. Sir Alistair Fleetwood, I guess he is now. I never met him. Never heard Bert mention him." She drained her glass and looked up.

"Maybe he knows where Bert is?"

Blackford volunteered to drive her the five miles to Old Windsor, but Renira Williams said no, she would prefer to take the taxi, as she had done in getting here. "The school always uses Fred's taxi. He is very obliging and doesn't charge much." And then, on reaching the outdoors, where the taxi was waiting, "I hope I have given you useful information, because I am making payments on the cottage." Blackford told her the supplementary payment would be forthcoming, and they shook hands. She looked him squarely in the eyes for just a moment, before opening the door of the taxi and sitting down in front with Fred, and heading out toward Runnymede.

EIGHTEEN

THEY MET IN THE office of Sir Eugene Attwood. Three Americans, two Britishers. Ellery Blass, tall, scrawny, silver-haired, as head of MI6 was responsible for international security. "We clearly have here," Rufus had said to Blackford in the car driving over to Leconfield House, "a case that blends the responsibilities of the two agencies, domestic and foreign security." He had studied, in Washington, the report of Blackford's month-long exertions. The covering note had ended:

I tell you, Rufus, I am convinced of two things. One of them is that Fleetwood is our man. The second is that he has come up with some devilish device that managed to crack our code on Tirana and everything we exchanged before then with the Brits through the embassy. We've got to play my hunch. And to do this, obviously, we need the full cooperation of MI5 and MI6. What do you say?

Attwood and Blass had known Rufus since the war. Attwood and Trust had had extensive dealings since Trust became the chief of station for the CIA in London. Trust was now introduced to Ellery Blass, and both the Englishmen to Blackford Oakes for the first time.

They sat around a table in a soundproofed, bug-proof room situated within a carapace especially designed to frustrate any efforts at electronic intrusion. It was in that room, at MI5, that all conversations of a highly secret nature were carried on. There was always the slight hum from the sonic detectors. The room was air-conditioned but it was warm, and before too long even the British had taken off their jackets.

Rufus was seated at the center, and gave a quick summary of the reasons for Blackford Oakes's manhunt, and then he turned the floor over to him.

Blackford Oakes stood up.

He began factually. He spoke of his conversations with "Henry," the commando put in charge of the destinies of forty American and British commandos. He reminded them of the grisly photo album they were all familiar with, and then told of his encounter at the airport, the surveillance by Anthony Trust of "Henry," and the man's disappearance the following morning.

He gave what he judged to be the relevant details in his painstaking reconstruction of the life of Bertram Oliver Heath. He stressed, when he came to the Cambridge days, the central role of Alistair Fleetwood, to whom everyone had pointed as the formative influence in Bertram Heath's life. He underlined the adamantine refusal of Fleetwood to any interview concerning Bertram Heath. He spoke then of the girlfriend, Renira Williams, and, finally, of the interview at Nell Gwynne's Tavern three nights before. By the time he reached the account of the insurance policy, Blackford's narrative had created a measure of excitement.

But when he ended the story, with its increasingly predictable request, the ice water began to drip.

Attwood: "You do not mean to tell me that that is all you have?"

Blackford replied that, yes, he had recited all the evidence he had accumulated, and that he thought it was sufficient to justify a full-scale investigation of Fleetwood including "the works"—bugging his phone, examining his mail, night-and-day surveillance.

There was silence.

Blass spoke. "You do realize, Mr. Oakes, of course, that Fleetwood is a Nobel laureate—yes, you of all people I need not instruct in Fleetwood's accomplishments. But one simply does not, on the basis of such information as you have given us, treat a British citizen as in effect a— a—"

Blackford endeavored to help him, "—possible traitor."

"Possible traitor," Blass echoed.

Blackford looked at Rufus. Did he wish Blackford to carry the ball or did he wish to do it himself? Rufus caught the signal, and Blackford in turn caught his quiet nod.

"If I may say so, sir, whatever standards the British are observing are clearly insufficient. There is absolutely no doubt that a hyper-secret operation resulted in an ambush of forty American, British, and Albanian commandos. There is absolutely no doubt that the man who was picked to lead those men is in fact in collusion with the enemy. There is absolutely no doubt that the radio operator at Camp Cromwell, which Winston Churchill would have needed a pass to get into, was in regular radio communication with the enemy, right there at the training camp. There is absolutely no doubt that secrets transmitted from Washington to MI6 via our own embassy were known in detail to the enemy, from which we deduce that that information is being got by *somebody*, by *some* means. And there is no accounting for the mysterious reluctance of Alistair Fleetwood to consent to see people innocently, so far as he knew, interested in Bertram Heath—"

"I would venture," Sir Eugene Attwood said,

"that Sir Alistair Fleetwood would not decline to see me, if I were to ask him."

"No, I am sure he would not, Sir Eugene. But that is exactly what I would argue one should not at this point do, namely give him any reason to suppose that he is under suspicion. What we need is evidence, and the way to get it in my opinion is the way I suggest. It is how we would proceed in America—is that correct, Rufus?"

Rufus said that that was indeed correct, and reminded his colleagues that a full security investigation had been undertaken in America of someone "as eminent in our society as Fleetwood is in yours. I speak of J. Robert Oppenheimer." The mention of the security investigation of the same American who had headed the Manhattan Project, which produced the atomic bomb, had an effect, though not a decisive one since it was supposed that any security investigation in America was the infamous result of the infamous McCarthy.

It lasted an hour and a half, at the end of which Attwood asked Rufus if he would "mind very much" if the two British consulted with one another . . . privately? Rufus made a gesture to leave the room, but Attwood insisted that the Americans stay, and instead of dislocating his guests, he left the electronic cocoon with Blass.

The Americans engaged quickly in conversation. "What are we going to do if they say no, Rufus?"

"They have problems. For one thing there is their pride. The Brits are first-rate at intelligence. And quite inept at security, paradoxical though that may sound. But remember, they are suffering more than they let on from the suspension of security traffic from the U. S. Their nuclear plant people, through the British Ambassador, have begged for the next scheduled shipment of technical information. They have not got it—Ike's orders. Be patient."

MI5 and 6 were back in a half hour.

Attwood spoke. "Very well. Round-the-clock surveillance we can agree on. And examining his mail. But tapping his telephone—that we could not agree to do unless further evidence is developed." Attwood paused here, as if to ask, "Is that satisfactory?"

Rufus spoke. "I think that is a very good beginning, Gene. But we must bear in mind that both parties to this—pursuit—are anxious. It is inconvenient, to say the least, for us to suspend strategic traffic between our country and yours, and presumably it is also inconvenient for Great Britain."

"It most certainly is," Attwood snapped.

Blackford broke in. "And it was very inconvenient for our agents to drop by parachute onto Soviet gibbets in Albania."

The British dubbed it Operation Oxford, which at first struck Blackford as rather a naïve way to seek to conceal, should anyone happen on the operation's name, that in fact it was a member of the Cambridge community that MI5 was interested in. He would not have recommended as a code name for an investigation of Harvard University, "Operation Yale." But soon the little piquancy amused him.

It was agreed that Blackford would continue to operate in the same safe house on James Street he had been using, and that the surveillance team, under the management of Superintendent Roberts, after reporting to MI5 would immediately relay the same findings to Blackford. Meanwhile, all available records on the background of Alistair Fleetwood would be examined, and brought in to Blackford's study-lab.

NINETEEN

DURING THE ENSUING fortnight, Sir Alistair Fleetwood spent much time at the Greenwich Royal Observatory, the great observatory where his Zirca had originally been assembled, the Fleetwood Zirca now scanning the heavens and bringing in great, detailed deposits of information concerning the surface of the moon, after which it was scheduled to train one by one on the other planets, reaching, in six months or so, to an examination of the stars themselves.

The observatory was a large installation located two hours from Cambridge at Herstmonceux Castle near Hailsham. While supervising the construction of the Zirca, Fleetwood had built and experimented with a miniature of it; this model had since been disassembled. He announced to the technicians in permanent residence at Herstmonceux Castle that he had had a fresh insight into the Zirca, the result of which might permit him to enhance its efficiency, and that for that reason he was going to reconstitute the model with the view to making certain adjustments.

This accounted for the numerous hours he spent at Herstmonceux, and by the end of September any technician who had reason to go into Sir Alistair's laboratory would see there the equivalent of a mini-Zirca, about three feet long, perched as a play cannon might be perched, aimed at an angle. The cannon was surrounded by wires and circuitry.

On two occasions Fleetwood drove, by himself, from Hailsham to London, both times to 48 Grosvenor Square, a six-story building. He went to the fifth floor and let himself in, using his own key. The first time, he stayed only a half hour at Grosvenor Square. The second time, it was for very nearly four hours. The building's commercial ledger indicated that the large apartment 516 was rented to one Robert Editta, who gave his profession as "photographer." The rent was always paid on time. "A thoroughly satisfactory relationship," the estate agent said, looking up at Superintendent Roberts and closing the ledger that recorded his transactions with clients.

Later in the month Fleetwood said to a technician at the observatory that he had decided to take the mini-Zirca to his rooms in Cambridge, further to reflect on its potential, as he had not quite solved the problem he had hoped to crack.

Accordingly, the following day one of the technicians helped Fleetwood first to crate the mini-Zirca, and then to lift it into the back of a rented Rover station wagon. It was heavy, perhaps eighty pounds, but not, for two men, unmanageable. Fleetwood thanked his helper and drove off, alone.

He stopped for a cup of tea at a café at Robertsbridge. When he had finished, he walked to the corner where he had parked the station wagon.

It was no longer there. But his own Ford sedan was in its place. He got in, reached under the seat, and took the key. He was in his quarters in Cambridge an hour and a half later.

Before retiring, he did his packing. A large suitcase, into which he stuffed apparel suitable for sailing at sea: foul-weather gear, rubber boots, thick sweaters, bosun's hat. He had spoken with his colleagues about how much he was looking forward to a week's sail in and around the islands east and northeast of Stockholm, a trip to which he had been invited by a friend in Sweden who had chartered a boat perfect for such a trip—a forty-foot yawl, Sir Alistair said happily at dinner on Fellows' Night, "without even a radio. If we need help, we'll simply have to fire distress signals. It will be fine to be away from Instant Communicability. Though as a ham radio operator I have no right to say that."

He took another glass of wine and smiled, and his friends, on leaving, wished him a splendid holiday.

In Stockholm, he checked into the Grand Hotel. He went through the identical ritual as before. And it all worked as before. Alice Goodyear Corbett was very excited by the adventure. "Everything has been thought of, my dear Alistair, everything." Fleetwood replied coyly that Alice had certainly thought of everything in bed before dinner. "All I ask is that this operation be as successful!" he replied, filling their liqueur glasses.

The following morning, dressed in a heavy sweater and cap and wearing seaboots, Sir Alistair Fleetwood, a green seabag in hand, told the concierge that he would be gone for a week and wished to check his principal suitcase until his return. The concierge instructed the porter to take the suitcase and give Sir Alistair a claim check. Fleetwood signed the hotel bill. The porter, carrying the seabag, opened the door of the taxi. Sir Alistair tipped the porter and asked him kindly to recite in Swedish the instructions on a card he showed him. The porter read out the number of a wharf and its location, the driver nodded in acknowledgment, and the porter returned the card to Sir Alistair.

A half hour later, Alistair was greeted by a young, bearded Swede. They spoke in English and boarded the boat. A few minutes later, back in the marina, Fleetwood called his secretary at Trinity, reversing the charges, to remind her to assemble the material he had outlined last August for the Rede lectures, as he would need to get to work on them as soon as he returned from his week's sailing holiday on which he would embark "as soon as I put this phone down." She wished him fine weather and good relaxation.

They boarded the *Fernbrook* and headed out of the prosperous harbor, the last of the summer's cruising boats here and there in evidence. Though it was early October, there were still a few sailing boats responding briskly to the gusty autumn winds. They headed out close-hauled past Lidingö. A southeasterly wind gave them a nice reach past the Djursholm strait, where the skipper turned north toward Österskär. Just after sundown, he maneuvered into the little harbor.

At seven the dinghy was lowered, the little Seagull motor fastened to its transom. The bearded skipper climbed down into the dinghy with his passenger, now also bearded and wearing a raincoat over a three-piece suit. They were met a few hundred yards from their anchorage at the commercial wharf by a large man and a woman, both wearing raincoats. The bearded passenger climbed the ladder onto the wharf, and the skipper lifted the seabag to the large man. The captain then reentered the dinghy, started up the quiet little outboard, and headed back to the *Fernbrook*.

Alice Goodyear Corbett did not introduce the large man who drove the car. "He does not speak English," she said. "You have your papers?" Alistair responded by patting his left hand against his right jacket pocket. They drove to the airport and at 9:15 checked in on the Finnair 10 P.M. flight to Helsinki: a contented Finnish couple completing their week-long holiday in Sweden and returning home to Finland.

At midnight the telex in Blackford's study at James Street came to life. Blackford sat up and read:

SUBJECT LEFT HOTEL 10 A.M. BOARDED SAILING YACHT FERNBROOK. DEPARTED HARBOR 1115, PUT IN AT OSTERSKAR HARBOR AT 1915. DEPARTED, WEARING BEARD, BY DINGHY TO TOWN WHARF. THEN BY AUTO LICENSE PLATE AA11864 TO BROMMA AIRPORT. BOARDED FINNAIR FLIGHT 221 TO HELSINKI AS BJORN HENNINGSEN MR. AND MRS. HAVE CONTACTED HELSINKI. OP OX.

TWENTY

THE PREPARATIONS TO penetrate apartment 516—Rufus had tabled his grander plans to penetrate the Soviet Embassy—consumed two days. They required the cooperation of technicians who acquainted themselves with the electrical morphology of 48 Grosvenor Square. "The requirement," Hallam Spring said, going over the plans with Jimmy Moser, the MI5 electrician, at the safe house, "is to blow the juice in Apartment 516 without simultaneously doing it in adjacent apartments, and that" —he pointed to the electrical schematics—"is going to require some re-circuitry, with a very brief interruption of power in the entire building. I figure maybe five, ten minutes, outside. That shouldn't get anybody too terribly excited."

Meanwhile Bruce Pulling had put together the camera apparatus to be used by Moser, whose responsibility it would be to inspect number 516, the mysterious apartment to which Alistair Fleetwood had twice repaired before leaving for Stockholm. It was a relatively simple device: a high-powered lens looking out the back end of a large, three-battery flashlight of the kind widely associated with electricians. Jimmy Moser's instructions were to handle the flashlight as though it were an extension of an expressive hand, gesturing to accompany his words and thoughts. The flashlight was equipped to take an infrared exposure every time the thumb slid its switch backward. Pushed forward, it caused the light to function as a conventional flashlight.

On Tuesday morning the technicians parked their small van with the electrical equipment at the corner of the basement garage and finished their preparatory work in the bowels of the building's cellar, laying out the wires as required to facilitate a quick reassembly.

At ten in the morning the lights went out in the entire western end of the building. The recircuiting required less than ten minutes, after which the lights went on again.

Only one tenant called down to Brian Larwill at the janitor's office during the interval to complain about the power failure. The switchboard revealed that it was not apartment 516 calling in. The janitor told him that the problem was being looked into, that he was confident the breakdown would be corrected quickly. As indeed it was.

*   *   *

A few minutes after two in the afternoon of the same day, Blackford Oakes, Superintendent Roberts, and Jimmy Moser sat in Brian Larwill's little bedroom behind his office. At a nod from Roberts, Blackford radioed on his walkie-talkie to the electrician in the basement, standing by the controls.

"Ready Op Ox, go."

On receipt of the signal, the electrician flipped the switch and the electricity to apartment 516 was cut off.

They waited in silence for the inevitable telephone call. Presumably it would take more than the few-minute cutoff such as had been endured that morning without protest, before apartment 516 called in to complain.

They waited, nervously.

The call came seven minutes after the blackout. On the switchboard, number 516 flashed on. Superintendent Roberts's recording machine taped the exchange.

"Is this Mr. Larwill? . . . Ah yes. Well, Mr. Larwill, the electricity has gone off in my apartment. It happened also this morning, but the lights came back on in about five minutes. In my business—I am Mr. Editta, and a professional photographer, you may recall—undependable electricity is very serious. Is the whole building without electricity?"

Brian Larwill said not so far as he knew, having received no other complaints. But he would telephone the occupants of apartments 514 and 518 and see if they too were out of lights. "Whatever the problem, Mr. Editta, we will check on it and call you back."

He waited five minutes and then dialed 516. "It appears to be a problem in your apartment alone, sir. I mean, localized there; 514 and 518 are getting current. I shall send an electrician up to have a look."

There was a moment's pause. "Surely the problem has got to lie elsewhere, Mr. Larwill? I have checked our fuse box in the kitchen, and the fuses are in good condition."

"Well, sir, I'll consult with the electrician before I send him up. I am not an electrical expert myself, but I don't see how the difficulty could be down here if your neighbors are getting power. Let me talk with him and call you back."

They had prepared for such a contingency. They would take pains not to show any inappropriate curiosity to visit the apartment. Ten minutes later Larwill dialed 516 again, but this time he said, "I'm going to put the electrician on. He can speak with you. Here is Mr. Moser."

Jimmy Moser took the telephone. "Moser 'ere, sir, 'Malgamated 'Lectrical Company. Checked below, nothing out of order there—'as to be a shorted circuit up where you are. I can come up, sir, but there will be a few minutes' delay. I need to go to the shop and fetch up my toolbox."

"Hang on a minute." Mr. Editta evidently wished to consult with someone. In short order he was back on the phone. "Very well. But in that case please do hurry up. It is very inconvenient."

"Righto, guv. Won't be long."

He waited twenty-five minutes. In his toolbox was a microphone, buried among the expected wires and plugs and tapes and sundry electrical parts. In the little bedroom behind the office of Brian Larwill, Superintendent Roberts and Blackford Oakes could listen in on the receiver to what was about to happen in apartment number 516.

Jimmy Moser was a short man with a full mustache. He wore a white cotton jacket with deep pockets in which he carried various tools of the trade, and rough brown corduroy pants. He had spots of grease on his left forehead and over his left arm. In his left hand he carried the large toolbox. In his right, the flashlight, which he held bottom side up.

The ring was answered by a large, dark-haired man wearing a sports shirt and tortoiseshell spectacles. A second man, tall and brawny, was sitting in the corner of the room, his newspaper —in the absence of a functioning reading lamp

—angled to receive light from the window. He did not look up when his fellow tenant said, "I am Mr. Editta. You are Mr. Moser?"

"At's right, guv," said Jimmy Moser, swinging his flashlight about as he spoke and affecting an air faintly dismissive. "Sorry about all this. But we'll 'ave it fixed up in a bit now. Now, if you'd just show me the fuse box."

Robert Editta led Moser through to the center of the living room and opened the door to the adjacent room. "This is my darkroom—my study. Usually"—he pointed to the large window at the far end of the room—"usually that blind is drawn. But of course right now we need what light we can get." The window looked out across Grosvenor Square. Large, cumbersome instruments of varied description cluttered up the room. One, pointing toward the window, had the general shape of a cannon and was held in place by metal scaffolding, to the right of which were several large tin receptacles. "Enlarger here," Editta muttered, ducking his head under a wire on which negatives, suspended by clothespins, were strung out. Jimmy Moser flashed his light about as though to make sure he would not bump into anything and cause disturbance.

"Here," Editta said, opening a door into the kitchen. "This is the fuse box."

Moser shone his flashlight and looked

thoughtfully at the fuses, unscrewing them one by one and checking them on his voltmeter. "Hmm. These 'ere seem all right. What I need to do now is check the indivigil outlets, see where the trouble is . . . um . . . No doubt about it, there's somethin' trippin' up the central power supply. Might as well be systematic and start in the living room."

Editta seemed fatalistic about it all. "Very well."

They walked back, Moser's flashlight jerking here and there, much as a bobby's nightstick pirouettes about as he does his rounds.

Moser went to the entrance door and said, "Right, we'll proceed clockwise." He got down on his hands and knees, pulled out the plug that led to a floor lamp, and inserted the prong of his voltmeter into the openings, all the while putting his flashlight to prodigious use. Editta had lost interest, retiring to the desk next to his silent companion and reading, from daylight, the sports pages of the newspaper.

Jimmy Moser moved to the next wall socket. And, a few minutes after testing it, to the socket directly left of where Editta's companion was sitting.

He looked up, "Excuse me, guv. I 'ave to ask you to move your chair, just a few inches. There we go."

In Brian Larwill's bedroom they could hear

the sound of a chair grating across the floor, but no voice. Jimmy Moser was clearly attempting to induce Editta's companion to say something.

"Bit of a bother all this, in'it? You also a photographer?"

"Get on with your work," was the abrupt answer.

"No offense, guvnor," Jimmy Moser said, involving himself entirely in the test of the circuit. "Nothin' wrong 'ere, not that I can see." And, a few minutes later, "This one neither, and that's the last outlet in the living room, Mr. Editta . . . We'll 'ave to test the outlets in the darkroom. I can find 'em. No need to disturb yourself."

Editta rose quickly from his chair. "No. I will point them out. I—we—must be careful of my equipment."

And so the tour proceeded. There were a half-dozen outlets, one of them reinforced with what appeared to be a large battery complex. "Wot's this 'ere, a juice-booster?"

"Yes. For when I need a very bright light for the enlarger mechanism."

"Righto. You see a lot a those round these days. But they shouldn't cause any trouble." Jimmy Moser, again on his hands and knees, plying his flashlight and using the small screwdriver and his voltmeter, said, "Aha! I think . . . I think maybe I found the bugger. But I'll need to remove the fuses to test it." He rose, used the flashlight to go back to the kitchen, loosened the fuses, returned to the socket from which the enlarger and its apparatus were fed, and, his head only inches from his toolbox, said bouncily, "If I'm right, your lights oughta go on in 'af a mo."

In Brian Larwill's bedroom Superintendent Roberts spoke in husky whisper into the walkie-talkie to the electrician in the basement. "Countdown, countdown. When I say go—" his face was turned to Blackford. Blackford, his ear on the little receiver, had his arm held high. He could hear Jimmy's voice sounding a little dimmer as he walked away from the toolbox, where the little microphone lay, to the fuse box.

"Here we go now, hold your breath." The word "breath" uttered, Oakes brought down his hand sharply, and Superintendent Roberts spoke into the walkie-talkie, "Now!"

The lights in the darkroom flashed on.

"*Well* 'en," said Jimmy Moser, beaming with an I-told-you-so look. "There we are. A short circuit in that socket. The wirin' for the booster wasn't quite tight enough. No problem now. I've checked all the others—they're all secure."

He was putting his tools back in the box, still on his knees. His eyes suddenly riveted on a pair of stocky brown leather shoes, inches from his face. He looked up into the face of the silent companion of Robert Editta. The man addressed Moser in terse tones.

"Are you the electrician for this building, Moser?"

"Our firm looks after this building, guv. I mean, also lotta other buildings," he smiled confidently.

"Let me see your card."

"Pleasure. Just let me . . ." He closed his toolbox, inserting his flashlight in it. He stood up, reached into his back pocket, and pulled out a card.

" 'Ere you are, and at your service, anytime."

He handed over to the large man the card, but did not wait for him to examine it, heading instead cheerfully to the apartment door, opening it. He said then without turning around:

"Afternoon, gentlemen."

Below, in the crowded little bedroom, Blackford Oakes said to Superintendent Roberts, "That was Bertram Heath."

TWENTY-ONE

THE RUSSIAN TRANSPORT landed at Sheremetyevo Airport sometime after three in the morning, and Fleetwood and Alice Goodyear Corbett did not disguise that they were very fatigued. A car was waiting and drove them to the National Hotel, where Bjorn Henningsen had been preregistered. After establishing that all was in order, Alice, in the presence of the concierge, said a formal good-night. But he caught the little wink. She would call him at noon the following day, she said.

Alistair Fleetwood and the porter carrying his bag entered the elevator. The young man languidly pushed the button marked "6." The elevator rose and in due course stopped. But when the door slid open it was obvious that the elevator had stopped not at the sixth floor but, so to speak, at floor five and one half. Sir Alistair breathed heavily his exasperation. The porter got down on his knees, pushed open the elevator door on the fifth floor, vaulted down to the fifth-floor landing, and signaled to Sir Alistair that he should do the same, first of all pushing out his bag, which the porter caught in his arms. There being no apparent alternative, Sir Alistair Fleetwood got down on his rump and ejected himself, feet first, through the open cavity, leaping four or five feet to the floor. The porter grabbed him on landing, which was quick thinking because otherwise Sir Alistair Fleetwood would have fallen back under the cab and down five and one half flights of elevator shaft.

He entered his room wearily, tried to remember whether tipping was frowned on in Moscow, decided he might as well take the risk since his life had, arguably, been saved, so he gave the porter a ruble and inspected his quarters.

The living room was equipped with heavy furniture, two armchairs, one couch, a heavy bureau of sorts, a solid wooden desk, and three lights, none of them bright enough to suit Fleetwood. Well, he would order larger bulbs in the morning. He went into the bedroom next to the living room and looked out on the few lights then still on, in the city he had not seen since finishing his first year at Cambridge. Wearily he began to undress, first removing the beard in front of the mirror and staring fondly at his repristinated face. It had been rather exciting at first, the beard business. He had been slightly dismayed to learn from Alice that it was expected that he should wear the beard everywhere outside his own room, "just in case some-one is around who knows you or would recognize you—remember you are a very famous man, my darling." Well, he would certainly not wear his beard when he was with Beria. When in the inner sanctum, he would take it off and put it in his pocket.

He woke earlier than expected. His watch showed nine o'clock. He struggled, unsuccessfully, to recall the Russian he had so doggedly, under discipline, made himself forget. He picked up the telephone and asked for room service. The operator evidently knew only a single word of English, which sounded like, "Outzide outzide." He essayed first French and then German, to no better end, and then the cinders of his Russian. He thought back to procedures followed on his first trip, put on his bathrobe, and peered outside the door. He saw, sitting at a desk opposite the elevator doors and the staircase, a matronly woman, and recalled the system of mini-concierges at every floor. He grabbed the key to his suite, put it in the pocket of his dressing gown, and approached the woman: "Do you speak English?"

"I understand," she said.

"I wish some breakfast. Can you order it brought to my room?"

"Downstairs," she replied. "Floor three."

"Yes, I am sure you have a nice dining room.

But I am asking whether you can have my breakfast brought up to my room." He was pronouncing his words very slowly.

The woman turned her head back to the newspaper she had been reading and said, "Floor three, breakfast."

With some exasperation he dressed and, eschewing the elevator, walked down to the third floor. He saw, on the right, the glass door that opened onto a cafeteria. He walked in. A dozen men and women were seated here and there, some of them talking, some reading the paper, others doing nothing except eating and drinking their tea. His hand instinctively ran to his chin: Yes, he had remembered to put on his beard. He picked up a tray and walked along the open platters, surveying the choice of fare. There was cheese, and bread, and a hot cereal, and ham, and what looked like goose liver, and cold hard-boiled eggs. He saw no fruit, and so took cheese, ham, a hard roll, paused over the coffee, deciding instead to take tea. He paid the bill and considered for a moment the option of taking the tray back to his suite, deciding against it lest the cashier raise a fuss. And in any event, Sir Alistair Fleetwood was not used to going up three flights of hotel with a tray of food in his hand as if he were a hotel steward.

He returned to his room not in the best of moods, and wondered what to do during the two hours before hearing from Alice. He would have liked to wander about the city to view the changes during twenty years and a world war, but thought it best not to do such a thing without first checking with his guide. In the general turmoil of leaving the *Fernbrook,* he had left behind not only his sailing clothes but the satchel with the books he always had in hand: two or three scientific treatises, a novel by Graham Greene, the current issue of *The Economist,* a new biography of Lloyd George, and Kingsley Amis's *Lucky Jim.* That precious satchel, he thought, sitting in that sailboat! In his briefcase he had only technical papers and plans of the mini-Zirca. What would he do?

There was nothing for it but to go down to the lobby of the hotel and see what he could find on the newsstand. He walked to the elevator, reasoning that the defective unit must either have been fixed or taken out of business. There were, after all, three to choose from. He pressed the button and presently the indicator showed that the elevator was there, so he opened the door, entered it, and pushed the button marked "Lobby." Arriving, somewhat to his relief, he saw again the great area he had first seen the night before, except that now it was full of what seemed to be Russian businessmen, except of course that there were no Russian businessmen. But there were a lot of men in their thirties, forties, and fifties, wearing mostly ill-fitting gray suits, bustling here and there. Fleetwood heard mostly Russian, but now and again some German and some French. No one, as he crossed the lobby walking in the direction of the concierge, was speaking in English. Too proud to use his neglected Russian, he decided that he would speak in French to the concierge, pending an update in workaday Russian from Alice Goodyear Corbett. So he asked for *"les journaux—où se trouvent-ils les journaux?"* The concierge pointed back to the elevators, and then indicated with his finger that on reaching them, the inquirer should turn sharp left.

On reaching the newsstand, Fleetwood first eyed matter-of-factly the several rows of Russian papers and magazines, and then looked about for books and magazines in foreign languages. But in English he saw only theoretical and historical works on the Soviet Union. No magazines whatever. It was so in French—and in German. He picked up a guide to Moscow in English, paid two rubles for it, and went discontentedly back to his room. The maps in the guidebook gave the names in Russian of everything about which he read in English. He remembered with remorse Alice's instruction, when she recruited him, to cease instantly his study of the Russian language with which he had got conversationally quite far during that golden summer twenty years ago. His resourceful mind now began the act of reconstruction, and by the time the telephone rang some of it was beginning to ooze back into memory, quickening his circulation, a feeling he had got used to over many years as he trained his powerful mind on scientific problems.

But he was happy to hear her voice, and he told her to come right up.

Dressed in heavy brown wool and a beret, she asked after his state of health and he told her that it had not been an ideal morning, but he was anxious to get on with the project. He looked at his watch: "At what time are we meeting with Comrade Beria?"

She hesitated. Her embarrassment was palpable. "I called on Comrade Abakumov—he is, as you know, State Security Minister, and the right-hand man of Comrade Beria. I must confess, Alistair, I was very much surprised. He told me that Comrade Beria has . . . he said that . . . schedule problems—that he hopes to see you before you leave but cannot undertake to make any commitment. You are to proceed immediately with the installation," she finally blurted out.

Alistair Fleetwood got up from his chair. He removed his beard. His complexion was white.

"I—I find this quite inconceivable, Alice. How is it possible, what you say? I am perhaps the most eminent living scientist after Einstein. I have devised an instrument that has already done historic work for the socialist revolution. I have stopped all my own work now for five weeks in order to meet Beria's special request. I cannot believe what you are telling me."

Alice Goodyear Corbett broke out into tears. She rushed over to Fleetwood and hugged him, and cried convulsively. She too, she said, could not believe it. But—attempting to control herself—but, she said, there must be a reason. There is always a reason. And by training they had to accept the decision and—

"My dear Alice," Fleetwood said. "I understand Bolshevik theory, and do not need your exegetical help in this matter. Here is my answer to Comrade Abakumov. Inform him that I shall proceed with the installation only after I have had a good"—Alistair Fleetwood stopped, and thought for a moment—"until after I have had a good one hour with Comrade Beria, during which I shall discuss common concerns, and public policies, and perhaps even Soviet developments. Tell Comrade Abakumov"—Alistair Fleetwood was beginning to enjoy his massive retaliation—"tell him that I shall stay in these quarters until I have visited with Comrade Beria. And"—Fleetwood was now walking up and down the living room, his hands clutched behind him, in the manner of Napoleon—"tell

him, further, that there is not one living soul in
Great Russia who can make the mini-Zirca work
for him other than me. Tell him that I am here
for exactly seven days, as per our arrangement."
Fleetwood was now standing on tiptoe, his arms
akimbo, looking down as though at a threaten-
ing bully. "Oh yes. And tell him that if on the
seventh day I am not back in Stockholm, why, I
shall have no alternative than to march over to
the British Embassy and complain."

She stood up and gave a short cry. "Alistair!
Stop! Stop, I say!" She looked about the room,
her eyes hysterical. She raised her finger to her
lips. She beckoned to him to go with her to the
bathroom. There she turned on the water taps
at full force, and in a low voice whispered
hoarsely, "My darling Alistair! One doesn't talk
that way about Comrade Beria! Not even *you*
can talk that way about Comrade Beria! And this
business of going to the British Embassy . . . I
mean, Alistair, don't *ever* say such a thing, not
even in levity." Alice Goodyear Corbett was
weeping like a baby.

Fleetwood had calmed down, but he was not
about to reverse the thrust of his comment. He
put his hands on both her cheeks and pressed
them together. He spoke in a low tone of voice.

"Very well, Alice. And on no account would I
make trouble for you. But my message stands.
No visit with Beria, no mini-Zirca. Now you go

and tell them that. They can hardly blame what I say and do on you. If I knew how to communicate with them directly I should do so.—And listen, dear Alice, when you come back, whatever you do, bring me something to read. And not something about the Soviet Union. No offense intended, you understand: The Lord knows, I am concerned with the Soviet Union, interested in the Soviet Union, obsessed by the cause of the Soviet Union, honored to be a servant of the Soviet Union. But right now, in my present mood, I want to read something. In English. Bring me some Trollope. Or Jane Austen. Or Dickens. Hemingway is legal here, isn't he? Well, bring me some Hemingway, then. And I am never averse to a little literate erotica, if there is any of that about. Now hurry away, my darling Alice."

He turned off the water and led her back into the living room. She powdered her nose in front of the mirror, picked up her handbag, blew him a silent kiss and left, her countenance grave as she contemplated the heavy message she was to deliver.

TWENTY-TWO

WHEN, THREE MONTHS EARLIER, the Office of the Director was advised that a communication had come in from someone who described himself as a "middle-aged Italian gentleman" with "very interesting information" which information, however, he would divulge only to the Director himself and to no one else, the request had received routine handling: The letter was turned over to an aide.

The aide wrote back to the box number designated on the letter to say that unfortunately the Director was busy, but that he, the aide, would be glad to see "Mr. Mussolini"—as the letter had been signed—anytime, at any reasonable place. That letter got back an urbane letter advising the aide that if the Director was not interested in knowing what the internal fighting within the Kremlin was all about, perhaps the Director should resign his position as head of the Central Intelligence Agency and perhaps become Baseball Commissioner? The aide pondered the communication, its rather special élan, and

238

made the decision to put the whole dossier into the Director's In box. The Director studied it, sighed, said to his aide that the chances were ninety-nine out of one hundred that Mr. Mussolini was a crackpot, but—well. He told his aide to set up a meeting at a safe house.

And so it was that Allen Dulles met Mr. Mussolini. Within five minutes the Director knew that he had drawn the one-hundredth straw. The man he was speaking to was not there in jest, or to announce that he had invented an ingenious means of keeping the sun from shining over the Soviet Union until they all said Uncle.

Mr. Mussolini was in his mid-forties, tall and angular. His hair was full and black. His eyes were always amused, even when his features were solemnly set. He was well dressed; the Director—dressed in his customary tweeds— thought him even rather foppish. And there was even a hint of fragrance there. Cologne of some sort? Not the kind of thing the Director found endearing in men. But he had become resigned to it, gradually, after discovering that young members of his own immediate and nonimmediate family, of inescapable masculinity, were going in for the new convention.

Mr. Mussolini spoke flawless English, accented as if he had spent years in a British public school.

Seated in the small Victorian drawing room with the two sofas, the coffee table, the fireplace, the bookshelves, the heavy oak doors, he began directly, autobiographically.

"I was a communist when I was a young man in Padua, and I went to Spain to fight with the Loyalists. While there, I became very good friends with a young Russian. We were over two years in that long war, and we saw everything" —he paused—"absolutely everything," Mr. Mussolini said, was the best way he could put it.

Mr. Mussolini had immediately volunteered, on returning to Italy, to divulge what he knew about the cynical nature of Soviet operations in Spain—"They cared not a bit for Spanish democracy; they cared to govern Spain"—to the Italian government, notwithstanding his loathing of Il Duce, its fascist dictator. The communists were onto him, but for several years were powerless to act. Finally they caught up with him when the partisan movement had begun to prevail; and, in December of 1943, he was sentenced to execution by a partisan firing squad— from which he was saved by an unexpected directive that came in through the communist hierarchy.

"And the man who signed that directive was —my old friend from Spain!"

His old friend was in the KGB, Mr. Mussolini explained. And once or twice a year he would hear from him, through channels now consolidated, channels the details of which "I would not tell to my father confessor, even though I tell him the most fearful things!" Mr. Mussolini smiled.

The Director thanked him for the background and said that he must be aware that in the trade the Director was engaged in, the counterintelligence people want "what we call 'earnest money' "—did Mr. Mussolini know what that term meant?

Again Mr. Mussolini smiled. Yes, he knew about "earnest money." He assumed that the Director wanted a scrap of valuable information to establish that Mr. Mussolini was on the level. "And incidentally, Mr. Director, speaking of 'earnest money' reminds me of just plain money. There will have to be some of that. Not king's ransoms, but not pocket money, either. My friend needs to look out for the inevitable day when, if he is not shot, he will escape that dreadful country, in which event he would not wish to spend the rest of his life as a common laborer. And that day is not far off."

The Director replied without reference to the matter Mr. Mussolini had brought up. "Let's begin with the earnest money," he said.

Mr. Mussolini's accents were now clipped, utilitarian. "At the last meeting of the Politburo, it was decided that the Foreign Minister should attack the American hegemony in Japan and propose a separate arrangement between the U.S.S.R. and Japan."

"You are telling me that Foreign Minister Molotov will make that public proposal soon? Or that it will be confided to Japan's Prime Minister?"

"The first. Something else. This is Tuesday. Before this week is out, *Pravda* will attack British Labor leader Clement Attlee for the criticisms he has made of the People's Republic of China since returning from his tour.

"That, Mr. Director, is your earnest money."

When, the next day, the attack on Attlee appeared in *Pravda* and, on Saturday, Molotov delivered a speech on the subject of the iniquitously close relationship between the U. S. and Japan, Dulles probed his staff to ascertain whether there had been any advance tips anywhere respecting the two events. The answer was negative.

From that moment on, the Director never hesitated to answer personally a call from Mr. Mussolini. These calls came irregularly, every two weeks or so, and each one of them cost the Director—this only after a little haggling—four thousand dollars in cash.

"Today"—Mr. Mussolini, meeting with the Director in the designated safe house, was dressed in Austrian loden, positively gleaming in green and pigskin leather buttons and a huge belt—"I have very important news from my friend."

The Director, a little deaf, removed his pipe from his mouth and leaned forward.

"The Politburo is divided on how to react to the American plan to recognize West Germany. The section headed by Beria wants to retaliate by recognizing East Germany's independence and then having East Germany take over the government of Berlin. Yes, *West* Berlin. Take over, in other words, what you, the British, and the French now control. Malenkov opposes this. But Malenkov needs, as I have told you before, shoring up. There must be, my friend informs me, some sense that he is making progress in his negotiations with the Western powers, even if that progress is measured only in terms of socio-political recognition."

"You are not suggesting we give up our plans to recognize a West German government?"

"Of course not. But Malenkov—and Bulganin, and Khrushchev—need *a response* that suggests you fully acknowledge Malenkov as the legitimate successor to Stalin—in the sense that no foreign country ever disputed that Stalin was the leader of the Soviet Union.

"And here, Mr. Director, is something else. And though I do not wish to be crude about it, for purposes of our calculations what follows will count as a separate communication; you understand my point?"

"I understand that my agency will be paying twice for this visit."

"Exactly. Now: Comrade Beria is actively engaged in spying on Malenkov, by means not disclosed to me. But he is actually reading Malenkov's cables. That would appear to me as though he were ready to strike."

"Is Malenkov aware of this?"

"Certainly not. If he were aware of it, he would presumably strike first. No. Only you are aware of it." Mr. Mussolini smiled. "Ironic, no?"

"Very ironic," said the Director, picking up his pipe. "In fact, quite incredible."

Mr. Mussolini drew his head back coldly on hearing the word "incredible."

"Now, now, Mr. Mussolini, I hope you don't mean me to take what you just said *literally?* I meant 'incredible' in the sense of something very difficult to believe. But that does not mean that I don't believe it: merely that it is *objectively* difficult to believe. You understand the difference?"

Mr. Mussolini said he did understand the difference.

The Director pursued his point. "You have told me on several occasions that Malenkov needs shoring up, and we have taken steps to attempt to do this, though public announcements have not been made. But you are telling me now something very concrete and very dangerous, namely that Beria may be planning a coup against Malenkov, and that if he took power he would proceed to communize Berlin and resist by force of arms any attempt by the West to keep this from happening?"

"That is how I read the message from my friend."

Allen Dulles rose. "The money will be deposited as usual. Meanwhile, let me know instantly when you hear again from your friend."

Mr. Mussolini bowed, his breezy smile dissolving any suggestion of servile deference.

This was the fifth visit in which the Director had met face to face with his informer. And he had made plans this time: to have his valuable friend tracked. Accordingly, when he left the safe house, Mr. Mussolini was followed discreetly by two agents of the Director. Mr. Mussolini walked circuitously, but soon entered nonchalantly 1601 Fuller Street. The Italian Embassy.

It did not take long, in the CIA Laboratory's file of pictures of registered diplomats, to establish that Mr. Mussolini was in fact Giuseppe Angelo, deputy chief of mission of the Italian Embassy.

"And that," Allen Dulles said to his brother

later that evening after divulging his news, "settles exactly nothing. If Mr. Mussolini-Angelo's game has been to tip us off to interesting but hardly earthshaking advance information ('PRAVDA ATTACKS ATTLEE'—I mean, so what?) in order to establish his credibility for the purpose of misleading us concerning a serious matter, then he has made just the right gestures. If Mussolini is a direct agent of Beria, then friendly gestures by us to Malenkov will hurt Malenkov rather than help him."

"That might have been so under Stalin," his brother, the Secretary of State, said. "Sounds too farfetched to me to suppose it's true this time around. I would guess the best interests of the United States clearly lie in helping torpedo Comrade Beria."

"I agree. But how're we going to persuade the President to make up his mind?"

"Nothing to it, Foster. All we need to do is get Joe McCarthy censured. Then Ike will let you go to Moscow to romance Malenkov."

That was a wisecrack, but it happened that the following morning the Senate, by a vote of 67–22, censured Joe McCarthy. That afternoon President Dwight David Eisenhower authorized Secretary of State John Foster Dulles to announce that he would travel the following week to Moscow to confer with Premier Georgi

Malenkov respecting West Germany and other matters.

Moreover, the President telephoned to Prime Minister Anthony Brogan, told him what he had agreed to do on the recommendation of his Secretary of State, and got assurances that under the circumstances the British would proceed forthwith to invite Mr. Malenkov to address Parliament, and that in due course it would be discreetly revealed that, while in Great Britain, Premier Georgi Maximilianovich Malenkov would be received by the Queen.

TWENTY-THREE

THE MEETING THAT afternoon had been
exciting: progress was in the air. The feel of the
chase. The pictorial bombardment by Jimmy
Moser was judged, however early (the enlarge-
ments were not yet ready), to have been a
smashing success: seventy ("seven zero!" Jimmy
Moser exclaimed) negatives had been got from
the flashlight-camera, and these were viewed on
a small screen by six spectators: the three Americans, Rufus, Anthony, Blackford; Sir Gene (as
they now called him, at his urging) and Superintendent Roberts; plus a photographic technician
with MI5.

More, the technician three times said, might
be discerned on the following day, after enlarge-
ment of the negatives was arranged. But in the
meantime one finding was conclusive: After
hungrily examining the pictures of the silent co-
resident, Blackford pronounced, in accents that
didn't invite contradiction, that the other man
in apartment 516 was indeed Henry, Bertram
Oliver Heath. The other finding of interest

made by the photographic technician was to the effect that he knew of no photographic assembly remotely like that which he now examined. He was eager, he said, for the session the next morning, with the negatives enlarged.

Rufus suggested, in an aside to Blackford, that the American party might dine informally together for professional purposes, and Blackford, in a telephone call to James Street, arranged for cold beef and chicken, red wine and cheese, fruit and coffee. They sat around the living room outside Blackford's Op-Ox study. The strain of the afternoon's proceedings—the quiet but tense disagreement with the two Britishers on how to proceed—almost required that during the eating hour, the compressed ensemble should give over a relaxing half hour to irrelevancies. And so Blackford reminisced about his first meeting with Anthony Trust ("He was a seventeen-year-old prefect at Greyburn College, Rufus, and we were all supposed to be frightened of prefects, but it took me a while to catch on"). Trust began to recount the awe he felt on first meeting Rufus, and was joyously embarked on the intimidating briefing given him by his CIA training officer on the subject of what was all right and what was not all right in the company of Rufus, and about Rufus's spectacular achievements during the war, when Rufus interrupted: a raised hand, the shy but authoritative smile: "No need to go into my background, Anthony." That much from Rufus was definitive; on to the next subject.

Was there a subject contiguous to Rufus's mystique? Blackford elided into eccentricity as a universal phenomenon. They laughed together over some of the mannerisms of their British colleagues. Blackford: "Sir Gene, have you noticed? A nose-picker, but he seems to think nose-picking becomes invisible" (Blackford, contorting himself, gave a demonstration) "if he bends his right arm behind his head to pick at his left nostril; and then, later, his left arm behind his head to pick at his right nostril. He figures this makes the whole maneuver socially invisible." Anthony laughed heartily. Rufus smiled; he enjoyed the banter, but left it to his young colleagues to practice it.

Inevitably the discussion turned serious. Professional agents of counterintelligence don't usually ask wide-eyed questions on the order of "How do you suppose Bertram Heath became what he is?" But, in a reflective frame of mind, Blackford now asked Rufus if he had gotten anything of universal application from his knowledge of the literature of communist apostates? "I mean, learned anything from the defectors beyond what we all know from reading their books, what I call The God That Failed books?" Rufus said that however perverse, it was still a form of idealism that kept many communists in the system. He cited the comment made by an Englishman within the KGB to a British mole who had given his colleague to read an account of what the communists had done to destroy Warsaw. "After reading the book," Rufus related, "he said words to this effect, that there were two alternatives facing Western communists. The first is to say, We were wrong! We'll chuck it all! And go back to the bourgeois world even though we know they haven't changed. The other is to acknowledge that human nature affects also the leadership of the communist movement, and that there will be purge trials and Nazi-Soviet pacts and Warsaw uprisings: but that also one day there will be a dream realized. He said he was choosing the second alternative. With that kind of thinking, one doesn't argue."

"What do you do?" Blackford asked.

"You wait. You fight." Rufus paused. And added quietly, "and you pray." Rufus stood up and walked toward the coffeepot. "Meanwhile we have the problem of the Brits."

That problem, which had been discussed endlessly during the afternoon, had to do with how to proceed on the matter of apartment 516. Sir Gene and Roberts were emphatic in recommending instant penetration with search and arrest warrants. Rufus had argued for a delay. His problem was in making his case for the delay without divulging his most valuable secret, namely the mole within the walls of the Kremlin now relaying vital information via Mr. Mussolini. Mussolini's bulletins might prompt action by Washington, the success of which would depend on Washington-London communications' being regularly intercepted by Moscow. Rufus had told neither Trust nor Blackford about Mr. Mussolini, and would not do so unless it proved necessary, so his arguments against immediate entry into apartment 516 were hard to sustain whether talking with the British or with his own colleagues. But at least with the latter he could say some things he couldn't to his British counterparts. And now he did so:

"I was not able, with the British, to go as far as I'd have liked in explaining why we want to consult other factors in deciding when to abort apartment 516. They would ask, 'What other factors?' I would be put in the position of saying, 'Other factors we elect not to tell you about at this point.' To you I can say merely that there *are* other factors which you do not know about."

Trust said, "This is their country, Rufus. And British laws have been broken. It's their call, isn't it?"

"Yes it is. But we have leverage, and we will use it. The two big actors in this episode are both British. The damage was done primarily to Americans. Something can be got out of that.

And they need our technical information. But it is getting late," Rufus said, picking up his hat and umbrella. "And we have an engagement tomorrow." He walked to the door. "Good night, gentlemen."

Blackford brought out a bottle of scotch, Anthony leaned back in his chair and said, "I got to admit it, Black, my instincts are for a quick kill. Get in there, put an end to the business. Haul 'em in. Examine The Spook. What do you think?"

"My instincts," Blackford said, standing now in his shirtsleeves, his back to the gas fire, and speaking with unwonted solemnity, "are to apply pressure through Henry. Henry: Bertram Oliver Heath. The young sadist of Winchester. Heath, the sycophantic lover of Fleetwood. Granted, we don't know whether their relations went in that direction. We know that kind of thing hasn't been exactly uncommon in Cambridge in the set that considers itself emancipated. Heath the mistress-beater. Heath, the man who led the forty-one commandos with whom he trained, who trusted him, to the gallows, then faked pictures of his own martyrdom. I'd like to go after him. But I confess that's in part because I don't much care what would happen to him if he didn't yield his secrets."

Anthony Trust recognized in his old friend the uncompromising determination that he had experienced in Blackford once before. He contented himself to say, in accents studiedly unpatronizing, "Black, we're involved in a joint venture. Remember, what *you* feel about Heath can't govern the thinking behind that operation."

Finishing his highball, Trust said, "Did you see the *Daily Mail* today? About Queen Caroline at the Covent Garden opening? An American reporter leaned over the royal box and said, 'Ma'am, is it true there might be a summit conference? And if so, would you be willing to greet Premier Malenkov?' Well of course normally the Queen simply doesn't answer questions shouted out at her that way, but she turned in his direction—can you see it, Black?—and said, 'I shall greet my horse Steadfast if he wins the Derby. Should I do less for Soviet leaders?' Bloody joy, that woman. But you know that, from 1951."

"Yes," Blackford said. "She is certainly something."

TWENTY-FOUR

AT THREE-FIFTEEN THAT afternoon
there was a knock on the door of Fleetwood's
hotel suite. Hastily he donned his beard and
went over to open the door. He was confronted
by a stout woman of businesslike manner followed by a young man carrying, or attempting
to do so—the object was half-lifted, half-pushed
into the hotel room—a large suitcase.

"You are Mr. Bjorn Henningsen," she stated in
declaratory English.

"Yes," he said.

"I am Nadya Balenkov, assistant librarian,
University of Moscow, at your service."

She did not introduce her young man. She
simply motioned him to lug the suitcase into the
living room.

"Where would you like it?"

Alistair Fleetwood, for the moment confused,
pointed vaguely at a corner of the room. Thither
the porter went.

"I hope, Mr. Henningsen, that these titles are
to your liking." Comrade Balenkov approached

the heavy cardboard suitcase, opened her handbag, and took out a key. She opened it, kneeling down on the floor. Inside the suitcase were about fifty books. Fleetwood approached it, took up one of them, Jane Austen's *Emma*. And another: *Moby Dick*. A third: *For Whom the Bell Tolls*.

He turned to Comrade Balenkov. "That is most kind of you to look after me. I shall take good care of these books, and of course you will have them back. How—do I—arrange to call you?"

Comrade Balenkov pulled a card from her handbag, gave it to Fleetwood and said, "When you are ready for us to come to take the books back, you will simply inform the concierge on your floor and she will notify us."

Alistair Fleetwood bowed. And without further ado, motioning to the young man to follow her, Comrade Balenkov walked to the door, opened it, and left.

At six o'clock the telephone rang. He had been expecting the ring with feverish anxiety, sedated only after the books came, which had made the last few hours pass by more quickly. Alice Goodyear Corbett was manifestly excited, but she was being cryptic, leaving it to Alistair Fleetwood to piece together the meaning of what she said. She spoke with unusual formality.

"Bjorn," she said, with heavy accent on his

pseudonymous first name, "I have had a very pleasant afternoon visiting with . . . old friends. We talked at great length about you, and my friends are great admirers of yours. That is the first thing I wanted to tell you. And one of those friends, the, the . . . senior of those friends, is most anxious to meet you and to have a nice visit with you. He is not at this moment in Moscow, but will be here later on this evening, and he hopes—I hope—you will not object to meeting with him at a rather . . . unusual hour. He would be available shortly after midnight."

Alistair Fleetwood had several reactions to what he had been told. Triumph, clearly. Unless he had drastically misunderstood the anfractuous message of Alice Goodyear Corbett, the Great God Beria had backed down and agreed to see him. But immediately following that agreeable sensation of victory it came to him that Beria was clearly imposing his own idiosyncratic schedule on his distinguished British visitor. A means of domesticating me, Fleetwood immediately thought.

He paused.

He was tempted to tell Alice that, really, at midnight he would be much too tired to keep spirited company with her "friend." . . . But a third reaction, modifying the second, rescued him from humiliation. He could accept the midnight meeting hour in the spirit of—security! After all, he was here in order to consummate a most private commission. Under the circumstances he might, without loss of dignity, respond to a midnight invitation as though he thought the hour selected with the single purpose in mind of maximizing security. All this was done with only a moment's hesitation. And so he answered her:

"Why of course, Alice. Midnight is fine with me. I understand the requirements." (Dramatic pause.) "There is of course a condition to all of this, which is that you and I will dine together in our accustomed, civilized way. Only I fear it will be up to you to cope with the requirements of Room Service here. My Russian is not up to it."

Alice Goodyear Corbett, manifestly relieved by his reaction, smiled. "Of course, my darling. I will be with you at eight, and I'll make all the arrangements."

"You did get the books?" Alice called back, a half hour later.

"I did get the books, and I thank you most heartily for them."

"I am so glad. Well, of course I have made the arrangements. You do like caviar, do you not—Bjorn?"

"I like caviar very much, never mind that I

disapprove of anything that costs one hundred pounds per kilo. Plutocratic, conspicuous consumption; but since it needs to be consumed, I shall make the sacrifice."

"You will see me at eight o'clock"—she permitted herself an indiscretion, Alistair thought, by closing, "entirely prepared for you, dear Bjorn." On the other hand, he supposed the KGB, judging from her fright earlier in the day, knew everything. They are, after all, supposed to know everything, he reminded himself, though he did not very much relish that anyone else should know everything about himself and Alice.

She had arrived at eight, told Alistair Fleetwood that the dinner would arrive at nine, they had both reenacted their rituals and were in bed, in intimate union, when the doorbell rang. Rang once, paused only momentarily, rang again, followed by peremptory, persistent use of the brass door knocker.

"Oh dear! Oh dear! Oh dear!" Alice Goodyear Corbett said, her voice a tangle of emotions. "I will go to the door. Oh-h, darling—forgive all of this." Disengaged, she got up, and then said, "My goodness! I have no robe! I must dress!"

She sprinted to the bathroom while the knocking on the door proceeded at progressively imperious tempo. In record time Alice Goodyear Corbett, her dress on, sped past the bedroom into the living room and opened the door. Through the slight opening of the bedroom door, Alistair Fleetwood could see three Russian waiters wheeling a huge trolley of foods into the living room, accompanying it with heated conversation. Alice was evidently reproaching them for bringing the dinner a full forty-five minutes before it had been expected, the headwaiter protesting something or other, all of it in energetic polemical tones; and then, suddenly, the three waiters were gone, the food and the large tray of bottles left on the table.

Fleetwood got up out of bed, dressed himself with only absolutely essential attire, and walked into the living room. "Really, Alice, I do think these arrangements most awfully . . . clumsy."

She explained that evidently the management of National Hotel had been instructed to pay such special attention to the desires of Mr. Bjorn Henningsen that in the eagerness to please, the management had advanced the schedule she had stipulated. Her voice was soothing, and the odor of the Chicken Kiev, and the sight of the rare (in Russia) white French burgundy in the ice cooler soothed Alistair Fleetwood. He even permitted himself a laugh. "I think I shall propose a new maxim to the lexicographers," he said. He drew his head back a bit, closing his eyes—a posture he used frequently in class, when he struggled visibly to decoct from the tumult of his stochastic knowledge a special truth—"a fresh formulation, even. *'Coitus interruptus causa splendidissimi convivii.'* 'The act of love interrupted by reason of the most splendid feast.' Do you like that, Alice my dear?" She said she did like it, and admired it, and that it confirmed everything she thought about him, including his wonderful good sportsmanship, and so they began their dinner as usual, except that when time came for the traditional liqueur, she cautioned, finger to her lips, "Let's not tonight, darling, not until after our meeting with our friend. I think we had better be very careful until then." Alistair Fleetwood nodded good-naturedly, and put the top back on the bottle of kirsch.

It had really gone splendidly, Alistair reflected the following morning when he woke at 8:30. The car had been there waiting for them at 11:15. They were in the waiting room at the Lubyanka at 11:45. And at exactly midnight, they were called into the office.

Beria had risen and walked over toward Alistair Fleetwood as though he were a close friend, arrived on a surprise visit. Beria kissed Fleetwood on both cheeks, threw his arms about him, and walked him toward the chair by his desk. He was talking rapidly, Alice struggling in spurts to interpret. He had been most fearfully embarrassed and put out on learning that his Minister of State Security had dealt so—offhandedly—with Beria's distinguished guest. What had happened was a reflection of the top security status of the operation in which "Comrade Bjorn"—this was followed by a heh-heh-heh and a wink at Alice Goodyear Corbett—was "playing so vital a role."

At that moment the door had opened and two trolleys were wheeled in with vodka and caviar and hot onion soup, and in moments the four of them—"Josef," a youngish, tall, sallow blond man wearing a double-breasted black suit, who had kept seated in the corner of the room during the whole period, was perfunctorily introduced as "my aide Comrade Josef"—were seated around the table. And Beria was telling Comrade Bjorn how highly he was prized in the Kremlin and how vital was his current mission.

After vodka had been poured for the third time and the trolleys removed, Lavrenti Pavlovich addressed Fleetwood. The operation, he said, needed to go forward immediately.

He showed—and for this Fleetwood was grateful and impressed—a meticulous knowledge of the physical requirements of the mini-Zirca, as Fleetwood had described them in the several sessions, personal and by radio, with Alice Goodyear Corbett. The requisite space had been located. It was appropriately situated to provide the mini-Zirca with a line of sight to a certain office. Fleetwood had said that an intervening structure would not in fact interdict the desired communications, but that a slight blur might result, so that the operation was best carried out between a building and the Kremlin window without "great steel things in between," as Fleetwood had put it in an idiomatic communication to Alice Goodyear Corbett.

The mini-Zirca was situated, Lavrenti Pavlovich advised Fleetwood, in exactly such a situation. The specified electrical requirements had been met. "All that is now needed," Beria said, wrinkling his face into a composite of fleshly wickedness force-fed by the demands of amiability—all that was now needed, in fact, was the "enabling" of the machine, and instructions to the technician on how to maintain it in operation.

"Here," Lavrenti Pavlovich smiled, "I have a wonderful surprise for you. Not only a wonderful surprise for you, Comrade Bjorn. But a wonderful surprise for our friend here—" he pointed to Alice.

"The technician in charge of the Zirca will be: Comrade Belushi!"

Alice Goodyear Corbett turned sharply to Beria, exclaiming in rapid Russian, causing Beria to reply in rapid Russian, leaving Alistair Fleetwood with little to contribute, though he sensed that Comrade Belushi was somebody very important or somehow controversial. In due course Beria turned to his guest, waiting for his interpreter to speak. Alice found it difficult to interpret a passage at once so impersonal, and so personal.

"Comrade Belushi," Alice exactly relayed the words spoken slowly by Beria, "is the proud husband of—no less—" and Beria raised his vodka glass and bowed in the direction of Alice Goodyear Corbett.

Alistair Fleetwood had not supposed that his visit in Moscow would involve an acquaintance with the creature Alice had been required as a matter of administrative convenience to marry. He did not look forward to receiving as his pupil the man he had cuckolded. But on the other hand war was war, so to speak. And his happening physically on Comrade Belushi would not in any way interfere with the large hold on his emotions that Alice Goodyear Corbett occupied. So all he could think to say was:

"How convenient, Lavrenti Pavlovich." And, looking to one side at Alice, a tiny shrug of the shoulders: So what? She returned the gesture with a suddenly affected indifference.

As they were being driven back to the hotel, Fleetwood reminded himself that he had intended to ask Beria some direct questions about the implications of this rather serious gesture of intra-Kremlin politics. But, he confessed to himself, he had been so much taken by the hospitality, Beria's gratitude for favors past, Beria's admiration of Fleetwood's continuing work for the revolution—all of this had caused Fleetwood to put aside pronouncing questions his curiosity had prompted him to ask.

And so as, wearily, he slid into bed at three in the morning for the second successive night, he blanked out what his musical colleague at Trinity liked to call the "hemidemisemiquavers." What mattered was that the revolution marched forward, and that unquestionably the most brilliant young scientist in the Western world was performing indispensable services for that revolution. It was, of course, comforting to know that the full measure of his importance was known to the chief of the KGB: that vast, vital system geared to contend with the subtle fascist machinations of reactionaries inside and outside the boundaries of the Soviet Socialist Republic. And that evening Sir Alistair Fleetwood, Nobel laureate, pride of British science, the envy of lesser men all over the world, had dined in the sanctum sanctorum of Revolutionary Intelligence in intimate contact with its head: that squat, ugly, fleshy little man who, Alistair Fleetwood was convinced, was the principal custodian of Soviet security.

TWENTY-FIVE

BLACKFORD HAD A telephone call from his mother early that afternoon. She told him that a messenger had delivered an envelope for him. "Really all very spooky, darling, because the envelope is addressed in red ink with very wide lettering, and it says: 'For the attention only of Blackford Oakes, Esquire.' I am of course very proud to know that others are aware that you can be reached through your mother. Will you drop around for it, dear, or shall I just post it?"

"No no," Blackford said. "Does it have any return address on it?"

"No, nothing. Nothing at all."

"I'll come by, Mother—" he thought for a moment. The day, as planned, was crowded, and it was not easy simply to go in and then out of his mother's house. "No. Mother, I'll send someone by for it. He will identify himself as Mr. Brown. Give him the package, all right? I look forward to our outing tomorrow." He pursed his lips to make the sound of kisses and hung up.

And so a young aide from James Street was dispatched. He was back within a half hour. Blackford was alone at his desk, studying the plans of the building where, he now knew, Henry lived and worked in apartment 516. He waited to open the envelope until the aide had removed himself.

He stared at the piece of paper, unbelieving. The brief message was signed merely *BB*. Written in German, in neat block letters, was:

Mr. Oakes. You remember that confessional that was very useful three years ago?

I shall be the priest, at 9:03 P.M. You the penitent. This is most urgent business of mutual concern. I shall wait only three minutes. I cannot overestimate the importance. If there are interruptions of any kind, the benefit to both parties will be eliminated.

It hadn't required him to speculate about the location of the proposed rendezvous. Three years before, Boris Bolgin would meet his British informer, when there was traffic to be exchanged, at the fourth confessional stall back from the altar, on the left side of the church at Farm Street. Blackford Oakes had worked on the case, and in due course the clandestine arrangement became known to him.

The meeting place had the obvious advantages, the church being dimly lit; and at that hour priests were not hearing regular confessions, so that any odd-hour worshippers, remarking a priest enter the stall, would reason simply that special arrangements had been made, somebody sick or in imminent danger of going to hell or off the following day on a trip around the world single-handed on a sailboat—whatever.

A private meeting with Bolgin! His chief antagonist for three years now. Head of KGB-Britain. The very idea of such a meeting intrigued Blackford, who in the three years they had battled each other, so to speak in the dark, had come to know something of the background of Boris Andreyvich Bolgin. Several times Blackford had stared probingly at the single photograph the archives possessed of the man who posed as military attaché at the Soviet Embassy, who never attended any public function, and was never present at any of the very few social functions held at the embassy.

Rufus. He must consult with him, Blackford thought.

And thought again. He did not doubt that Rufus would authorize him to cooperate. But Rufus might stipulate certain precautions that Bolgin would interpret as a breach of trust . . . Blackford's esteem for Rufus was such that he asked himself, finally, whether Rufus, in Blackford's shoes, would report to Rufus: and decided, although with misgivings, that Rufus would *not* report to Rufus. And so Blackford would not.

He picked up the telephone to cancel his scheduled meeting with Minerva, who wept over the telephone until Blackford promised that he would telephone her if he found himself free later in the evening. "No matter how late?" she pleaded. "No matter how late," Blackford promised.

It proved to be much later than he expected.

At exactly 9:04 Blackford got up from the pew where he had sat for ten minutes, and where he had most fervently prayed for guidance, prayed also that the Lord would intervene in the affairs of man sufficiently to rid the world of the curse around which he had built his professional career. He could discern the confessional, but was far enough away from it to avert any suspicion that he was engaged in trying to memorize the features of the stocky man wearing a cassock who, at three minutes after nine, walked through the entrance to the church directly to the confessional, opening the priest's door, entering it, and quietly closing it again.

Blackford rose, entered the penitent's booth, and drew shut the curtain. The priest opened the sliding partition. They could not, in the dark, see each other, but their heads were inches away. Boris spoke softly: "I shall speak to you in German. You are fluent in German and I am more comfortable in it than in English. And besides, it is not a bad idea to speak in a foreign tongue."

"What do you want, Bolgin?" Blackford replied.

"I want to spend one hour with you, and I have a suggestion that I think you will find professionally acceptable. We will both leave the confessional together. We will walk out the rear door and across Mount Street to the Connaught Hotel. There we will ask the doorman to get us a taxi. Whichever taxi is at the head of the line is the taxi we will take. We will then ask the taxi driver to take us to his favorite pub. If it proves entirely unsuitable for our conversation I will give you a list of recommended pubs I have in my pocket, and you will select the pub we shall go to. Are these precautions satisfactory?"

Blackford thought. The suggested schedule was not the way to trap an American CIA agent. Moreover, it made no sense, having got this far, to be querulous.

"That is satisfactory. Except omit the driver's pub. When we get into the cab, give me your list and I shall select one."

"Very well. You are ready?"

"I am ready."

They both got up and walked out. Bolgin led the way to the church door. Silently they walked over to the Connaught. Three cabs were in line, and as they approached the hotel entrance, the first one was summoned by the doorman for a middle-aged woman who was waiting. Boris Bolgin, carrying an umbrella which had suddenly materialized from inside his cassock and which he used now as a walking stick, hailed the doorman: A taxi, please?

The doorman pocketed the half-crown piece Bolgin tendered him and whistled for the next cab, which drove up the hotel's miniature half-moon drive. The doorman addressed Bolgin.

"You are going . . . sir?"

"Ah, yes," Bolgin said in a guttural English. "I have it written down in my pocket. Mr. Chestnut, sir, can you read the address? I do not have on my glasses."

Blackford used the light from the hotel's huge brass lamp and read a page cut out from the current issue of *What's On* magazine, giving the names of a dozen bar-restaurants. He was familiar with several of them. He selected the Queen's Arms, which was quiet; indeed, it had several private rooms. He gave the name and address to the doorman, who called it out to the driver.

In the cab Bolgin, while removing his cassock and tucking it into his large briefcase, spoke, as ever in German: spoke of the summer weather, of the indifferent quality of British food, of the

WILLIAM F. BUCKLEY, JR.

fact that as a boy, his mother had made him use
the confessional, but that it had become increasingly dangerous to do so, and how greatly relieved he was, on reaching fourteen, that his
mother thought it in fact too dangerous and so
ceased going to church. "The revolution's first
flower in my young life," Bolgin chuckled, "rescued me from compulsory churchgoing with my
mother."

They pulled up at the Queen's Arms, Bolgin
took out a ten-shilling note, carefully counted
out the tip, and they went in. Bolgin turned to
Blackford and, still in German, said, "You make
the arrangements."

In a few minutes they were in a small private
room. A table with two comfortable chairs, a
couch at one end of the room, and as much or as
little lamplight as they chose, done by rheostat.
The waiter took their orders. Blackford asked
for a pint of beer and some chips. Somewhat to
his surprise, Boris ordered a pint of vodka; and
then asked for cheese and sausage and hard
rolls.

"I have not eaten. You have eaten?"

"Yes," Blackford said. Bolgin continued with
the badinage until the food and drink came.

Bolgin poured himself a half glass of vodka
and placed a sausage into half a roll, squeezing it
together. He took a deep draft of his drink and
then bit a large hunk from his roll. It occurred to

Blackford that he looked not unlike Khrushchev: small, sharp eyes; jowls, wattles, teeth
separated, nose squat, though Bolgin had more
hair, which he wore in a crew cut. His nose was
dappled and slightly pink. Bolgin caught Blackford's eye: "Frostbite. Courtesy of Siberia. It is
there, too, that I learned not to postpone eating.
Bad habit," he took another large swallow of
vodka. He leaned back in his chair.

"I don't often drink while doing business. In
fact I never do. On the other hand, I don't often
have a meal with a fascist imperialist." He chortled. Blackford half smiled.

"Let's get on with it, Bolgin."

"Yes. Yes." He grew, suddenly, serious. He
looked about him cautiously. The small uphol-
stered room was secure. They could hear the
hum of voices from the bar and dining room
outside. Boris turned to Blackford. "You will
perhaps understand my request if I tell you that
my life depends on it?"

"What is it, Bolgin?"

"Would you not consent to call me Comrade
Bolgin? Or perhaps Mr. Bolgin? You may of
course call me just Boris, though perhaps you
will find that too familiar."

Blackford detected a creeping mellowness in
voice and manner.

"I shall call you anything you like," he said.

"In that case, call me Boris. If you think of it as

273

too familiar, you can excuse it by appealing to the protocols of the world we operate in, where everyone has only a single name. A false name. My name actually is Boris, but you can use it as though it were a pseudonym. What shall I call you?"

"Whatever you like."

Bolgin chortled. "You heard me refer to you outside the hotel as Herr Chestnut? Oak? Chestnut? Birch? Maple?" He laughed, and drank again from his refilled glass. "The 'Chestnut' came first to my mind, so I shall call you that: Mr. Chestnut." He laughed again. "But I must get on with my request. I wish, please, to search you to make certain that you are not carrying one of those wire recorders."

"Of course." Blackford rose, extended his arms upward, while Bolgin quickly and expertly frisked him.

"Thank you," Bolgin sat down, and drank again. "Do you know the Russian authors, Mr. Chestnut?"

Blackford said that he had read much of Dostoevski, and a little Chekhov and Tolstoi.

"Ah!" Bolgin responded. "What treasures we have given to the world! I have read them all—Turgenev! My God, you did not mention Turgenev! Or Gogol! Or Pushkin! I have read them all—and when I finish, I begin again!" Blackford noticed the sudden change in his voice, which had become lyrical. "Ah, Mr. Chestnut, if only we lived in a world in which everyone spent time reading, instead of killing."

"That would put most of your friends out of work," Blackford permitted himself.

Bolgin arrested his hand, which was halfway to his mouth. "You talk about killing, my dear Mr. Chestnut. You who invented the atomic bomb. You who plundered the Indians and the Mexicans. You whose folk heroes are Billy the Kid and Jesse James! You lecture *us* about killing!"

"You certainly do not sound, Boris, like a graduate of Gulag."

"Ah!" The tone now was conspiratorial. "I will confide to you that *I* did *not* admire Comrade Stalin. No, not at all. I worked for him, yes. There was no other way than to work for Comrade Stalin. But I think things will be different. But I have certain fears. These are what I am here to talk to you about. And please, let us not talk about the imperialists until we do our business, shall we, Mr. Chestnut?"

"Sie sind dran—It's your call, Boris. So what did bring you out tonight? We have not spoken once in the three years—"

"In the three years in which I have kept pace with your perfidious activities. No, we have not spoken, Mr. Chestnut. But"—he was serious again—"I come to you with the gravest intelligence. Something even I am not supposed to know. Perhaps only four, five people know it."

Blackford waited.

In hushed tones Bolgin said: "When Comrade Malenkov comes to visit England, it is planned that a bomb will explode in his car. The English will be publicly blamed. And Beria will take over the government in Moscow."

Blackford found himself breathing slowly. Bolgin drank again.

Blackford: "Why are you telling me?"

"Because I do not want another Stalin," Bolgin said simply, his eyes downcast.

"What use did you expect me to make of this information?"

"Have security forestall the accident. I would expect to be able, from my source, to supply you with more detailed information before the event. Quick preventive measures would frustrate Beria's entire plan. Perhaps weaken him decisively."

"When would you expect to have this more . . . detailed information?"

"In time. There is no secret more carefully guarded, but I will have it. If I do not have it twenty-four hours before the visit is scheduled, then you must abort that visit, on whatever pretext. I know that that would be difficult. But the alternative would be disastrous—if Malenkov is killed by a bomb while visiting this country."

"You realize, of course, that this is information I shall need to report to my superiors. Your proposals are hardly of the order I have the personal resources to implement."

"I know that. I expect that you will share your information with your superior, Rufus. And if it becomes necessary, of course, the Prime Minister and the President will need to concert the postponement. *I* am safe so long as Beria does not discover my source. If he does, and it becomes plain that British Intelligence was on to the plan, I have the choice of committing suicide or of being shot. Beria would find me anywhere else."

Blackford didn't know quite how to respond to what Bolgin had just now told him. "You would of course be given sanctuary."

"There is no sanctuary from Beria."

Best not to pursue the question. Blackford asked, instead, how Bolgin proposed to communicate with him in the critical days ahead.

"Give me a private telephone number. If I need to meet with you I will give 'Mr. Chestnut' the exact time that 'confessions will be heard.' "

Blackford scratched out on a matchbox the number of the telephone on his desk at James Street. Bolgin drained his glass—the pint of vodka was empty. Blackford made an effort to drink down his beer. Bolgin leaned back, flushed. His hand, lighting a cigarette, was not entirely steady.

"The next few days, at most two weeks, will tell. If all goes well, we will be fighting each other again." He beamed. "But I will then be something else than the agent of Beria."

Blackford thought it best not to say what was on his mind, that Malenkov and Khrushchev and Bulganin had not got where they had got except by satisfying the same monster, Stalin. Better, he thought, to be passive. He called for the bill, and presently they walked out together. Bolgin did not extend his hand, satisfying himself merely with, *"Auf Wiedersehen."* Bolgin hailed the first cab, Blackford the next.

He gave the address of Rufus. His heart pounded. From the corner of Rufus's block, in the pub, he called. Rufus answered his phone pursuant to the convention—two rings, hang up, ring back, answer on the fourth ring. Upstairs in the apartment, he listened exactly to the exactly recounted story.

Blackford was wide awake. He went back to the pub and dialed a number and was greatly pleased to hear Minerva's voice. "Are you busy, Minerva?" he asked.

"Never too busy for my golden boy. When will you be 'ere?"

"I should say in twenty minutes. I could use a little champagne."

"Is that all you could use, dove?"

"That's all I can use that you might not have on you," Blackford said, smiling into the phone. He had, in visiting Rufus, discharged his nervous exhilaration. With Minerva, of whom he had grown passionately fond, he hoped also to discharge his physical exhilaration. And to please her, at which he had become accomplished.

He was back at his desk at James Street at seven in the morning.

TWENTY-SIX

No, Blackford had said to his mother, no, under *no circumstances* would he be late. Yes, he said to his mother, he *did* realize how very interesting it would be to attend the garden party the Queen was giving for what she termed "the academic elite" of "Oxford and Cambridge etc.," including the trustees and their families, and yes, he was very pleased to have been invited, *ex officio* as the stepson of the chairman of the board of trustees of Cavendish Laboratories. "And as your dutiful son, Mother."

"You are more than my dutiful son, darling," Lady Sharkey had said. "You are my beautiful, wonderful boy." Blackford, at the other end of the telephone, closed his eyes in exasperation but let it pass. He would rather suffer than reprimand his gentle mother. His stepfather, Sir Alec Sharkey, was similarly disposed. Not that putting up with Carol was difficult: she was the most obliging, most retiring, devoted, affectionate woman, so unlike Americans Sir Alec had both known and become familiar with in books and movies: the brassy, hard-boiled types. There was nothing hard-boiled about Carol Oakes Sharkey, but after her divorce and remarriage to an Englishman, in 1941, she had made it a point to live as the British did, and a royal garden party was no mere frivolity on her social schedule.

Blackford wondered vaguely whether, given that there were over a thousand guests scheduled to be there, his path and the Queen's would even cross. He half hoped they would not; half hoped they would, three years having passed since their fleeting, fleeted encounter, first at Buckingham Palace, then at Windsor Castle, including the time spent entirely alone . . . There had been no communication of any sort since that time, and Blackford had never even been tempted to take the initiative. Indeed he thought twice before accepting his mother's invitation. But curiosity and nostalgia, even a kind of loyalty, prompted him to accept the invitation of the most glamorous woman in the world.

And now they were bound, the three of them, for the palace, in the limousine rented by Sir Alec. As they drove through the park, their limousine, so bright and spectacular when it set out from Portland Place, became just one of many limousines, rented for the bright occasion, in that long caravan headed for Buckingham Palace.

Nature, that day in London, was being fully

cooperative with the Queen. It was warm and sunny, there was a light breeze, the children were playing in the park, and the tourists were ogling outside the palace gates. When, still a few hundred yards from the gates, their vehicle almost ceased to move under the constipating press of luxury cars, and promenaders. Sir Alec said abruptly that they should leave the motorcar and walk—"It is too beautiful outside to sit in the car." Lady Sharkey said something or other about her new shoes not being very fit for walking, but it was said routinely. Sir Alec exchanged an understanding with the driver on where they should look out for him on leaving the palace a couple of hours later, and soon they were walking, Lady Carol Sharkey with one arm clasping her husband's elbow, the other eased between her son's arm and his side. Blackford suddenly realized that he was quite nervous.

They arrived, their credentials having been examined, in the garden well ahead of the Queen's appearance. They were served a fruit punch and finger sandwiches and they strolled about the garden here and there, Sir Alec pausing to greet fellow trustees of Cavendish Laboratories. The garden was not exactly full—it would have needed an additional ten thousand guests to fill the garden of Buckingham Palace.

Suddenly the orchestra stopped its afternoon music. There was a pause, and then "God Save the Queen" as, at a distance, from the garden entrance to the palace, the Queen emerged, followed by Prince Richard and a half-dozen brightly attired ladies-in-waiting and aides. She wore a pale yellow pleated chiffon dress and a perky little veiled hat of the same material, perched on her blond hair at an angle. She looked directly ahead and smiled, rather absently, but after a few steps she stopped suddenly, stooped over, and lifted up from the lawn a little boy—evidently an old affection, because even at a distance one could hear his giggles at being kissed so resoundingly. She let him down with a gentle pat on his silk-clad bottom and was quickly surrounded by his parents and other adoring subjects. And from that moment on, what had begun as a procession relaxed into the informality of another garden party, though it was plain that guests at the party attempted, without ostentation, so to maneuver as to be in the way of the casual circle the Queen was engaged in describing.

It was while she was addressing the rector of St. Andrews, Sir John Appleton, that she caught his eye. Blackford was chatting with one of his stepfather's elderly friends. The Queen, on seeing him, began to fan herself briskly with the antique yellow ivory instrument she carried sometimes as if a scepter, sometimes as a ferule, sometimes as an adornment. She continued her conversation, and there was a little pause, pending which Blackford might have taken the initiative in approaching her, but did not. Queen Caroline smiled at Sir John and walked, followed by two aides—Prince Richard had left the Queen to make his own, counterclockwise circuit, and the young princes, with their nannies, were playing with other children—toward Blackford.

"Why, Mr. Oakes. How very nice to see you again," nodding her head ever so slightly and smiling warmly, but also warily, though there was no disguising the brightness of her eyes.

"Ma'am, may I present my mother, Lady Sharkey, and my stepfather, Sir Alec Sharkey?"

The lady curtsied, the gentleman bowed deeply, the Queen acknowledged them. "I am very pleased to meet you." And, to Lady Sharkey, "Your son engaged in some architectural research several years ago that led him to Windsor Castle, where along with a few other guests he stayed for a day or two." And to Blackford, "Did you complete your project, Mr. Oakes? Did you find the secret to the Great Wall of China? Do we know why it survives, while so many other structures do not? This is the sort of thing the Massachusetts Institute of Technology specializes in, is it not?"

"It was Yale I came from, ma'am."

"Indeed. Yale. It is in California, isn't it? Yes, of course. San Francisco. Silly of me to forget."

Blackford smiled. She had not changed. "Yes ma'am. But don't be embarrassed. I know some Californians who don't realize that Yale is in San Francisco."

Queen Caroline looked Blackford directly in the eyes, and there was a trace of an amused wink, an amusement at the play. There was a brief pause, after which nothing the Queen might have said would have surprised Blackford. What she said was:

"Good afternoon, Mr. Oakes. Sir Alec. Lady Sharkey." She smiled and, her entourage alongside, resumed her casual round.

Lady Sharkey was ecstatic. "How nice, darling, that she remembers your visit. But you know, dear, she is quite wrong about Yale. Evidently she confused you. I couldn't quite understand your reply . . ." But Blackford had been accosted by a meteorologist who had worked side by side with Rufus during the war. If he heard his mother's question, he did not heed it. And she did not repeat it, her mind wandering to other of the visual delights, that sunny afternoon at Buckingham Palace.

TWENTY-SEVEN

IT WAS A YEAR and a half before Nikita
Khrushchev, addressing the Twentieth Con-
gress of the Communist Party, would coin the
phrase "the cult of personality" to describe one
of the lesser sins of Josef Stalin. But well before
the phrase was formulated, its coils embraced
the minds of Soviet leaders even though they
went to extravagant lengths to conceal this.
More time was given to the factor of precedence
than at the court of the Sun King, and almost as
much time to concealing this concern. So that
when the regular Thursday morning meeting of
the Politburo convened early in October, Georgi Malenkov, whose post was that of First Secretary and who was therefore the senior member of the body, didn't stride into the chamber
like Stalin, approaching the chairman's seat as if
he had grown up sitting on it. Rather he approached it, so to speak, sideways, as if always in
need of orientation in the matter of which was
his seat. And his companion members of the
Politburo crowded at either side, not noticeably

behind him, confirming, if by no means as stridently as they had with Stalin, their acceptance of their subordination.

He approached the chair, which an aide drew back to permit him comfortably to sit, and found himself facing the nine other members of the Presidium of the Party Central Committee, generally referred to as the Politburo.

He greeted them amiably, fraternally, and told them they all knew that there was one major question on the agenda—namely, how should the Soviet Union react in the matter of the scheduled recognition by the Western powers of the sovereignty of the state of West Germany? As they all knew, he said, looking away from Lavrenti Beria who was seated directly opposite, he had issued invitations to the principal Western powers to a summit meeting to consider the implications of the planned diplomatic step, but although there were encouraging signs, he could not now report that his diplomatic initiative had worked—had worked, that is, in such a way as to give the Soviet Union the opportunity to use its great resources to stall the German demarche planned by the Western powers—

He was interrupted. It was Beria. "My dear Georgi Maximilianovich, you must understand that there is only a single way in which to deal with the West in this matter, and moreover we have the advantage here of its being singularly plausible. If they exercise the power to declare West Germany a sovereign state, we quickly and instantly retaliate by declaring East Germany a sovereign state. We then declare that it is up to East Germany to decide the status of Berlin. Ulbricht instantly announces that immediately on the formal recognition of East Germany, his government will incorporate Berlin as a part of its territory.

"And that means"—Beria leaned back, triumphant—"that means, gentlemen, that the same day President Eisenhower signs the diplomatic instrument recognizing the sovereign state of the German Federal Republic, we shall sign a complementary instrument declaring the Democratic Republic of Germany an independent state. And that same afternoon, Herr Ulbricht will sign an instrument declaring that Berlin, as a part of East Germany, is hereinafter under the political domination of the government of the Democratic Republic of Germany!"

Beria all but stood at this moment, as though promulgating his great geopolitical coup to a huge admiring throng. Instead he got from Malenkov:

"But Lavrenti Pavlovich, you are aware that the West has frequently reiterated rights of conquest in the matter of Berlin, denying to any single co-liberator the right to dispose of the area without the agreement of the others—"

Beria laughed. His laugh was a blend of truculence and condescension. "I am aware, Georgi Maximilianovich, of the legal wiles by which the imperialist powers further their designs. We paid no attention to those when the time came to face up to *their* objections over *our* understanding of the Yalta treaty, at which point our great Comrade Josef Stalin"—he paused here, as if invoking a moment's reverence in memory of his mentor—"waived the little legal points and kept his eye on the main business. Our main business in Germany, gentlemen, is to incorporate Berlin, which is a seedbed of bourgeois poison in our system."

Nikita Khrushchev intervened. "But listen, Lavrenti Pavlovich, even if it is true that you are correct about what should ultimately be done on the Berlin question, it is not a position we can take now unless we are prepared to counter the probable response of the West, which would be military."

There was whispering about the long table, much of it animated. Beria broke in: "I answer you in this way, Nikita Sergeyevich. In the first place, it is doubtful that the West would mobilize the will to fight for Berlin. In the second place, it is totally unlikely that they would resort to nuclear force. And in the third place, if they do not, our own tactical preponderance on the ground is more than sufficient to deal with the puny NATO forces."

Marshal Voroshilov at this point intervened. He said: "Comrade Beria, I would not dispute that the Soviet forces would triumph. But surely it is wrong to designate as 'puny' a NATO ground force west of Berlin that consists of forty-eight active divisions, over five hundred tanks, and one half again as many bombers as we command. To overcome such a force would require a major, protracted effort."

"So who is against a major effort in behalf of socialism?" Beria asked. He snapped his fingers at an aide sitting behind him. The aide rose, presented him with a cigar, and lit a match under it. Beria puffed. "The point is, surely," he addressed himself to Malenkov, "that if we permit the West to get away with this—this—rape of West Germany, there is no knowing where they will stop. I say *stop them now!*" There was muted applause from three or four members of the assembly.

Malenkov looked pleadingly to Bulganin. The marshal rose and spoke. He said that these were difficult times, that the paramount need was for unity, that nothing could so greatly jeopardize the great Soviet endeavor as to get into a war at a moment when the Soviet Union was not really prepared for war. Under the circumstances, he concluded, sitting down, "as a marshal of the Soviet Union, whose patriotism has been extensively tested, I would vote in favor of Comrade Malenkov's plan, and resist the temptation to use force over Berlin."

Malenkov tormented himself, wondering whether to take a vote. During the first few self-conscious months when they met without Stalin they made it almost a sacramental point to take a vote, subtly to distinguish between the ways of the new order of the Soviet Union and the old. But gradually the habit of a single dominance had made the vote less and less frequent. And now, Malenkov thought, was hardly the moment to revive the moribund tradition.

Accordingly, after an hour's discussion during which almost everyone contributed views on the question, he said that as chairman of the Council of Ministers, he had been very glad to have the invaluable advice of his invaluable colleagues, which advice he would take thoroughly into account before deciding on a course of action.

Malenkov paused. He sensed that if there was to be mutiny, this would be the moment for it. But Beria sat still, puffing on his cigar and making notes. Malenkov involuntarily shivered at the thought of the use those notes might one day be put to.

He called the meeting to an end, quickly involved himself in conversation with Bulganin, and walked out of the velvet-curtained room feigning a self-confidence he did not feel. He sensed that Beria would make his move soon.

It was ten that evening, Eastern Daylight Time, that the Director was finally reached by Rufus with the news of Blackford Oakes's meeting with Bolgin. On hearing it he drew a deep breath. He had been many years in the intelligence system. He had never before come across high jinx at such a high level.

TWENTY-EIGHT

NEITHER BLACKFORD nor Anthony Trust
was present during the wrangling between CIA
and MI5, though Rufus reported on it when he
got back, acknowledging, in his fatalistic way,
his frustration. Privately, Rufus had told Blackford that the Director had agreed that no one—
no one at all—should be told of Bolgin's conversation until Blackford heard again from him: or,
in the unlikely event he did not, until a few
hours before the scheduled visit by Malenkov.
Attention once again focused on apartment 516,
its secrets, and its nefarious occupant.

But Blackford absolutely had to break away,
he explained to Anthony. He had to go to dinner
with his mother. He could not, he excused himself to Anthony, put this off. "Besides, there isn't
anything I can think to do until Rufus brings our
friend Sir Gene around. Fleetwood is due back
from Stockholm in five days. We've got to get
into apartment 516 before that, I'd say—but
what the hell."

He was tired. Anthony Trust attempted to

WILLIAM F. BUCKLEY, JR.

cheer him up. Sprawled out on the couch, he
raised his head as if addressing the cracked ceiling and said, "Remember. The Brits have promised to keep round-the-clock surveillance on
apartment 516. And if anyone tries to jump ship,
they'll arrest him: they've got the warrants. We
shouldn't be faulting those guys after the job
they did shadowing Fleetwood. Attwood is anxious to move. He doesn't like Rufus's idea of
waiting. Too dangerous, he says. Might jeopardize the whole operation."

"Well," Blackford said. "Round and round we
go." He said good night and told Trust he would
be at James Street early in the morning. But the
following morning he did not appear at all at
James Street. He did not appear until the late
afternoon, shortly before dinner.

Carol Oakes had married Sir Alec Sharkey after divorcing, as she had more than once described him, her "gifted, wayward, sweet, irre-
sponsible flyboy"—Blackford's father—after he
had disappeared one too many times. He was
always away—in search of an odd airplane design he triumphantly announced he would sell
to some country or other in order to make the
million dollars he had been certain—absolutely,
volubly certain—he would make "any day
now."

It had been so every month during their eighteen-year marriage. By contrast, Alec Sharkey was a tidy man. Portly, formal, shrewd, civic-minded, a British architect who kept teemingly alive any number of associations: with his old public school, Greyburn College; with Jesus College at Cambridge, of which he was a trustee; with Cambridge's scientific center, Cavendish Laboratories; and, always, the Coldstream Guards, in which he had served as a major and artillery officer during the First World War. He was intensely patriotic, a fervent royalist, an intense student of public affairs.

He was very fond of his stepson, though occasionally put off by his disheveled—though never rude—informality. And although habituated to Carol's demonstrative, indeed melodramatic, fondness for her boy (almost unseemly by British standards), he was always faintly unnerved by it. Carol was capable of making her son positively blush listening to her discourse on his courage, intelligence, physical beauty, his feats as a fighter pilot during the war, the grades he achieved at Scarsdale High School and Yale. Sometimes Sir Alec simply had to stop her. Blackford, as at the garden party a few days earlier, always attempted halfheartedly to do so, but after years of trying he would, with doleful eyes, dumbly acknowledge his inability to restrain her.

As usual, it was black tie. There were three

couples invited. Blackford brightened on learning that one of the guests would be a professor under whom he had studied at Yale, a gifted particle physicist, Drummond Weiss, whose most endearing pedagogical manner—widely imitated, and caricatured, at Yale, by students and professors alike—was the heated argument he would stage with himself during his lectures, arguments that sometimes reached insane *ad hominem* levels: arguments so robust that students were often genuinely baffled as to which of the two sides of the vivid dialectical exchange was the one that Professor Weiss himself believed in. He gave the lie to Max Beerbohm's *bon mot*, that the Socratic manner is not a game at which two people can play. Professor Weiss, Blackford learned, was a visiting fellow at the Cavendish Laboratories, where he had met Sir Alec at one of the joint meetings of trustees and fellows. They had become friends.

Blackford loved his mother dearly, and permitted a half minute of her dizzy shower of affectionate and admiring garlands, congratulating himself on his prudence in arriving ahead of the guests. "But, darling, I told you just the other day at the garden party that you are thin. I knew you would get thin, spending so much time in Germany." Blackford asked why she came to that conclusion, given that German food is widely associated with the high incidence of obesity, and she replied with that sweet vague smile that all that was before the war, but that food in Germany was very scarce, that everything had been rationed since V-E Day, "Isn't that right, Alec?" Sir Alec Sharkey had long since abandoned any effort to impose chronological order on the mind of his wife, who last week was overheard in a conversation over the telephone with an old friend to say that she could not exactly remember when it was that Charles Lindbergh—"my Blackie's godfather, you know, Mildred"—had crossed the ocean, but she thought it was "at least seven or eight years ago."

Blackford contented himself to pat his mother on the head, hug her again, and tell her not to worry about food in West Germany, that they were eating very well there now, and that the reason he had lost a few pounds was that he had been doing a great deal of traveling. She let it go.

Professor Drummond Weiss greeted his former student with great enthusiasm, demanding to know in detail what he had been doing during the four years since "we studied together." Blackford was well trained in handling such queries, but he was not often questioned by such a searching curiosity as that of Drummond Weiss, who, after listening to the boilerplate about foundation work and reports on antique architecture for an engineering society, sniffed, in a low voice, that he guessed Blackford was engaged in confidential work of some sort— never mind, Drummond Weiss would not rat on him.

The other guests were also associated with the Cavendish Laboratories, two of them fellow trustees. One was a banker who liked to tell jokes about bankers, and exhausted on Blackford what Blackford hoped was most of his repertoire. His wife smiled wanly through it all, refilled her glass of sherry, and eventually eased herself away to talk to the wife of the third member of the Cambridge community, the loquacious Mrs. Floreat England. Mrs. England was as animated as her husband—a researcher in chemistry looking forward to his retirement the following year—was laconic.

It was quite suddenly, when the gentlemen were seated languorously about the table with their brandy, that the thought occurred to Blackford. "Mr. Weiss," he said quietly, as at the other end of the table the banker told the dismayingly familiar story of what Willie Sutton, the bank robber, said to the judge when asked why he robbed banks, which was on the order of asking what had Little Red Riding Hood found on approaching her grandmother.

"Call me Drummond."

"Uh. Okay, thanks—Drummond. Are you familiar with the work of Alistair Fleetwood?"

"Haven't personally examined his Zirca over at the observatory, but I am of course familiar with the papers published on it. Before you get a Nobel Prize, Blackford, the community of your peers needs to know what it is you're getting it for."

On impulse Blackford said, "Will you be in your office tomorrow?"

Drummond Weiss slipped his hand into his pocket and pulled out his calendar. "All day. What do you have in mind?"

"Might I come to see you? It is very important, actually."

Drummond Weiss's pen was in his hand. "What time?"

"Ten o'clock?"

Professor Weiss wrote down the hour on his book. "You will of course stay for lunch?"

"Thanks."

Sir Alec Sharkey had risen. "Shall we join the ladies? That really was a most amusing story, Allan, most amusing. I shall remember to tell it to Carol." He led the company into the pleasant padded Victorian living room, with the hunting prints and the signed picture of George V decorating Sir Alec for conspicuous bravery on the field of battle at Ypres.

*   *   *

Blackford left 50 Portland Place at 10:45 as the other guests were leaving, went back to the safe house at James Street, opened the door, disarmed the burglar system, and climbed the stairs to his Op-Ox office. He leafed rapidly through the log record of Alistair Fleetwood's visits to the Greenwich Royal Observatory. He ran down his finger to where the agent, on his first visit, had written the nature of the conversations Fleetwood had had with his colleagues. He came to the references to the "model," or "mini-Zirca," which Fleetwood had said he intended to reassemble in order to probe an insight that was scratching at his consciousness. And then, six pages later, to the passage in the log that related to the loading of the crate with the mini-Zirca, and the stopover at Robertsbridge where two men had appeared, driving off in the large station wagon with the crate, leaving Fleetwood's Ford car, the driver's seat of which Fleetwood had casually slipped into on leaving the café. What MI5 had not done was follow the station wagon that drove off with the crate. Their orders had been to stick with Fleetwood.

It must be so, Blackford thought. The mini-Zirca must be the key.

He needed to take one formal precaution,

silly though it seemed, but a hard and fast rule within the Agency.

And so he looked at his watch. It would be seven at night in Washington. He called the special number, and gave his identification. And then spelled out "W-e-i-s-s, Drummond. Professor of physics, Yale University." He waited impatiently, but in a few minutes the voice came in, "Nothing negative." "Thanks," and he put down the telephone.

Drummond Weiss sat in his office wearing a sweater and gray flannel pants, his unruly red hair falling over his black-framed glasses. His welcome was warm but also functional, distinguished from the kind of welcome Blackford had been given the evening before, about which all Professor Weiss now said was, "Awful bore, that banker." Motioning Blackford to sit down opposite, he turned his ruddy face down to a journal on his desk, open where a paper clip had been inserted.

"I gathered you wanted to talk about Fleetwood and his Zirca, so I got out the journal *Astronomischer Jahresbericht*—April, 1953—which has the most comprehensive treatment of it. What is it you have in mind?"

"I am wondering," said Blackford, who, having experienced the directness of his old teacher, had taken care to rehearse his questions, "whether a miniature form of the Zirca, using the same principles, could be got to read—" he reached into his pocket and pulled out a roll of paper three inches wide with dots punctuating it. It looked like a narrow player piano roll. He identified it as eight-channel punched tape, produced by a special teletype, which in due course was fed into an encoding machine.

"At what distance did you have in mind?"

"Concretely, we harbor a suspicion of an apartment ostensibly being used as a photographer's darkroom. It is four hundred feet between the window of the darkroom and the window of the cable office of the United States Embassy."

Drummond Weiss began his characteristic self-examination. But since he was not in class he spoke less didactically than Blackford was used to hearing him speak. It sounded rather like this:

"Hmm. You could, with the Zirca, project a very fine high-frequency non-visible beam of small-circumference cross section—" He twisted around his fingers the paper roll Blackford had handed to him, staring at its small punched holes—"like holes the size of a pencil lead. We know the Zirca incorporates enough electronics to fill many equipment chests, implying an extraordinary capacity for accuracy. The beam's aim—" he paused and looked down at the journal, "and focus—and movement—are each under ultra-precise control of these electronics.

"On the big Zirca, the beam would be wider. On a small model it could be made as small as one wished. The beam moves from left to right across the target area in a perfectly straight line. Then it drops down one beam's thickness, then sweeps right to left across the target in another straight line—on and on until the target has been totally swept . . ."

Professor Weiss suddenly forgot the presence of Blackford. He was speaking now to himself, but speaking words Blackford could hear. "Let's see—but the paper is coming out of the machine the whole time. No matter, no matter. The Zirca's scanning speed would prevail. Hmm. The whole thing then repeats from top down again, on and on."

And then again to Blackford, his eyes suggesting the excitement he felt—"Like the scanning beam in the TV tube, it excites the phosphors on the tube face, but this beam wouldn't change in intensity. The Zirca's beam emits in intense, discrete bursts. So—you would aim it onto this paper here, the punched tape, as it exits automatically from the machine, as the clerk is typing out the message. Yes." He paused for a moment. "As it sweeps the target its emission level is constant. Each burst is the same intensity as any other, all electronically monitored. The sweeps completely cover whatever size target area is set."

He stood up and began to pace behind the desk, turning his head now to Blackford in exegetical fervor. "The sweeping pattern, you understand, is one of successive discrete XY bursts. Each space is hit by a Zirca burst. So, for instance, the fifth space over on the tenth line down would be Zirca Burst number 5.10. Each discrete burst becomes an XY coordinate. Now," his voice became low, thoughtful, inquisitive, "the electronic brain keeps these each in mind waiting the return by reflectance. Gauging the difference in energy between what went out and what came back, you adjust for the constant loss—window glass, smog, distance, whatever the beam goes through both going and coming. So," he sat down again, "so each individual burst is thus fired and recovered, with the difference— *adjusted by the constant*—" he looked up as though to admonish his student, "recorded in sequence as perhaps something of an analog recording of intensity. Those intensity levels could later be converted into digital codes. That would be it."

He paused again.

"Subsequent processing equipment would take the analog tape and crudely say to itself: if the intensity is over such-and-such a level of decibels, but not below this other level, then it's a '5', and so forth. And the output of this, composited by whatever means, could *flow* the target area past in time frames. You would need overlays of some kind of additional signal on the recording tape identifying exactly where you've recorded the results of the last burst of a given total target frame scan, completing a given total target area frame before the next total scan begins." He stopped and was silent.

He looked up at Blackford.

"Yes," he said. "Yes. I can see that it would be theoretically possible to do what you say: at a distance of several hundred feet, to discern electronically the configurations of the punched tape that issues out of a teletype. I have to admit I would be astonished to see it actually work. But not surprised. As I say, theoretically it is possible. Quite possible. Practically—I simply don't know."

Drummond Weiss was arguing with himself.

Blackford felt as he imagined Newton felt when the apple dropped on his head. Not to *break* the code, but to read the message before it became coded.

TWENTY-NINE

GEORGI Maximilianovich Malenkov had accepted immediately the invitation to address Parliament, to which had been quietly added, by the British Ambassador, the assurance that Queen Caroline would receive him in Windsor Castle. On the very same day, the U.S. Ambassador called on Foreign Minister Molotov to say that the Secretary of State would be willing to travel to Moscow to confer with Soviet leaders about a number of questions. Malenkov summoned the Politburo and gave them the news, together with his interpretation of its meaning —which attested, he said, to the objective recognition by the West of the growing power of the Soviet Union and the stability of the post-Stalin leadership, whence the decision to sue for a conciliatory relationship. "Which means, of course, that we can press our plans under more auspicious circumstances than if the hostility of the West were totally mobilized." Malenkov was clearly exuberant.

Marshal Voroshilov wanted to know, Did the

British Ambassador really say, in as many words, that Queen Caroline of England would actually receive the Soviet Premier? —After all, that would be the first meeting between the Soviet chief of government and a Western chief of state since Potsdam.

"Those were his exact words, Kliment Yefremovich," Malenkov beamed.

There was light banter about the Queen, while several members of the Politburo stole glances at Beria, who finally spoke up:

"Tell us, Georgi Maximilianovich, did you make any concessions to the British or the Americans in order to—to bring on these developments?"

"Certainly not, Lavrenti Pavlovich, certainly not. Clearly they are the result of our stable policies—"

"Nothing on West Germany?"

"Nothing on West Germany." Malenkov quickly changed the subject, and slid into a related matter on the agenda—namely, what kind of a reception was it advisable to give to the American Secretary of State, renowned for his primitive anticommunism. . . .

In Washington and in London the principal players were well rehearsed. It had been decided that since the Queen was involved, however tangentially, the critical cable would go out of Whitehall. The exact contents of that cable, discussed in personal sessions and by telephone through the scrambler system between Anthony Brogan and John Foster Dulles, were dutifully transmitted by the State Department to the United States Embassy in London by cable, confident that it would be intercepted by the Soviet mechanism they were hunting down. The cable was addressed to the U.S. Ambassador in London:

"LATER TODAY WHITEHALL WILL CABLE MALENKOV ALL PLANNED DIPLOMATIC VISITS ARE OFF UNLESS WE RECEIVE EXPLICIT ASSURANCES THAT IN OCTOBER WHEN WHITE HOUSE AND EUROPEAN POWERS MEET TO SIGN ACCORD ON WEST GERMANY SOVIET PROTESTS WILL BE NON-MILITARY. WILL ADVISE RESULTS." It was signed, as such cables are, simply, "DULLES."

That afternoon, two days before his scheduled departure for London, Georgi Malenkov sat in his office staring at the cable freshly received from London. Granted it had none of the terseness of the American cable to the ambassador in London, the pirated text of which Malenkov had seen a few hours earlier. Still, it demanded assurances about Soviet behavior after the forthcoming recognition of West Germany. The cable read, "YOUR EXCELLENCY MUST REALIZE THAT REPORTS HAVING REACHED US IN THE PAST FEW DAYS THAT THERE IS A POSSIBILITY

OF ARMED RESISTANCE TO ALLIED POLICIES RE-
SPECTING WEST GERMANY H. M. GOVERNMENT
WOULD NEED TO HAVE NEGATIVE ASSURANCES
BEFORE YOUR EXCELLENCY'S ARRIVAL AS IT
WOULD GREATLY EMBARRASS THE GOVERN-
MENT IF YOUR VISIT WERE FOLLOWED SO
QUICKLY BY ARMED ACTION. AND NEEDLESS TO
SAY WE COULD NOT EXPOSE HER MAJESTY TO
ANY SUCH POSSIBLE EMBARRASSMENT." The
earlier part of the telegram had stated that the
two governments were acting in unison, and
that the trip by the Secretary of State would also
be put off in the absence of such assurances.

He summoned his two closest associates. Nikita Khrushchev's reaction was that he didn't
like to be pushed around like that. But Bulganin,
concurring with Malenkov, said that the request
was in fact reasonable, and since the Politburo
had already decided that no military resistance
would be put in the way of West German recognition, actually the Soviet Union was not giving
up any alternative it hadn't already agreed to
discard. "Moreover, we need to act quickly. It
would hurt us even if the rumor got out that
there might be a postponement."

Malenkov rang for his secretary.

After the proposed cable was typed out, Malenkov read it again, out loud, to Khrushchev
and Bulganin, and they concurred that it was

wise, dignified and, though conciliatory, uncompromising.

"What about the Politburo?" Malenkov asked.

Khrushchev used a vernacular Russian expression, a rough translation of which was, "Fuck the Politburo."

"And Beria?"

The mention of Beria's name always brought a pause. But they all knew that to bring Beria into the picture would merely mean incessant delays and recriminations. They felt sure that they had the backing of the majority in the Politburo.

Orders were given to dispatch the cable.

Within one hour of reading the cabled assurance to Whitehall from Malenkov through the mini-Zirca, Comrade Belushi made his transmission to his old friend Mr. Mussolini in the Italian Embassy.

He then went to the processing machine and managed to move the date and hour of the cable he had just recorded for Malenkov exactly twenty-four hours forward. He would take it to Beria tomorrow. That would give the Americans time to act. And give Beria time to act. But less time. And indeed they did act.

The next morning, early on Tuesday, U.S. Ambassador Charles Bohlen sent his deputy to the

Kremlin with the message that it was vital that he confer with the Premier, that a great deal hung on the immediacy of that meeting.

When word of this request was given to Malenkov a few minutes later he groaned, wondering what new conditions might now be imposed on the carefully planned itinerary, scheduled to begin on the following day with his departure for England, and to be followed next week by the reception in Moscow of the American Secretary of State.

He nodded to his aide to have the ambassador admitted. In the incredibly short time of fifteen minutes, the ambassador was shown in. He shook hands all the way around—Nikita Khrushchev and Marshal Bulganin were also in the room—and in his fluent Russian, smiling, said that he was authorized by the Secretary of State to give this communication only to Premier Malenkov, in the presence of absolutely no one else, and he did not have the authority to modify these instructions, even in behalf of such illustrious members of the Politburo as Comrades Khrushchev and Bulganin.

Malenkov looked at Khrushchev, who paused, then shrugged his shoulders, signaling to Bulganin. The two men left. Ambassador Bohlen delicately pointed to the interpreter. "You have never had any problem with my Russian, Your Excellency." Malenkov motioned to his aide to leave. The two men were alone in a hall once used by the Czar to meet ambassadors. The large vaulted windows high above their heads introduced daylight, but it was supplemented by the yellow light of the heavy crystal chandeliers overhead.

"Well, Mr. Ambassador," Malenkov pointed to the couch to one side of the huge desk, and Charles Bohlen sat down. "You may proceed."

"Your Excellency, we have received word in Washington from a source that has never proved wrong in any particular that a coup is being planned against you, possibly even before you leave tomorrow for Great Britain, by Comrade Beria."

Malenkov turned white. But said nothing.

"Comrade Beria has procured an instrument, developed in Great Britain for the purposes of astronomical research, to spy on you. That instrument was activated two days ago by the English inventor Sir Alistair Fleetwood, who is staying here at the National Hotel under the pseudonym of Bjorn Henningsen." Ambassador Bohlen passed Premier Malenkov a 3 × 5 card on which the name was written. "The instrument has been installed at an office in the War Ministry on Kuibysheva Street, which is of course directly opposite the Kremlin. Indeed," Ambassador Bohlen pointed his hand toward the outside wall of the office, "the machine sits directly over there." Bohlen paused. "It is not our function to interfere in Soviet politics, but this gesture of goodwill perhaps will be recorded in your memory on future occasions."

Malenkov hardly knew how to act. On such occasions, he quickly decided, extreme formality is the best guide. Accordingly he rose, walked slowly toward the entrance door in such a way as clearly to indicate to the ambassador that the conference was over and, as he walked, said stonily, "Thank you, Mr. Ambassador, for your trouble. I shall certainly take what you say under advisement." The door had no sooner shut than he rang his aide and told him to advise Khrushchev and Bulganin that they were needed urgently—"At once! They should both still be in the building!"

As the aide rushed out he thought to himself he had never ever seen Georgi Maximilianovich so excited.

V. S. Abakumov, State Security Minister, and Josef, Beria's closest personal aide, were in the office of the Lubyanka with him. Beria held up triumphantly a copy of the cable dispatched by Malenkov to Whitehall. "This does it! This does it! Malenkov can be charged with 58! Article 58!" Beria proceeded by heart: " 'Section One, Treason against the homeland; Section Three, Maintenance of relations for counterrevolutionary purposes with foreign states; Section Four, The rendering of assistance, by any means whatsoever, to that section of the international bourgeoisie which is endeavoring to overthrow the communist system!' He is ours! Ours! We can demand a closed, summary court martial, and instant execution! It will not be necessary to proceed with what we had planned for London. Malenkov will not arrive in London!"

Abakumov stared at the cable. "That is certainly the meat and potatoes, Lavrenti Pavlovich. A flat promise in effect to *cooperate* with the enemy in making an arrangement that strips us of any formal voice over the future of West Germany—in the teeth of his guarantee to the Council of Ministers that no concession was being made in the matter of West Germany in connection with his visit. Well done, Lavrenti Pavlovich, well done!" Josef said he too thought it was well done.

Lavrenti Beria sat down. "Let us make our plans."

He was a very happy man.

THIRTY

SIR ALISTAIR FLEETWOOD leaned back in the comfortable reclining chair aboard the Soviet Antonov AN-2 transport. It had ten seats but Fleetwood was the only passenger, with the exception of the escort officer, Major Somebody —Fleetwood had not caught his name when, at the very last minute, he arrived with instructions to be of any necessary service to "Comrade Henningsen." Already Fleetwood had waved goodbye to Alice Goodyear Corbett, after a mutual pledge of an early rendezvous in Stockholm, perhaps right after the New Year. The heavily bearded major, before motioning Fleetwood up the ramp into the airplane, asked him for his passport, "so that I can take care of the formalities for you, sir." He spoke in German, and Fleetwood answered him in German, reaching into his jacket pocket and handing him the Finnish passport made out to Bjorn Henningsen.

The major sat in the forwardmost window seat, so that Fleetwood was spared the nuisance of having to make conversation with him, or sharing a meal. The male steward offered Fleetwood cakes, tea, Russian wine, beer, and vodka. Fleetwood settled for the tea and cakes, it being only just after lunch. He leaned back contentedly and opened *The Forsyte Saga*, a book he had never got around to reading. He simply hadn't bothered to return it to Comrade Balenkov, the thoughtful librarian of the University of Moscow to whom he had dispatched, via the concierge, the suitcase full of the other books brought in a week ago.

The ceremony in the inner sanctum of the Director of the KGB had really been quite touching. And entirely unexpected. Alice Goodyear Corbett had telephoned him early and said that a little surprise was in store for him on his last full day in Moscow.

And there Beria was, as also the two principal deputies of "Lavrenti Pavlovich," as he had been instructed to call Comrade Beria. And with great solemnity Alistair Fleetwood had been presented with the Order of Lenin, "for conspicuous contributions to the cause of international socialism and devoted service to peace and the liberation of the working man everywhere." It was a beautiful gold medal, with of course the profile of Lenin and, on the back, the inscription that had been read out to him. "But we left out your name—the space is there for it.

Security. When the climate is propitious, you may take it to a jeweler and have your name inscribed. Meanwhile, in our safe, is the authorization. We cannot for obvious reasons publicly decorate you, Sir Alistair"—once again, Alice was rattling along to keep up her all but simultaneous translation of the fast-talking Beria—"but your constructive deeds, creative genius, and loyalty will forever be inscribed in the annals of Soviet heroism."

That was quite a presentation, Sir Alistair Fleetwood reminisced proudly, looking down at the patches of clouds covering the endless snowfields. It was good, he thought, that he had been critically helpful in penetrating a plot that might have brought the Soviet Union international disgrace, as Beria had explained it to him, among the legions who had worked throughout their adult lives, as he had done, for the cause of brotherhood.

He wondered whether, when the revolution came, he would need to give up his knighthood? He supposed so. And it was true he had got rather used to it. But there were other rewards. After all, Lenin was never Sir Vladimir Ilyich Lenin, let alone Lord Lenin—Alistair Fleetwood had to acknowledge that the possibility was overwhelming that sometime in the not remote future he would be given a seat in the House of Lords, where in fact he belonged—

that is to say, where he belonged in a society so
structured. There would of course be no such
thing in the future. Not the immediate future.
The forces of fascism were not quite ready to
give up, but that would come. Meanwhile, if he
had to serve as a lord—Lord Fleetwood? Rather
euphonious—why, he would simply do so.

He began to doze; as he did so, a tiny grain of
sand entered his scientific mind—the mildest
little irritant, lodging itself in the subconscious
of the Nobel laureate. That little irritant said,
yawningly, *How odd that, flying northwest from
Moscow to Helsinki, the gradually setting sun is
behind the porthole, rather than abeam of it*
. . . But not an irritant quite compelling
enough to wake him up.

They landed at 3:30. It was extremely cold
and blustery and Alistair Fleetwood had to lean
heavily into the wind to make headway down
the companionway. He did not recognize the
profile of the Helsinki airport, but of course he
had seen it a week ago only during the midnight
hours. He was vaguely surprised that an officer,
indeed an officer and six armed men, were there
to escort him to the terminal, where presumably they would disengage, leaving him to embark the commercial airliner to Stockholm as
that perennial tourist Bjorn Henningsen. He
smiled in the teeth of the wind, holding down
his furry cap, the present Alice had given him

the day before. The officer at the airfield spoke briefly with Fleetwood's bearded escort, who thereupon reentered the plane, which taxied to the end of the runway and, before Fleetwood had reached the building toward which they were headed, was airborne.

It was only then that he felt a twinge.

Within three hours Alistair Fleetwood had been court-martialed; sentenced to twenty years at hard labor for spying on the Soviet Union; informed that no, he would not be permitted, given the sensitive nature of his offense, to communicate with the British Embassy; put in a cold cell without light or window, having first been stripped of his wallet, watch, and briefcase. He pounded the heavy wooden door of the prison until his hands were swollen. He crawled then on his hands and knees to the thin mattress, wrapped his coat about himself, and wept hysterically until utter exhaustion took over, allowing him to imagine fleetingly that he was in thrall to a nightmare that would surely pass the next morning.

As Fleetwood, exhausted, was finally dozing, the passenger from Helsinki showed his passport at Immigration in Stockholm, having flown in from Helsinki to which the army transport, by special orders from the Kremlin, had taken him, on the understanding that he would first deliver the prisoner—who would learn now the high cost of facilitating an act of espionage against the duly constituted government of the Soviet Union—to the concentration camp whose director had been instructed on how to deal with him. All this a reward for very special services to the Kremlin: no less than the revelation of Zirca spying on the Premier himself. A contrivance, ironically, invented by the same man recruited and managed by the informer's own American-born wife! Ah, the ironies were wonderful.

He would miss Alice, really, though he would get over it. And of course she, as an accomplice, would be purged. But such was life: some people win, some people lose; and Alice knew that—big girl, Alice. The immigration officer, examining the passport, commented, "Well, Herr Henningsen, you evidently like our country. Second visit in just a week, I see." He stamped the passport and returned it, disdaining to examine closely the passport photo of a heavily bearded man in his late thirties. The following morning, at a hotel suite where the Bank of Zurich kept an agent with a teletype machine, the Swiss agent confirmed, after a teletyped exchange with Switzerland, that the number given to him by the customer entitled him to the instant payment of the five thousand dollars he requested, against the balance waiting for him in Zurich, one half of which, he kept reminding himself sorrowfully, belonged to his old friend—he was amused as he reflected on the name his friend had given himself, "Mr. Mussolini."

Vladimir Belushi counted the notes carefully, pocketed them, and walked out, checking his city map for the location of the Swiss Embassy, where certain formalities would need to be undertaken.

THIRTY-ONE

A FAREWELL MEETING of the Politburo was scheduled for nine that night. It was intended as a celebration, beginning, to be sure, with a brief business meeting. No outsiders had been invited, not even wives. For that reason it had been designated as a meeting rather than as a social event.

While Stalin was alive, Politburo members always arrived early. As much as an hour early. In recent months that punctilio had been in decline. At one session a month or so ago Beria had actually arrived late, though only by ten minutes; and he had excused himself, an act of contrition that caught his colleagues, unprepared to believe that Comrade Beria could, after Stalin's departure, apologize to anyone for anything, by surprise. Most of them assumed it was a tactic, an effort to ingratiate.

They came, always, in their limousines, through the Borovitsky Gate. Their Zis limousines, the Soviet Union's bulky 110-horsepower imitations of a prewar American Packard, moved at top speed through the gate, coming in through the very center of the most heavily guarded streets in the world. During the period of their arrival the principal street through which they would travel was blocked off by police, who received elaborate warnings in time to clear all pedestrians and other vehicles. The cars were followed by touring cars loaded with armed guards. Warning bells went off at the Borovitsky Gate as each car approached.

Tonight the ten ministers of state began to straggle into the Kremlin's interior through the East Door after passing through the Borovitsky Gate. They arrived with one or more aides, and were brought in by guards.

Marshal Bulganin loitered at the entrance to the East Door, chatting with his own aide, his eye out on who was coming and going, interrupting himself to greet the ministers casually but warmly as one by one they came in.

When Lavrenti Beria arrived, Bulganin waved his aide to one side and approached him, speaking matter-of-factly.

"Georgi Maximilianovich requests that you stop by his office on the way to the meeting. He wants you to look at his proposed statement at the London airport before he reads it to the whole Council."

"Very well," Beria said, removing his gloves and handing them, together with his overcoat, to his aide. He did not wait for Bulganin to lead the way. Instead he strode directly toward Malenkov's office. Arriving at the Premier's office he paused, undecided whether to knock. He simply opened the door.

Two guards grabbed him, one by each arm.

Premier Malenkov was standing grim-faced in front of his imposing desk.

"As Premier and Commander-in-Chief of the Soviet Army," he said metallically, "and having surveyed the evidence, I accuse you of high treason against constituted authority. You have been tried by an executive committee of the Presidium and been sentenced to death, the sentence to proceed immediately."

From the corner of the room Nikita Khrushchev bounded forward. He drew a 9 mm. Makarov from his right jacket pocket, aimed it at Beria's head, and pulled the trigger.

The guards had been preinstructed on the matter of the disposition of the corpse. The three deputies of Beria would be arrested within the hour.

Orders would issue simultaneously that until further notice all KGB orders would file through the office of the Premier.

The three men—Malenkov, Bulganin, Khrushchev—walked, with strict attention to rank, into the Ministers' Council Room. On noting the expression on their faces there was instant silence.

Georgi Malenkov opted for the identical formulation they had all heard so often, so stunningly often, from Josef Stalin; so casually delivered. The communication was straightforward, unadorned:

"Gentlemen. Comrade Lavrenti Pavlovitch Beria was apprehended while engaged in treasonable activity against the State. He has been tried and executed.

"We will get on with the agenda."

Premier Malenkov proceeded to read aloud the short statement he would deliver at the airport in London the following afternoon.

There was no comment—until Marshal Voroshilov spoke up: "I think it is absolutely excellent, Georgi Maximilianovich."

One by one the other members concurred.

"Excellent."

"Just right."

"Very good."

"Bravo, Georgi Maximilianovich."

THIRTY-TWO

In Brian Larwill's office and in his now crowded bedroom it was the same cast. But only a few yards away, in one of the indoor garage's parking spaces, was the lorry, in the rear section of which sat silently the four men brought in from Camp Cromwell, at Colonel Mac's direction, by Joe Louis: trained commandos. At exactly fifteen minutes after 8 P.M. on that warm night in the late London fall, Superintendent Roberts called down on the walkie-talkie to the technician standing by the main fuses in the basement.

"Ready out Op Ox."

"Roger out."

They waited.

They did not need to wait seven minutes this time. Almost immediately the telephone rang. It was Robert Editta.

"Is this Larwill?"

"Yes, sir."

"Well, this is Robert Editta, apartment 516.

Goddammit Larwill, our fucking lights are out again. I was just developing a film."

"I'm most awfully sorry," Larwill said. "I'll have to call Jimmy Moser. I have his home telephone number. It will take him ten, fifteen minutes to get here. Do you have torches, sir?"

"We've got exactly one torch, and the batteries are weak."

"In that case, sir, would you like me to bring you a couple of extras while you wait for Moser?"

There was a pause. Clearly Editta was soliciting the advice of his companion.

"Yes. Call Moser first, then get up here fast with those torches."

"Very well, sir. Won't be a minute."

In apartment 516 Bertram Heath suddenly stood up and wrenched the flashlight from Editta. "I don't like this. It could be all right but I'm not going to risk it. You stay here. I'll go out the hall to the other side of the elevator. Just in case."

Without further exchange he shone the light on the doorknob, opened the door, and went out, down the dark hall toward the elevator. He opened the door to the emergency staircase, leaving it ajar just enough to keep his eyes on the elevator. He waited. Not long.

A few seconds later the elevator light advised that the cab was coming to a halt at the fifth floor. Bertram Heath saw five men emerging, four of them in commando garb. He waited two, three seconds, and then began on tiptoe to walk away. Moments later he was racing down the five flights of stairs.

The five men walked noiselessly to apartment 516. Two commandos flattened themselves on either side of the door. Each was carrying a huge flashlight in his left hand, a pistol in the other.

Brian Larwill, carrying two powerful searchlights, knocked on the door with his toe. And said, "The torches here, Mr. Editta."

The sound of the chain being unfastened and the lock being turned was easy to make out.

The door opened, Moser jumped back, beaming his blinding lights into the darkness. The first commando lunged at the door, knocking Editta down. The second and third cast their glaring lights about the room. "Where's the other one?" one of them said.

"Look in there."

. They rushed into the darkroom. And then into the bathroom. They searched the closets and the kitchenette. The leader shone his light into the face of Editta, seated on the floor, his hands handcuffed behind him. "Where is he?"

"I wouldn't know, guv'nor. Mr.—Harrison, he left here this morning." The squad leader was on the phone to Larwill's office. Less than a minute had gone by.

Blackford Oakes, left below with the technicians, posted himself restlessly by the adjacent door of the elevator at the basement-garage level. Blackford wanted to stare into the face of "Henry" when, secured by four commandos he had neglected to execute, he came down. He gripped his right hand with his left. He would need to restrain himself.

At that moment the door around the corner burst open and a large hurtling figure ran out toward the street.

At the same time the door of Brian Larwill's office opened—they had got the radio signal from apartment 516. One man apprehended, one man missing. Superintendent Roberts's staccato report to Blackford caused a moment's hesitation. But an instant later Blackford had bounded from his post, tearing through the garage toward the entrance through which Heath —Blackford assumed it was he—had just gone. He spotted the figure running on the other side of the street toward a line of taxis. He was fifty yards ahead of Blackford when the cab he had got into pulled out into Upper Grosvenor Street. Blackford jumped into the back of the second taxi and said fiercely: *"Don't lose that cab!"* The driver, a heavy, younger man of dour countenance, turned his head slightly and said through the crack in the glass, "Easy come, easy go. I ain't chysin ahfter no one, guv'nor." Blackford opened the right-hand door, then the driver's door, reached in and grabbed the driver by the neck of his coat. With all his strength he sprawled the driver onto the street, and with a single motion seated himself in his place. The motor was already running and Blackford slipped into first gear and careered into the dark street, racing to catch sight of the first car.

He did. Two blocks along Upper Grosvenor. It was traveling at abnormal speed—clearly Heath had bribed the driver to go beyond the conventional speed limit. Blackford slowed, leaving fifty yards between himself and his prey: he would tackle Heath when he left the cab.

But the fast speed of the first vehicle, after it turned right on Park Lane, made conspicuous the speed of the second, and by the time the lead car had passed Speakers' Corner in Hyde Park it was traveling at over fifty miles per hour. The lead car turned through Cumberland Gate to Bayswater Road and began to race alongside Kensington Gardens. Still Blackford kept his distance, electing, instead of running into the car, to keep it in sight. At Kensington Palace Gardens, it took a left turn.

Suddenly it was clear where Heath was headed. To sanctuary.

There it was, the Soviet Embassy, within view. With the armed guard posted outside. An English policeman, to be sure, but not one likely to permit Blackford to apprehend a gentleman authorized to proceed into the embassy. Blackford made the decision quickly. He jammed the accelerator to the floor. As the first cab slowed to approach the embassy gate, Blackford swung left, tearing into the broad right side of his quarry, bringing it to a dead halt with a screech of rubber, and turning it over on its side.

The crowd formed instantly, with the usual confusion and excitement. There were shouts of "Ambulance! Ambulance!" Police hedged in. A half dozen of them and a few volunteers concerted to pull the two bodies from the car. The driver presented special problems because of the bent steering wheel. The passenger appeared comatose, and the door, facing skyward, was inoperable.

Blackford had shielded himself by crossing his arms over his wheel at the moment of collision. Stepping out of the car, he mingled quickly with the crowd. Both driver and passenger were dazed, though the passenger showed signs of recovery, and by the time the window had been broken, its edges scraped and insulated so that he might be pulled through without being cut up, he was talking. It was then that the ambulance arrived, and two men carrying stretchers laid first the driver on a stretcher and into the ambulance, and then Heath, who now was beginning to protest, insisting that he was well

WILLIAM F. BUCKLEY, JR.

enough; he would be on his way. But the police doctor motioned to the assistants to get him into the ambulance. "We'll need to check you out, sir. Won't take long." With no further attention paid to his expostulations, his arms were strapped to his sides with the stretcher's harness and he was lifted into the ambulance and deposited alongside the cab driver. Then the door was made fast with the outside latch.

It is now or not at all, Blackford decided; and so, as the orderlies began to walk up to the front seat, Blackford shouted out, "You forgot him! The third man! He's over there! Bleeding!" He pointed excitedly toward the densest part of the crowd. Both orderlies instinctively turned to search for the third victim. As they did so Blackford sprang into the driver's seat and brought the ambulance to life.

He was grateful for being shielded from the back of the ambulance by a steel grille: through his mirror he could see Heath struggling. In a few minutes he had made his way free of the leather straps. He tried to open the ambulance door from the end, wrestling for access to the front seat, and attempting with an aluminum first-aid box to bang open the rear window. Blackford spotted the ambulance's siren toggle switch on the dashboard and quickly activated it, giving him license to drive quickly through the traffic. He saw also the radio and flicked it on. He was connected to the hospital dispatch center and spoke into the microphone. *"This is an emergency. Emergency. Emergency. Telephone instantly to TRA 5858, ask for the line for Superintendent Roberts. Tell Superintendent Roberts the prisoner who escaped is being brought back by ambulance to Grosvenor Square. Do you hear me, Emergency?"* An efficient woman's voice came in. "I hear you, whoever you are. I shall make the call instantly. After I have made it, identify yourself."

"Roger," Blackford answered. *"I'll stay on the line. Advise when contact is made."*

He had reached Park Lane before the woman's voice came in. "The number is radioing information to Superintendent Roberts. Now, sir, what vehicle are you calling from?" Blackford saw no reason to dissimulate, and gave the number of the ambulance, written large on the registration paper on the dashboard. But when the dispatcher asked for further details he did not answer. He was close now to Grosvenor Square.

Reaching the building, he swung into the garage through the same door through which both Heath and he had just fifteen minutes before run out. He tore into Brian Larwill's office. To his relief he saw, still there, Colonel Mac, Joe Louis, and the commandos.

Breathing heavily Blackford said, "I've got

him outside. Locked in an ambulance. There's another fellow in there too, cab driver. I had to run into them. They're shaken up, but not badly. Roberts here, or heard from?"

Colonel Mac exchanged a glance with Joe Louis, who said, "Yes, he telephoned ten minutes ago. We were heading back to Cromwell and he told us to take Heath with us. Said to lock him up; he'd be around tomorrow with the interrogators. Wants privacy, I guess."

"Let's get going," Mac said.

Blackford went to the back of the ambulance and turned the latch. The door flew open, knocking Blackford over onto the ground. A human cannonball shot out of the ambulance. Into the clenched fist of Joe Louis. Two commandos dragged Heath into the back of the army lorry. Joe Louis stepped into the driver's seat. Colonel Mac sat down next to him. Blackford climbed in next to the colonel.

"Hey there, wait one minute, Yank. This is our operation."

Blackford liked Colonel Mac, and had got on well with him during their days at Cromwell. But he did not wish to be misunderstood. "Mac," he said, his jaw set, "I caught this man. And he killed thirty-two American commandos, you will remember. Where he goes, I go, and that's the way it's going to be, period." Colonel

Mac looked over for a moment at Joe Louis, who nodded silently.

The lorry fired up. Three men in front, the prisoner and four commandos in back, it pulled out of the garage and began to head southwest toward the highway leading to Salisbury.

At first there was no conversation. But soon Colonel Mac made an effort to ease the tension. "That was nice work you did, Ernie"—Blackford, at Camp Cromwell, had been "Ernie."

"Thanks, Mac."

And then the grizzled commando went on. "There's something you ought to know. You might want to get out of the way, Ernie. Something I promised Joe Louis. You want to tell him, Joe?"

"Yuh. I don't mind telling you, Ernie. You're a good man. When I found out—It was only today. This afternoon. When I found out what happened. What happened to my brother Isaac Abraham. And to the other fellahs—the rest of the lads at Cromwell—I said to Mac, I said, Mac, if I find that man Henry, that man is *dead*. That's it, dead. Then they showed us . . . Then they showed us the pictures . . ." Joe Louis stopped talking. Colonel Mac took over.

Both officers, Blackford learned, had been called into MI5 that afternoon and briefed on the entire operation. It was done in the office of General Islington, with Sir Gene there. The briefing had included showing them The Album. Neither of the briefers had known that one of the victims was the younger brother of Major Louis. When the page in The Album turned on Joe Louis's younger brother, his inert head twisted in the noose, his tongue protruding, Joe Louis had had to leave the room. Through the wooden door they could hear his sobbing.

"There isn't going to be maybe twenty years or a life sentence and then a trade-off with a spy they got over there in Moscow, not with this chappy. I promised," Colonel Mac said.

Blackford's silence was taken by Colonel Mac as indecision. Blackford sensed this. He said, ambiguously:

"Mac. I'll stay with you. But do me a favor. This is very important. I must telephone my—chief. I must let him know we have the prisoner. It means a lot for him to know."

"Why wouldn't he learn that from Superintendent Roberts?"

"You don't understand the communications system in this business, Mac"—Blackford's tone of voice implied he was telling them deeply kept secrets. "My superior hears only from me," Blackford lied. "If he doesn't hear soon from me he will conclude the worst. And for very important reasons—a lot depends on this—we can't let that happen. If I give you my word I will say nothing of your—plans, can I telephone him?"

Colonel Mac turned his head inquiringly to Joe Louis at the wheel. He had sat ramrod-straight throughout the exchange.

Joe Louis grunted his assent. The lorry slowed a mile down the road, next to the entrance to the year-round carnival at Basingstoke, with its half-dozen acres of booths and amusement parks—not heavily patronized at this time of year, though it was warm tonight. Blackford bounded out of the car, told the ticket lady he merely wanted to use the public telephone, and was searching his pocket for change as he walked into the booth. He found the shilling— they were already thirty miles outside London —and gave the number to the operator, his fingers tapping the telephone impatiently. He suddenly reflected that he was not absolutely certain, though he expected to be hearing the voice of Rufus in seconds, whether he would keep his word to Colonel Mac or not.

"That number is busy, sir. Try again later."

Blackford raised his head, waiting for a minute to pass before dialing again. He reflected on what Joe Louis had gone through that afternoon. And on what his brother had gone through a few months before. He reflected on the end of the mystery, with the discovery of the Zirca.

It was then that the tent in the amusement park caught his attention. It was directly across from the telephone booth, a few feet away. He read the blazing sign across the top of the stand:

MAKE YOUR OWN HEADLINES! SURPRISE THE FOLKS BACK HOME! SURPRISE THE KIDDIES! SURPRISE YOUR LUV! ONLY THREE SHILLINGS!!

He looked under the big sign where a half-dozen specimens, home-oriented headlines framed in glass, were posted. The logo was that of the *Daily Express*. The first headline read, "SALLY SAMPLE MADE DUCHESS/QUEEN GIVES HER PALACE" Another read, "JOHNNY BURT SENTENCED TO HANG/ADMITS TO SLAUGHTER OF 500" Another, "DICK BETROTHED TO SHIRLEY/'NEVER LIKED LIZ TAYLOR' HE SAYS."

Blackford closed his eyes for a moment. He opened the door to the telephone booth and stepped across the way to the tent. Five minutes later he left it, a newspaper rolled in his right hand. He walked past the telephone booth, through the arcade's entrance, around the lorry to the left door, opened it, got in and slammed the door shut.

"Did you get through?" Colonel Mac asked as Joe Louis started the motor and began to move.

"No. But I got the morning paper." He handed it to Colonel Mac, who unrolled and read it. He tapped the shoulder of Joe Louis, indicating that he should read it now, and reached over to handle the wheel of the car while he did so.

It was nearly an hour and a half before they reached the gates of Camp Cromwell.

The guard shone his inquiring torch on the colonel's face, grunted, and waved him on.

They pulled up in front of the radio shed, opened the back of the van, and told the commandos to bring out the prisoner.

Bertram Oliver Heath spat when he saw Blackford Oakes. They brought him into the main room and sat him down on a chair. His torso, at Colonel Mac's direction, was strapped to the back of the chair, leaving his arms free. The commandos were dismissed.

Heath spoke. He had said nothing that surprised Blackford. Not after his six weeks' reconstruction of the life and character of Bertram Oliver Heath. "You should know you will never get anything out of me. And I know the rules that govern the use of torture. But if you want to ignore those rules, go ahead."

Colonel Mac spoke now.

"We didn't think you would suddenly be cooperative, Henry. For that reason we have made other plans." He turned to Blackford.

Blackford Oakes stepped forward, the newspaper in his hand. To Heath he said gruffly: "Take hold of this."

A puzzled expression crossed the face of Heath as he reached out for the newspaper.

The headline blazed across it read: "COUNTERREVOLUTIONARY PLOT FOILED/INVADERS AND TRAITORS FOUND, EXECUTED."

At that moment a flashbulb caught the picture.

And then the shot was fired. Through the newspaper, penetrating Heath's forehead. As he slumped forward, a new flashbulb lit the scene once more.

"Well," Colonel Mac said, putting down the camera as Joe Louis returned the gun to its holster, "now we have a complete album on Operation Tirana."

The men left the shed and headed for the bar. They would clean up in the morning.

EPILOGUE

THE CALL TO Blackford to come to the office of Anthony Trust was uncharacteristic. The summons, at James Street where Blackford was closing the file on Operation Oxford, was delivered through a junior officer, when normally Trust would have made the phone call himself. It specified a meeting that afternoon at 3:03, pursuant to the convention not to make appointments at round-numbered times. Blackford had an idea what it was all about, and wondered only at the delay. The end for Bert Heath had come on Tuesday, and it was already Thursday. Neither Rufus nor Anthony had called him when he got back to James Street. He had written out and sent to Trust, his next-in-command, a report on the events of Tuesday night.

And they were both there, Rufus and Anthony. Anthony Trust sat behind his desk, Rufus on the small couch to the right, Blackford on the couch opposite. Trust began:

"Nice going on following Heath."

"Thanks."

"Crowded day, it was."

"I gather it was crowded also in Moscow. Do we know anything about Fleetwood?"

"No. He has been reported missing at sea by the Swedes. The Brits haven't decided whether to tell them they know he got off that boat and flew to Helsinki and on to Moscow. They'll have to decide that: it was their men keeping an eye on him. We don't even know if the Swedes have located the boat captain. If they find him, they'll get it from him that he was just hired to take Fleetwood up to Österskär where Fleetwood disembarked that same afternoon."

"That means Fleetwood is still in Russia, obviously."

"Yes. No way of telling whether he is in or out of grace. If he was associated only with Beria, I pity him."

"Beria dead?"

"We think so, but we don't know."

Rufus spoke. "We had an asset in Moscow, but he's gone now, so we're only putting two and two together. Malenkov's speech yesterday to the Parliament didn't sound like the speech of somebody who is afraid to go home."

"Did you tell the Brits about the designs on him?"

"No, not after the message you got from Bolgin Monday that the plan was off. We interpret that as meaning that the Beria power play collapsed. But we did warn them that high security would be a good idea, as we had picked up 'rumors.' "

"Anything on the girl? Fleetwood's contact? The American?"

"No. We'll cool that one for a bit—wait to hear from her parents. They'll start asking about her, and then we can get our embassy to inquire."

"Exciting times," Blackford said.

"Right, Black. Exciting times at Cromwell too, I gather."

"Yes," was all that Blackford volunteered.

"Sir Gene told us yesterday they are going to hold a hearing. They want you there as a witness."

Blackford noticed that Rufus was looking at him with that pale blue X-ray look. He said, "When?"

"The meeting is scheduled for next Wednesday, 10 A.M."

"Well, you've seen my report."

Anthony opened the manila folder. "Yes." His eyes ran over it. "You say, quote, 'After the commandos left Heath in the radio shed there was a loud rumpus, and then a shot, and evidently Heath made a move to escape, but was shot by Joe Louis.' What did you mean by 'evidently'?"

Blackford pursed his lips. For a moment he had a wild desire to smile. Here he was, cat-and-mousing about the death of an acknowledged traitor with his oldest friend, both of them allies in a very tough business. But formalities were of substantive importance. In almost every situation. And so Blackford said, "I had the evidence of my ears. And there was no doubt there was a shot. I was there to see Heath's body, and there isn't any doubt there was a bullet in his head."

"Blackford," Rufus interrupted, "tell me yes or no, one thing. Did you kill Bertram Heath?"

"No, Rufus, I did not."

Rufus looked over at Anthony and gave a signal. Anthony responded: "Black, would you go out to the library, please?"

Blackford rose, opened the door, and walked into the dark library, with the bare empty desk and reading light. Spread over it was an open copy of the morning's *Times*. Blackford sat down and turned to the crossword puzzle, pulling a pencil out of his pocket.

He had no trouble with "Famous physicist," four letters. He tried "R A B I." And for "Govt. agency"—why not "C I A?" He loved "After zwei," writing in confidently, "D R E I." "Harem rooms?" . . . If he could only get that lollapaloosa, twelve letters down: "Like Pearl White's rescuers." Pearl White. Who in the hell was Pearl White? What might be said of her rescuers, whoever they were? Obviously the rescue operation had worked, if she was rescued . . . His pencil flew down to try it out.

"IN THE NICK OF TIME!" Anthony - was there. "Come on in, Black."

They sat down as before.

Rufus spoke. "Blackford, we had as you know intended that you should stay here for the next period to help out, to work with Anthony. But something has come up elsewhere, and you will need to go to Washington for a briefing."

"Yes, sir," Blackford said.

"I shall advise Sir Gene that unfortunately you will not be in London for the hearing, but that we have interrogated you, and that you had no hand in the killing of Bertram Heath."

"That you interrogated me and that I did not kill Bertram Heath."

"That you did not kill Bertram Heath, nor bore any responsibility for the accident."

Blackford let it rest.

Trust got up. "A little tea, gentlemen?"

"Oh, one thing, Rufus," Blackford said. "Though it's a gruesome reminder of what happened to his brother, Joe Louis would like a copy of The Album. MI6 told him that was up to us, that the original is U.S. property. Can I send him one?"

Rufus hesitated. "If he wants one, let him have it. He is security-cleared. Besides, there's nothing in The Album the Soviet Union doesn't know."

"That's right, Rufus. Nothing in The Album

right now they don't know about. Someday," he was following Anthony Trust and Rufus out the door, "we'll find out, maybe, how come they sent that thing in."

"Someday," Rufus said, "we will find out a lot of things. Someday, I hope, there'll be some things we still haven't found out."

During tea they watched on television Queen Caroline greeting Premier Malenkov at Windsor Castle. Queen Caroline looked radiant. So did Malenkov.

ACKNOWLEDGMENTS

STUDENTS OF TRIVIA may be amused to learn that when I decided to write about the year 1954, I looked at a standard reference book to reexamine the mischief done by the Soviet Union that year. One index notation caught my eye. It read, "BERIA, AIDES EXECUTED," going on to give the date in December. And so I composed the narrative, heading toward the execution of that awful man. The moment came when I needed to familiarize myself with the names of Beria's aides: only to discover that said aides were executed one year *after* Beria was executed. The index notation should have read, "BERIA AIDES EXECUTED," no comma. My friend Professor Hugh Kenner long ago warned me that journalism was a "low-definitional medium." Never, he warned, "rely for the exact communication of your thought on the correct placement of a comma." Well: I did, and learned my lesson . . . On the other hand it happened that while writing the book I came upon someone who told me he had it from (forgive me, but it is in fact in this way that much history gets written) someone who claims he was physically present when the deed was done that in fact Beria was executed as described in the novel. I checked a Khrushchev scholar (Strobe Talbott of *Time* magazine) who a) does not believe it is so; and b) advises me that it was Khrushchev himself who originated the fantasy. My principal regret is that this novel permits Beria to live one year longer than he actually did.

Dorothy McCartney, the research director of *National Review*, was, once again, invaluable in helping me to research the book. I thank her, and as always the indispensable Frances Bronson, who supervises my books and, substantially, my professional life. Important research was done for me on the spot, in London, by Camilla Horne (Mrs. Gerald Harford). Camilla is the daughter of the distinguished British historian Alistair Horne. She is my goddaughter, and he was my roommate at preparatory school. I dedicate the book to her, and to her mother and father, affectionately.

I was asked by Samuel Vaughan of Doubleday please not to mention yet again his extraordinary editorial ability, kindness, generosity, and care, so I won't. Mrs. Chaucy Bennetts is responsible for the best of the copy editing, residual grammatical anomalies being my own, intransigent responsibility. Joseph Isola did the proofreading, his twentieth for me, leaving me greatly indebted to him. And I thank them for their kindness in reading the manuscript and making suggestions: my wife Pat, my sister Priscilla, my brother Reid, my son Christopher, my friends Thomas Wendel, Jr., and Charles Wallen, Jr., and my friend and literary agent, Lois Wallace. As usual, my friend Sophie Wilkins gave me advice as invaluable as it was severe.

And of course no caper relying in part on technology could get off the ground without Alfred Aya, Jr. When I conceived the idea of the Zirca, I flashed him an MCI to Portland from Switzerland asking if he would be good enough to give my concept a moment's thought. Twenty-two hours later I had a fifteen-thousand-word MCI from him telling me how the thing might be done. I crossed out his name, substituted my own, and sent the paper to Stockholm. I expect, next time around, to become a Nobel laureate.

And, finally, I note that two critics of my last book wrote that Blackford Oakes was not interesting enough. I can't imagine how they came to this conclusion. I find him fascinating.

W. F. B.
Stamford, Connecticut
August 28, 1985